Cissy and Jack Galloway
August 1991

FREQUENT HEARSES

By the same Author:

THE MOVING TOYSHOP
HOLY DISORDERS
THE CASE OF THE GILDED FLY
SWAN SONG
LOVE LIES BLEEDING
BURIED FOR PLEASURE

FREQUENT HEARSES

A Detective Story

by

EDMUND CRISPIN, pseud.

On all the line a sudden vengeance waits,
And frequent hearses shall besiege your gates.
—*To the Memory of an Unfortunate Lady*

LONDON HOUSE & MAXWELL,
NEW YORK
1971

First published 1950
Reissued 1971

IMPORTANT NOTE

AFTER the first edition of this book had been printed, I happened to see in a newspaper that investigations in a case were being carried out by Superintendent Capstick of Scotland Yard. I need not say that the real Superintendent Capstick of Scotland Yard (to whom I apologise for my inadvertence) and *my* local Superintendent Capstick have no connection with each other whatsoever. I invented the name Capstick when I was meditating the story: but Nature had got in first.

E. C.

Published in the United States by the British Book Centre as a London House & Maxwell Mystery 1971. First published under the title SUDDEN VENGENCE.

Printed in Great Britain
08277-0251-5
Library Catalogue No. 72-146322

CHAPTER I

I

TAKING PICCADILLY CIRCUS as your centre, draw a circle of radius eighteen miles, and you will find the major film studios—Denham, Elstree and the rest—dotted about its circumference. Long Fulton lies to the north-west. Should you wish to travel to Long Fulton from Oxford, your best plan is to entrain for London, and on arrival there set out afresh from Marylebone. The cross-country journey is prolonged and tedious, involving four changes—at stations of progressively diminishing size and increasing antiquity, so that the effect is of witnessing a dramatised History of the Railways in reverse—and, in the upshot, a ruinous, draughty single-decker motor-bus. It is advisable, as a general rule, not to attempt this. That Gervase Fen persisted in doing so may be attributed first to his innate perversity and secondly to the fact that the spring season commonly made him torpid, so that to meander through the burgeoning March countryside at twenty miles an hour was an occupation which consorted well with his mood. By getting up at six he could be at Long Fulton comfortably by ten, the time at which script conferences were usually advertised to begin. And since in actual fact (the making of films being what it is) they never began until ten-thirty or eleven, there was ample opportunity for him to drink coffee in the canteen or to rove through the congeries of decrepit-looking structures in which the brain-children of the Leiper Combine were nursed from undisciplined infancy up to the final cutting, dubbing and reduplication which preceded their *début* on this or that West

End screen. The amusement which this afforded Fen was never more than tenuous. He was unable to regard British films as in any way indispensable to the Good Life, and his own temporary responsibility at the studios—which was to provide expert information about the life and works of the poet Pope—weighed very lightly on him in consequence.

It was on the occasion of his third visit—a day of flying clouds and clear equinoctial sunlight—that he first became aware of the existence of the girl who called herself Gloria Scott.

To all intents and purposes the studios had annihilated Long Fulton village, and there would have been a good deal of querulous correspondence about this in *The Times* had the evidence allowed anyone colourably to maintain that the process had been deleterious. It quickly proved, however, that regarded simply as a village there was little or nothing to be said in Long Fulton's favour; its architecture was uniformly undistinguished and its lack of historical and literary associations such as to strike even the most resolute and exhaustive guide-books dumb. Moreover, it is certain that the villagers themselves would have opposed any attempt to protect them from the invasion of the Leiper Combine, for the building of the studios not only permitted them intoxicating glimpses of those deities (as persons interchangeable, but as stimuli sempiternal) to whose worship they addressed themselves twice weekly in the Regent at Gisford, but also enabled them, by sundry rapacious, underhand devices, to derive much monetary profit from the incursion. Like some uncouth Danaë, Long Fulton was seduced by the irresistible amalgam of gold and godhead. And to the condition of helotry which inevitably followed, the villagers were by nature and instinct most admirably suited. Left to their own exiguous devices, they had mismanaged Long Fulton to the point of virtual extinction. They were only too glad to surrender their independence to the studios, and would have stood out in a body against any scheme that proposed restoring it to them.

The studios were as nearly in their midst as made no difference. They impended threateningly from behind the church—an extensive huddle of many disparate buildings which might have been the dolls' houses of some careless giant-child, kicked together anyhow in a corner of the nursery. Fronting the road there was an attempt at a façade, but its failure to impart coherence to the structures behind it was so patent that æsthetically it would have been a great deal preferable if the attempt had not been made at all. The road itself was decimated by a weight of traffic for which it had never been designed, and its air of dilapidation was echoed wherever you looked. The pervasive whitewash badly needed renewing; bomb damage (to the very last, German Intelligence had clung tenaciously to the conviction that the studios were an arms factory of some description)—bomb damage had been patched up rather than properly repaired; and the great stages, towering monolithically above the other buildings, looked quite capable of folding up at the advent of a high wind. For all this, economic considerations—the industry is for ever in the toils of one financial crisis or another—were no doubt responsible; but the general untidiness of the scene was accentuated by the surrounding estate, which was cluttered up with realistically wrecked aeroplanes, half-demolished plywood cottages, immense blue sky-screens, mystifying pyramids of sand, small lighthouses and all manner of other miscellaneous bric-à-brac.

Nor were matters very much improved when you got inside. There were large zigzag cracks in the walls; flakes of whitewash were liable to detach themselves from the ceilings and settle in your hair; dust was omnipresent and cleanliness doubtful; of the multiplicity of telephones which constituted the principal furnishings, at least a third were perpetually out of order. Moreover, the topography of the place was so irrational and obscure as to make it seem inchoate. It possessed, certainly, a few permanent landmarks such as the Music Department and the Script Department, but for the rest it appeared to be made up of numerous small, bare rooms, identically furnished with chairs, a table and the inevitable telephone, which were employed for official and unofficial confabulations and could be distinguished one from another only by a surrealist system of digits and letters of the alphabet; and to locate any particular one of these unaided was a considerable enterprise. More than anything else, perhaps, the studio lacked a focus. A decisive single main entrance might have provided this, but in fact there were three main entrances, severely egalitarian in their amenities and with nothing to choose between them except that one of them gave access to the place where you wanted to arrive and the other two did not; and in none of them was there anywhere where enquiries could be made and some species of orientation established. To the mere stranger it was all vastly confusing.

Mere strangers, however, were few and far between; for obvious reasons, the organisation did not encourage their presence. And it was to be presumed that Mr. Leiper's employees, set in their habitual orbits and pursuing their familiar avocations, could find their way about all right. Certainly they were a diverse community: innumerable technicians, meditating strikes; stenographers with impeccably dressed hair, as instinct with poise as the heroines of a woman novelist; camera crews; continuity girls; youngish directors; well-shaven, lounge-suited producers and executives, rather older; actors and actresses in their make-up; "extras", swathed in boredom as in a garment; canteen staff; porters and messengers. By their united labours romance would come to Wigan, to West Hartlepool overmastering adventure, to Birmingham and Aberystwyth an anodyne against the pains of living. Hand clutched in sticky hand, head against shoulder, Jane and George, Sally and Dick would for three hours at least snatch immunity, by the studios' contriving, from war and the rumours of war, from domestic contention and public strife, from tedium and malice and routine and the struggle to keep alive. . . . Long Fulton, in short, was a notable well-head of our most potent latter-day religion; and this being so, some degree of *hubris* might reasonably have been expected of its acolytes. Yet these studio people were not, on the whole, vainglorious. Like Gulliver among the Brobdingnagians, they were acutely conscious of the more squalid defects of that to which they ministered, and were therefore constantly surprised—if not, indeed, actively repelled—by the homage which it so unfailingly exacted from the millions of its worshippers. Only rarely did the glamour of "a job with films" go to anyone's head—and though the girl who called herself Gloria Scott may have suffered from such delusions of grandeur, she had the excuse of being young, and was in any case a person of very little consequence. Her death, and the appalling consequences which followed it, was perhaps shocking precisely because she *was* so unimportant; it was as if a bomb had gone off in an area confidently scheduled by the authorities as completely safe. . . .

2

The bus from Gisford went no farther than 'The Bear', a failing hostelry at the opposite end of the village from the studios. From that point, then, Fen was obliged to walk—and on the morning in question he was negotiating the main street, with a copy of *The Ambassadors* held open in front of his face, when a small saloon car pulled up beside him.

"The studios," said a voice from within it. "Can you tell me, please, if I'm right for the studios?"

Half of Fen's attention lingered on the unconscionable Strether; with the other half he delivered an affirmative. He was about to expand this with specific directions when an exclamation checked him.

"Professor Fen!" said the car's occupant cordially. "This is a very pleasant coincidence indeed. How are you?" And at this Fen shook himself hurriedly free of the stupor which the prose of Henry James invariably induced in him, stooped, and peered in at the car window.

Sitting benignantly at the wheel, like a well-disposed gnome, he saw a small, neat, dapper man of between fifty and sixty, with greying hair, a round, clean-shaven pink face, and innocent blue eyes. A slender cheroot was in the corner of his mouth; a grey Homburg hat surmounted him; shining brown shoes were on his feet. You would have put him down, perhaps, as a prosperous and engaging commercial traveller with mild pretensions to culture—and it may be that some such effect was what he aimed at, for the habit of camouflage had often been useful to him in dealing with the complexities of metropolitan crime. But his appearance expressed his true nature faithfully enough: he was in fact, and without affectation, tidy-minded, disarming, unaggressively cultivated; and although these traits were undeniably of assistance to him in his work at New Scotland Yard, he had always successfully resisted the temptation—a natural enough temptation in the circumstances—to gild the lily by exaggerating them into a pose.

"Humbleby," said Fen, enlightened; and extended a hand which Humbleby moved flaccidly up and down inside the car. "Two years, is it, or three?"

"A little less than two, I fancy." And Humbleby nodded approval of his own acumen. "The Sanford affair was in September of 1947. Have you been back there since that time? I understand that you didn't get into Parliament after all. What a good thing. Have you heard that Myra . . ."

For a minute or two they gossiped about the case which had brought them together. You may remember it—it was the business of the ex-prostitute who was poisoned through the post. Then Fen, suddenly tiring of these reminiscences, said:

"But why are you going to the studios? Police business?"

Humbleby nodded. "Of a sort. This is what you once, I believe, called a 'criminological holiday task'. But nothing very sensational—as far as you can tell at the moment . . . I *am* right for the studios, I suppose?"

"Those are they." Fen pointed. "Those fanciful white buildings behind the trees. The gate's about two hundred yards along on the left. I'm on the way there myself, so you can give me a lift."

"By all means." Humbleby opened the car door, and Fen climbed in. "What's that you're reading?"

"*The Ambassadors.*"

"Narcotic," said Humbleby. "I always feel that Henry James ought to be dealt with in the Dangerous Drugs Act, and perhaps used in childbirth as an alternative to trilene. . . . Here we go, then."

Humbleby had no talent for cars, and they moved off in spasms along the almost deserted street. The sun shone down on them with impersonal benevolence, and a dog, misdoubting their intentions, barked tremulously at them from the kerb. Humbleby put out his tongue at it as they passed.

"And you," he said "—are you just paying a visit to the studios, or are you professionally occupied there?"

"The latter." Fen stiffened as they approached a bend in the road, and did not relax until again they were safely round it. "But only as casual labour. I'm acting as literary adviser in connection with a film they're making."

"Bless us," said Humbleby. "A film about what?"

"It's based on the life of Pope." The final words of this statement were drowned out by an imperious, and apparently quite disinterested, blast on Humbleby's horn. "Based," Fen reiterated irritably, "on the life of Pope."

"The Pope?"

"*Pope.*"

"Now which Pope would that be, I wonder?" said Humbleby, with the air of one who tries to take an intelligent interest in what is going forward. "Pius, or Clement, or——"

Fen stared at him. "Alexander, of course."

"You mean"—Humbleby spoke with something of an effort—"you mean the Borgia?"

"Don't be so ridiculous, Humbleby," said Fen. "Do you really imagine they've called in a Professor of English to instruct them about the Borgias? No, I mean the poet, of course."

"That was my first thought"—Humbleby was aggrieved—"but naturally I rejected it out of hand. There's nothing in Pope's life that anyone could possibly make a commercial film of."

"So one would imagine." Fen shook his head gloomily. "None the less, a film is in fact going to be made. And the reason for that——"

He checked himself in order to flourish a mandatory

finger at the studio gate, where they had now arrived. They swerved in past the disregard of a gatekeeper in a sort of sentry-box. Passes were supposed to be shown, but except on the days when extras were being interviewed this rule was seldom enforced. "The reason for that," Fen repeated doggedly, "is as follows. A few months ago Andrew Leiper died, and his brother——"

But Humbleby was not attending. Instead, he was searching for a gap in the line of expensive-looking cars—monuments, many of these, to an involved scheme for hoodwinking the Inland Revenue Department—which were parked, nose inward, along the front of the studios. Presently he found one and scraped into it.

"Yes?" he said encouragingly. "You were saying?"

"I was saying that this company used to be owned by a man called Andrew Leiper. Andrew Leiper died recently, however, and the company, along with his other interests, was inherited by his elder brother Giles."

And Fen pointed to the façade above them, where a group of workmen were engaged—and in their leisurely way had been engaged for the past three weeks—in substituting, in the great gilt-letter sign ANDREW LEIPER FILMS INC., the word GILES for the word ANDREW. "*Si monumentum requiris . . .*"

"Just so." Humbleby switched off his engine, removed the cheroot from his mouth, and examined the end of it attentively. "But as to the immediate relevance of the situation you describe——"

"We're coming to that. . . . Now, Giles's sole claim to distinction is that he's a literary crank. He believes, for instance, that the Earl of Rutland wrote Shakespeare's plays (with the exception of *The Tempest*, which he ascribes to Beaumont and Fletcher), and he's published a nasty little book which purports to prove it. He believes that

Dryden was impotent, and that incestuous relations between Emily and Bramwell were responsible for *Wuthering Heights*. In fact, I'm inclined to think that he believes that it was Bramwell, and not Emily, who actually wrote *Wuthering Heights*. . . . But all that's by the way. The point is that Giles Leiper has ideas about Pope, too. Do you know the *Ode to the Memory of an Unfortunate Lady*?"

"Dr. Johnson," said Humbleby with the cautious deliberation of one who treads slippery conversational ground, "interpreted it as an apologia for suicide."

"So he did. And——"

"But I like it," said Humbleby, suddenly enthusiastic. "I like it very much indeed. '*What beck'ning ghost*,' " he intoned dramatically, " '*along the moonlight shade Invites my something something something glade. 'Tis she!—but why that bleeding—*' "

"Please, please." Fen fished a packet of cigarettes from the pocket of his coat and lit one. "Your recollection of the piece seems to be very indistinct. I'd better explain what it's about. It concerns——"

"There's not the least necessity——"

"It is an Elegy to a girl who has killed herself as a result of being—um—callously deserted by her husband. The poet——"

"I remember it very clearly," said Humbleby. "Very clearly indeed."

"The poet, in addition to deploring this situation, announces his belief that vengeance will overtake not only the husband, but the whole of his family as well."

" '*While the long funerals*,' " chanted Humbleby in solemn antiphon, " '*darken all the way*.' "

"*Blacken* all the way, *blacken*. . . . The girl may have been a Mrs. Weston, by birth a Miss Gage. But that's conjectural. The poem was almost certainly a mere imaginative exercise, and there's not the smallest evidence that Pope was in any way personally involved. Which brings us to Giles Leiper."

"Brings us, at long last, to Giles Leiper."

"Leiper believes, along with his other fatuities, that Pope *was* personally involved. Not long ago, in fact, he wrote an article in some tawdry journal or other stating his conviction that Pope had had an affair with this girl, and that that was why he was so upset about her death. '*Are we to understand*,' " Fen quoted with repugnance, " '*that a poem as deeply felt as this was no more than a callous exercise in versification? Is it not much more in accordance with our knowledge of poets and poetry to assume that Pope was intimately interested in the lady?*' "

"Well, isn't it?" said Humbleby, taken genuinely unawares.

"No, it isn't. And even if it were, there's not, in this case, the smallest justification for imagining that Pope's connection with the girl was anything but platonic. . . . Anyway, it's this supposititious affair that the film is chiefly about—though a lot of other things come into it, of course." Fen considered these, not without pleasure. "There's Lady Mary Wortley Montagu. There are Addison and Swift—Swift is depicted as walking about the country all day, writing *Gulliver*, thinking erotic thoughts about Stella, and having little preliminary or proleptic fits of madness. There's also, and somewhat anachronistically, Bolingbroke."

Humbleby chuckled. "And Dryden and Wycherley," he said, "and Handel and Gay and Queen Anne. I mustn't miss this film. How far has it got?"

"It's not on the floor yet."

"On the *floor*?"

"Yes, I'm sorry: their damnable jargon is infectious. I

mean that they haven't actually started making it yet. We're still at the stage of script conferences." And Fen glanced at his watch. "There's one this morning—which is why I'm here."

Humbleby threw the end of his cheroot out of the window. "You're not in a hurry, I hope?"

"Not specially, no. Before I go, tell me what you're doing here. If it isn't confidential, that is."

"No, it isn't confidential." At the reminder of his mission a certain sombreness had invaded Humbleby's bland countenance. "And knowing these people, you may possibly be able to help me."

"A crime?"

"Suicide is a crime, yes. But there's nothing special about this one, except that the poor wretch was so very young; and thought better of it at the last moment—though too late to save herself. . . ." And Humbleby braced himself, as a man braces himself when confronted with a necessary but wholly disagreeable task. "Tell me," he said, "have you ever come across a girl called Gloria Scott?"

3

A group of cleaners—stolid, morose, elderly women—drifted in at the studio gate; their voices, exchanging laborious witticisms with the gatekeeper, rasped unpleasantly through the limpid morning air. The men on the scaffolding had ceased work and were recouping their energies with cold tea. A distant succession of reverberating bumps suggested that someone was loading or unloading balks of timber. And as Humbleby spoke, the shadow of a great cloud curtained the studios from north to south, so that, by contrast, the low hills where the sun still shone glittered like polished metal.

"Gloria Scott?" Fen echoed. "No, I'm afraid the name doesn't convey anything to me."

Humbleby was absently fingering the lapel of his light-grey overcoat. "I'm not clear," he said, "as to whether she actually worked here or not. But it was from here that Miss—um"—he consulted with his memory—"Miss Flecker rang up to identify her. Perhaps you know Miss Flecker?"

"No, I don't," said Fen restively. "And all this means nothing to me, nothing. Explain, please."

"You've seen this morning's paper?"

"*The Times* and the *Mail* only."

"The *Mail* had it in. A photograph of this girl, with a request for identification."

Fen produced the paper from his pocket and hunted through it. "There," said Humbleby, pointing.

The photograph was of a pretty, sulky-looking girl in her late teens. It was a portrait of that contrived and glamorous sort favoured by the acting profession, with the lips, nose, neck, and breasts sharply outlined by careful lighting. The accompanying letterpress was scant, conveying no more than that the police wished to know who she was.

"There's a sense in which one recognises her, of course," said Fen thoughtfully. "You can see that photograph—or something pretty well indistinguishable from it—outside almost every repertory theatre in the country. . . . What was she—brunette, red-head, mousy? They all come out the same in black-and-white photographs."

"Auburn, when I saw her. Saturated auburn, with a dressing of Thames mud and Thames weed."

Fen glanced at him sympathetically. "Well?" he said. "What about it?"

"It happened early yesterday morning—that's to say,

during the night before last, at about 2 a.m. A taxi picked this girl up at the Piccadilly end of Half Moon Street, where she was talking to some man whom the driver didn't particularly notice. She asked to be taken to an address in Stamford Street, on the other side of the river. Then, when they were in the middle of Waterloo Bridge, she told the driver to stop. She was a good deal overwrought, it seems, and the driver didn't immediately start off again when she'd paid him. He watched her run towards the parapet, and as soon as he realised what she was going to do, he ran after her. The bridge was almost deserted, but there was a police-car coming across it, and the people in that saw what happened. The taxi-driver made a grab at her as she went over, but it was too late. She came up once, and screamed—she'd fallen flat on the surface of the water, and you know what that does to you when you fall from a height. One of the men in the police-car dived in after her, but she was dead when he got her ashore."

The cleaners had disappeared inside the studios. A shooting-brake, crammed with carpenters in overalls, emerged noisily from a hidden entrance to the left. But Fen hardly noticed it: in imagination he stood on the vacant, lamplit expanses of Waterloo Bridge, peering over the parapet at a figure which floundered through the shallows and the mud, dragging after him the limp, rent body of an auburn-haired girl. . . . The cloud, driven hapless towards the north-west, had unveiled the sun again; yet for all that Fen shivered slightly, feeling on his mouth the night wind and in his nostrils the smell of the river at low tide. Such visions were not, of course, germane to the matter in hand: they would certainly be distorted, certainly incomplete. But it was with a curious reluctance that he put them aside. . . .

"Yes," he said. "Go on."

Humbleby shifted uneasily—conscious, perhaps, that it is when a man is most sincere that he is apt to sound most histrionic.

"The whole business," he said, "was dealt with, of course, by the Divisional Superintendent. And he happens to be my brother-in-law—years ago, when he was only a sergeant, we were on a case together, and he met my sister at my flat and fell for her, God help him. . . . Anyway, I hadn't seen him for a long time, and being on holiday, I dropped in at the station yesterday morning, and he told me all about it. As you'll have guessed, it was identifying the girl that was the difficulty. She'd dropped her handbag on the bridge, but there wasn't anything at all revealing in it except for the photograph, and that didn't have the photographer's name on it. And her clothes were all new and not marked, so they didn't help either."

"But the address," said Fen, a little surprised at Humbleby's ignoring what seemed the first and most obvious line of approach to the problem. "The address she gave to the taxi-driver."

"Useless. We found it all right, but it didn't help us to identify her. She'd only moved in there the previous afternoon, and hadn't so far either signed the register or handed over her ration-book. She'd told the landlady her name, of course, but the landlady was deaf and didn't catch it. . . . It really looked as if the Fates were in a conspiracy to make trouble for us."

"But her belongings—papers and so forth. . . ."

"Ah, yes. This is where the one really odd feature of the affair comes in." And Humbleby paused, not displeased at having something mildly bizarre to relate. "By the time we got to it, her room and her things had been searched."

A ragged flight of blackbirds passed overhead, peering

inquisitively down at the studio roofs. In a window in the wall directly facing them a smooth-looking young man appeared, gazed at them suspiciously, muttered something to a companion invisible behind him, and vanished again. Humbleby, distrait, was playing with the door-handle. He was not normally a fidgety man, and Fen interpreted this as a sign of considerable perturbation.

"Searched?" he said. "Searched for what?"

"For signs of identification. Everything of that sort—papers, photographs, the fly-leaves of one or two books—had been removed and taken away. The laundry-marks had been cut out of all the clothes and the paper lining of the lid of a suit-case, which had obviously had a name and address on it, had been torn out. And whoever did it was thorough. We weren't able to find a single thing he'd missed."

"But that's extraordinary," said Fen rather blankly. "If she'd been murdered, now. . . . But I suppose there's no doubt——"

"None whatever. She killed herself all right. But mind you, there might quite well be someone who didn't want her motive for killing herself to become known, and chose this rather oblique way of—um—occluding it. . . . For instance, it's possible she was pregnant. We shall know about that when the autopsy report comes in."

Fen nodded. "Odd," he commented. "And interesting in so far as whoever was responsible must surely have realised that there was a very fair chance, in spite of all his efforts, of her being identified in the end. Unless . . ."

"Unless what?"

"You say you've now discovered that her name was Gloria Scott?"

"That's what this Miss Flecker said over the 'phone."

"Yes. Well, I don't want to put wrong ideas into your

head, but it sounds to me as if it might conceivably be a stage name."

Humbleby considered this. " 'Gloria'," he murmured. "Yes, I see what you mean. And in that case, it would probably be her real identity that the murderer was trying to conceal."

"Quite so. . . . But all this is hypothetical at present. Let me get one or two other things clear. For instance, is there any indication as to *when* this girl's room was searched?"

Humbleby had stopped fidgeting with the door-handle and was now manipulating the gear lever. "Yes," he said, "there's a pretty clear indication, as a matter of fact. It was almost certainly done during yesterday morning."

"*After* she killed herself?"

"After she killed herself, yes. I needn't go into all the details, but from the time when she arrived—Thursday, the day before yesterday, in the afternoon—until about nine o'clock yesterday morning, there really wasn't a chance for anyone to get in and out unobserved and at the same time remain there long enough to do what was done; anyone, that is, except the landlady, whom there's no possible reason to suspect. For one reason and another, the Super. and I weren't able to get down to making a search ourselves till yesterday afternoon, and by that time the mischief was done." And Humbleby paused expectantly. "Well," he said presently, "what do you make of it?"

"Very little." Fen sniffed deprecatorily and moved his long legs about in an attempt to mitigate the cramp which was stealing over them. "Very little indeed. This business of obliterating identity may not be connected with the suicide—in which case it's quite unfathomable at present. But if it *is* connected, there arises the question of how the person concerned knew the suicide had happened. Was it reported in yesterday's morning papers?"

"Only a brief paragraph. The picture wasn't published, and no names were given—since at that stage there weren't any names to give."

"Our *X* might, I suppose, have actually been present when this girl threw herself into the river. Or anyway when they were pulling her out. Were there many lookers-on, do you know?"

"A few. . . . Yes, that's a possibility." Humbleby had engaged the lever in first gear and was struggling to disengage it again. "Undeniably," he said, breathing heavily, "it's obscure."

"Do leave the car alone, Humbleby; you'll break something in a minute. . . . Yes, well, the only thing is to find out a bit more about the girl. And that, I take it, is why you're here."

Humbleby relinquished his efforts and gazed at the lever with distaste. He took a scrap of paper from his pocket, wrote on it the words "*Be careful—you have left this car in gear*", and propped it up against the windscreen.

"Yes," he agreed, "that's why I'm here. The call from this Flecker girl, who'd seen the picture in the papers, came through about half-past eight this morning, and I offered to drive here and interview her. . . . To tell you the truth," said Humbleby confidingly, "I've always wanted to see the inside of a film studio, and this is the first chance I've had."

In that confined space Fen's cramp was growing intolerable. He brought the colloquy to an abrupt conclusion by opening the door and getting out.

"Well, you'll be disappointed," he said unkindly. "And if I don't go now, I shall be late. Can we arrange to meet at lunch-time?"

"Wait a minute, wait a minute," said Humbleby, emerging hastily on the other side. "I'll come in with you, and you can help me locate this person I'm here to see."

"I very much doubt if I can. But I'll do my best."

They crossed the gravel to the nearest of the three entrances, mounted a short flight of steps and went inside. A circular vestibule received them. The monogram A.L.F. appeared in faded mosaic on its floor, and to the right of it, blocking the lower third of a Roman arch, was a species of reception desk with, however, no one behind it. The prospect beyond was of a corridor, bifurcating in the middle distance, with a number of doors marked PRIVATE on either side. Film studios go in terror of fire, and a great many buckets, coiled hoses and extinguishers were visible. But of other furnishing, and for that matter of human occupation, the place gave no sign. Abashed by its chilly quietude, Fen and Humbleby halted.

"In my simple-minded way," said Humbleby, "I had anticipated something like a cross between a *lupanar* and an automobile factory. No doubt we're as yet only on the outer fringes. But still——"

He broke off as footsteps, accompanied by a noisy, convulsive fit of coughing, burst upon them from a hitherto unnoticed passage to the left. This humanising influence materialised into a small, slim man of between thirty and forty, who strode into the vestibule with a handkerchief pressed to his mouth. He had a brown and humorously ugly face decorated with large and beautiful eyes, and Humbleby, who was a tolerably regular theatre-goer, recognised him at once.

So also, apparently, did Fen; he said unsympathetically: "You're ill."

"Like hell I am," the new-comer croaked back. "You haven't any whisky on you, by any chance?"

"None."

"You'd imagine that even in a God-awful hole like this whisky would be procurable somewhere or other, but it isn't. I'm going into the village to see if I can wangle some. . . . By the way, this morning's script conference has been postponed till eleven. And it's not in thirteen, it's in CC, wherever that may be. Oh, and Leiper *isn't* going to be there—which means that I'm not, either, if I can get out of it." The new-comer moved towards the door. "Of all the damned silly films ever contemplated. . . ."

"Just a moment," said Fen. "Do you know where we can find a Miss Flecker?"

The man paused. His face grew red and he sneezed twice before replying. "Flecker? Flecker? That's a girl who works in the Music Department, isn't it?"

"Well, where is the Music Department?"

"Oh, that's easy." He pointed. "You go along *there* and take the right fork, and then—oh no, blast it, I'm thinking of one of the sound stages. Well, let's see now. . . . I think if you take the left fork——"

"You haven't," said Fen coldly, "the slightest notion where it is."

"Oh, yes, I assure you. Curse it, I've *been* there. The trouble really is that though this place seems to reduplicate itself as you go about it, you never get an *exact* repetition: there's always a room or a corridor that's different. I tell you what"—a novel and satisfying idea occurred to him at this point—"you *ask* someone; that's your best plan." He moved towards the door again. "Yes, that's your best plan, I think. I may see you later." He departed in a fresh fit of coughing.

"Stuart North, wasn't it?" asked Humbleby; and he spoke the name with a good deal of respect. "I didn't know he'd taken to the films."

"He's made only one so far," said Fen. "*Visa for Heaven*, or some such trashy name. He's due to play Pope in this fantasy I've been telling you about, and after that he's going back to the stage."

"He'd be rather good as Pope, I should imagine. Given a little artificial deformity, he has the right physique. And facially he's not unlike, either."

"I don't think," said Fen vaguely, "that Pope's deformity is going to be stressed very much. . . . Well, we'd better find the Music Department, I suppose. As my conference has been postponed, I can come with you. Let's ask this girl."

"This girl", now approaching with the glazed, intent expression of an amateur juggler about to embark on the most precarious part of his act, was a blonde stenographer, so superlatively groomed that she looked as if she would crack open at a touch. ("*Lupanar*," said Humbleby with satisfaction. "We progress, then.") She proved willing enough to lead them to the Music Department, and in her charge they traversed a warren of bare corridors and staircases, eventually fetching up at an unmarked door which she earnestly assured them was what they wanted. They thanked her and went in, finding themselves in a small room with two desks and a large filing-cabinet, where some half-dozen young people were giggling together and consuming tea. An amiable-looking youth detached himself from this group and asked Fen and Humbleby what he could do for them.

"Miss Flecker," said Humbleby. "We're in search of a Miss Flecker."

"I'll see if she's busy." The youth put down his cup and opened a door which led to an adjoining room. "Judy," he said, "there's two men want to see you."

A girl's voice from within, pleasantly drawling and with a suspicion of a lisp, demanded to be told who they were.

"Who are you?" the youth enquired agreeably from the doorway.

"Detective-Inspector Humbleby," said Humbleby, "of Scotland Yard."

"Cripes. . . . I say, Judy, it's——"

"Yes, all right, I heard," said the voice. "Ask them to come in, please. . . . Come in, Inspector," she called. "And, Johnny, bring them some tea."

4

From behind a littered but business-like desk, as they went in, she got up to welcome them—a girl in her middle twenties with sleek black hair, cool grey eyes and a clear complexion. She possessed two of the rarest physical attributes of her sex, broad shoulders and long legs; and she wore a tailored navy-blue coat and skirt with an oyster-coloured blouse and a brooch of diamonds encircling a sapphire so dark as to be almost black. But for her intelligence, and the mildly sardonic look in her eye, she would have been what the *Sunday Pictorial* is apt to describe as "a lovely". Inside the room Humbleby halted, at gaze; and after no more than a second's calculation she addressed herself to him.

"Hello, Inspector," she said. "Do sit down, won't you?"

The windows looked out on to a crossing of asphalt paths, and you could glimpse a corner of the immense carpenters' shop, with a prospect of trees beyond. Near them was an arm-chair, and into this Humbleby cautiously lowered himself.

"This," he observed, "is Professor Gervase Fen. He is"—and Humbleby paused, momentarily perplexed—"he is assisting me, I suppose you might say."

"How do you do," said Miss Flecker civilly. "I have

heard of you, of course. And I was hoping that while you were working here we might be able to meet. How is the Pope film progressing?"

In default of a second chair, Fen had settled on the edge of the desk, and was regarding Miss Flecker with undisguised approval. "Very little, I should say; but as I'm not familiar with film-making I'm scarcely in a position to judge. . . . There's a lot," said Fen pensively, "of *quarrelling*."

"There would be." Miss Flecker grinned mischievously. "The Cranes *en famille* are not a very sedative influence, in my experience."

"Cranes?" echoed Humbleby in polite incomprehension.

"You must be aware of Madge Crane," said Miss Flecker, "even if you haven't heard of her brothers." She turned to Fen. "Madge is playing Lady Mary, isn't she?"

"Suitably bowdlerised," Fen agreed gravely, "and chiefly occupied, when not offering Pope wise and kindly advice about personal matters which are no possible concern of hers, in introducing inoculation against smallpox from Turkey."

And Humbleby nodded, enlightened. "Madge Crane is a Star, then?" he ventured.

"You really hadn't heard of her?" Miss Flecker chuckled maliciously. "She *would* be pleased. Madge is one of the First Ladies of British Films."

"First La——" Humbleby shook his head in bafflement. "Whatever can that mean?"

"Well, I think it means that she's no longer obliged to make films in which she has to show her legs." Miss Flecker delivered this judgment with notable dispassion. "And that saves everyone a lot of trouble, because they always did have to be filmed very carefully if they were going to come out looking like anything at all."

The door opened and the youth called Johnny appeared with two cups of tea, which he handed to Fen and Humbleby. "We've finished off the biscuits," he announced without visible remorse, "so I'm afraid you'll have to do without. . . . Judy, the L.S.O. is hanging about on Stage Two complaining because Griswold hasn't turned up. Where is he?"

"He had to go to Denham to see Muir about something or other, and he said he might be late. Calm them, Johnny, calm them. Tell them to sit down and practise a symphony. Has Ireland arrived yet?"

"Not yet."

"Well, mind you behave respectfully to him when he does."

"You don't think," said Johnny wistfully, "that it would be a good idea for me to run them through a few of the music sections while they're waiting?"

"No, I don't. Go away and get on with your work."

Johnny retired in dejection, and Miss Flecker was saying "Well now . . ." when the telephone rang. "Damn," she said. "Excuse me. . . . Yes, put him through. . . . Good morning, Dr. Bush—Geoffrey, I should say. . . . Triple woodwind? Well, I imagine it might be managed; I'll ask Mr. Griswold. . . . It'll be the Philharmonia, yes." Dr. Bush crackled prolongedly. "No measurements for reels four and five yet? All right, I'll nag them. . . . Yes, I know you can't be expected to write a score if you haven't got any measurements. . . . No, there's not the least chance of postponing the recording; you'll just have to work all night as well as all day. . . . Have you sent any of the score to the copyists yet? . . . Well, you'd better get on with it, hadn't you? . . . See you at the recording. . . . No. . . . Certainly not. Good-bye."

She put down the instrument. "A composer," she explained soberly, like one who refers to some necessary but unromantic bodily function. "I'm sorry things have to get hectic the moment you arrive. Perhaps now we shall have a few minutes' peace." She retrieved her cup and drank the tepid tea in it with a grimace. "Oh, Lord, measurements. . . . Johnny!" she called; and when that individual put his head hopefully in at the door: "Johnny, get on to Loring, will you, and tell him Dr. Bush is waiting for the measurements for reels four and five of *Escape to Purgatory*."

"He'll only go all pathetic on me," said Johnny, his optimism abating at this request, "and say they're doing their best."

"Tell him they must do better if they want any incidental music for those reels. . . . And, Johnny, see to it that I'm not disturbed for ten minutes, please."

With a doleful nod Johnny vanished, and Miss Flecker relaxed gratefully in her chair. "At last," she said. "And I really do apologise."

"Not at all," said Humbleby. "It's we who should apologise for interrupting you." He produced a notebook and a gold propelling pencil and cleared his throat premonitorily. "Now as regards this girl . . ."

"Are you in a position"—Miss Flecker spoke a trifle warily—"to tell me why you want to know about her?"

"Certainly." And Humbleby eyed her in an innocent-seeming way which in reality masked swift and shrewd powers of observation. "She has committed suicide."

For a moment there was silence. Clearly Miss Flecker was shocked, though the only sign she gave was a slight lifting of the eye-brows.

"Suicide," she murmured—and during a brief interval seemed preoccupied with rapid inward calculation. "Any reason given?"

"No. Can you yourself think of any?"

Miss Flecker hesitated. "The gossip is that she was going to have a baby, but I don't believe much of what I'm told in this place, so don't rely on it. In any case, I suppose that an autopsy——"

"Just so." Humbleby was at his most judicial. "But may we start at the beginning, please? Your name——" He poised his pencil expectantly.

"Is Judith Annecy Flecker. Age twenty-six. Occupation, Secretary to the Long Fulton Music Department."

"Good. And the name of this girl whose picture you saw in the paper is Gloria Scott."

"She called herself that, yes."

Humbleby glanced up from the notebook. "That was just a stage name, you mean?"

Miss Flecker crossed her admirable legs and contemplated them for a moment with a satisfaction in which Fen, who does not scorn simple pleasures, abundantly participated. "I *think* it was only a stage name," she said, "but you'll have to ask someone who knew her better than I did. And if it *was*, I've not the ghost of a notion about her real name, I'm afraid."

"You didn't know her well, then?"

"Only very casually. But I thought I'd better ring you up about her, because I know what the people here are like. Half a hundred of them will have seen and recognised that photograph, and they'll all be studiously engaged in leaving the job of communicating with you to someone else. So I thought I'd forestall their havering. *Did* anyone else from here telephone you, by the way?"

"No one had when I left," said Humbleby. "But mind you, that was some time ago, and you got in early. I shall ring up Charles in a moment—that's the Superintendent in charge of the case—and ask him if anything else has come through from here. In the meantime"—he smiled with real charm—"I'm very pleased to be able to talk to you. And if you'll just tell me anything you know about the girl . . ."

Miss Flecker nodded, and her gaze moved reflectively about the pleasant, untidy room, with its severely functional windows, its murmurous radiators, its book-case of manuscript musical scores. "Well, you won't want me to describe her," she said, "because you've got that photograph. It flatters her, of course, but it's a fair likeness. She was about—oh, nineteen, I imagine."

"Married, or engaged?"

"Neither."

"Any particular man?"

Miss Flecker smiled wryly. "Gossip ascribes her to Maurice Crane and Stuart North, but how much truth there is in it I don't know. Possibly none. I've seen her with both of them, but that means nothing."

"And to which of them does gossip ascribe her—um—hypothetical pregnancy?"

"As far as I know," said Miss Flecker decorously, "opinion is evenly divided. It's no use my pretending," she added with sudden candour, "that I don't listen to gossip, because I do. I pass it on, too—as you'll have noticed. But as to believing it, that's another matter. So I ought to warn you. . . . Oh, damn."

She broke off as the telephone rang again, and picked it up with a movement of irritation.

"Johnny, I thought I said I wasn't to be disturbed. . . . Oh. That's different. . . . Yes, you did quite right. Sorry." She held out the instrument to Humbleby. "It's for you."

"Hullo, Charles," said Humbleby. "What news?" And for a full minute he remained silent while the receiver, like a witch's familiar, muttered insinuatingly into his ear. "All right as far as it goes," he commented at last. "Have there been any further calls from here? None? . . . No"—he glanced at Miss Flecker—"apparently that was to be expected. . . . Yes, I'm enjoying myself very much, thank you. . . . Don't expect me till after lunch. If anything interesting develops I'll 'phone you. . . . No, not so far: we're only just getting down to it now. . . . Yes, all right. Good-bye."

He rang off. "Gossip was right in one respect, anyway," he said drily: "they've done the autopsy, and she was about three months on the way. . . . Poor silly child. Does that sort of thing happen very often in this profession?"

"No, it doesn't," said Judy. "In spite of popular superstition on the subject, we're a very respectable community, even if a rather simple-minded one. That's the reason, really, why there's been so much talk about Gloria Scott. . . . I suppose that now you'll be aiming to find out where Gloria and Stuart and Maurice were three months ago."

"Exactly. Christmas—which ought to make it a bit easier." Humbleby was tapping the end of his pencil meditatively against his thumb-nail. "From what you know of the girl, now, do you think this pregnancy could be a motive for her killing herself? Was she the sort of person to get hysterical over a thing like that?"

"M'm, that's awkward." Judy took a cigarette from the case which Fen offered her, and, murmuring thanks, lit it with a heavy table lighter. "You see, I didn't know her all that well: we had lunch together once or twice in the Club here, and that's about all. But from what I did see of her, I should say the answer to your question was No. She *was* emotionally unstable—or anyway, that was how she struck me—but not, I fancy, along quite those lines. . . . I'm afraid all this must sound very woolly and unsatisfactory, but you asked for my impression, and for what it's worth, that's it."

"But if the man concerned had refused to—to——"

"To make an honest woman of her? We-ell . . . She'd certainly have been *upset*, but I can't see her going so far as to kill herself."

Fen, who up to now had been unwontedly silent, said briefly and directly: "Why not?"

"Because—well, because she was one of those people whose emotional life is less important to them than—other things."

"Ah," said Fen, "this is more to the point. In her case, less important than what other things?"

"Well—than her career, say."

"She was very ambitious, then?"

"Oh, yes."

"Was she liked?"

"I'm afraid not."

"Why wasn't she liked?"

"She was conceited—aggressively conceited. A lot of people in this business are, but they mostly manage to conceal the fact. She didn't."

"And the faults we most dislike in others," Fen murmured, "are generally those we unwittingly display ourselves." He paused to consider this citation, and apparently found it, or his own gratuitous use of it, in some fashion distasteful. "But you yourself—did you like her?"

"Yes. I did." Miss Flecker made this admission with a certain reluctance. "She was very young"—Miss Flecker's twenty-six years were as she spoke mysteriously transmuted to an infinity of rich experience—"and very eager. Oddly defenceless, too, as single-minded people so often tend to be. Yes, I liked her. But there weren't many other people who did."

"With the exception, presumably"—Humbleby's intrusion on this nebulous duologue was clearly designed to restore a sense of realities—"of Mr. Crane and Mr. North." And he contemplated Fen with the satisfaction of a man who at one blow has expelled metaphysics with common sense. Fen, however, was unabashed.

"You miss the point, Humbleby," he said waspishly. "Sane people commit suicide only from motives which seem to them, rightly or wrongly, to be overwhelmingly important. And Miss Flecker, as a result of my own intelligent questioning, has indicated that in Gloria Scott's case those motives were probably bound up with her career."

"Which leads us," said Humbleby, not at all perturbed by this reproof, "to enquire what professional set-backs she has suffered just recently." And he looked enquiringly at Miss Flecker.

But she shook her head. "It's rather the reverse, I'm afraid. After she came here——"

"Wait, wait," said Humbleby, applying himself hurriedly to his notebook. "When *did* she come here?"

"About a year ago, I think. She was taken on as an extra, to start with."

"And where did she come *from*?"

"I've an idea she was in repertory, but which repertory I can't say."

"We ought to find that out easily enough. . . Sorry to interrupt. Go on."

"As I say, she was taken on as an extra. After that she got a cameo part in a film called—damn, what was it?" Judy flicked her fingers irritably. "Oh, I remember—*Visa for Heaven.*"

"A cameo part?"

"Yes, you know: the film equivalent of a bit part on the stage. Something just a little more important than merely walking on. And then the last thing I heard—though I wouldn't swear to its being true—is that Jocelyn Stafford signed her up for quite a good part in this Pope film."

Fen looked up. "Really? Do you know what part?"

"Martha Blount, she said."

"It's a role which gets more and more etiolated," said Fen cheerfully, "as one script conference follows another. But even so, not a bad chance for a girl who's virtually unknown. Have you any idea how she came by the job?"

"Yes, I rather fancy it was Maurice Crane's doing."

"We seem to be hearing a great deal about this fellow," Humbleby complained, "but I'm sorry to say that I for one haven't the remotest idea who or what he is. Do please explain."

"He's Madge Crane's youngest brother," said Judy, "the other two being Nicholas Crane, who's a director, and David Crane, who's something very minor in the Script Department. Maurice is a camera-man—and a very good one, which means that he's an influential person hereabouts."

"Do you suppose that his getting Gloria Scott this part would be an attempt at reparation for—um—coercing her into maternity?"

"It might be. If in fact he was responsible for that."

"There's another candidate, of course." And Humbleby sighed dejectedly. "Of the two men, which would be the more adversely affected by the publication of Miss Scott's —um—condition?"

"Stuart North, certainly. Camera-men, however good, aren't celebrities. Actors are." Judy replied so promptly that for a moment the tangential nature of the question did not strike her; when it did, she said inquisitively: "Why do you ask that?"

"It's possible," Humbleby answered with reserve, "that

someone may have made an attempt to conceal the motive for Gloria Scott's suicide."

"You mean torn up a suicide note, or something like that?"

"Something like that."

"Stuart North would certainly have more reason for doing that than Maurice Crane. On the other hand——" Judy's grey eyes widened suddenly. "Hell, what a fool I'm being! I've just remembered."

"Remembered what?"

"That Stuart North was in America during December and January, doing a short run of a Shaw play on Broadway. And Gloria was very definitely in England. So we've been maligning Stuart."

"You think, then, that Maurice Crane——"

"He or someone else."

"I suppose"—Humbleby scratched his nose ruefully—"that you can't think of anyone, Crane apart, who would be likely to *know*?"

"There's one possibility, yes—a girl called Valerie Bryant, who was Gloria's particular friend."

"Where can we find her?"

"I've an idea she's working on a film now—a musical comedy called *Gaiety Sue*."

"Lumme," said Humbleby; it was his affectation to relapse occasionally into the milder forms of plebeian slang. "Is she an actress, then?"

"A chorus girl."

"And it would be possible for me to meet her this morning, would it?"

"That depends on the shooting schedules. The film's on the floor all right, but they mayn't today be doing anything she's concerned in. I can find out for you."

"I wish you would."

Judy resorted to the telephone. "Johnny," she said,

"get me someone who's working on *Gaiety Sue*, will you? . . . Yes, Weinberg will probably do." There was a pause; with her hand over the microphone, "Weinberg is the jazz end of this department," Judy explained. "He's—— Oh, hello, Sam. I want to know what they're doing with *Sue* today. Is the chorus here? . . . It is? Good. What stage are they working on? . . . Five? Right. Thanks very much. Bye-bye."

She returned the instrument to its cradle. "All's well," she said. "Johnny'll take you across as soon as you want to go, and rout out the Bryant girl for you. I warn you, she's pretty dumb. . . . Well. Is there anything else?"

"Let's see where we've arrived." Ceremoniously Humbleby consulted his notebook. "Gloria Scott had been given this part in the Pope film. . . . Now, how long ago did that happen?"

"Not more than a fortnight ago," said Judy definitely. "Perhaps less."

"And she was pleased?"

"Lord, yes—on top of the world. A few days back I met her by chance on the way here, and she told me about it then. It had quite gone to her head, silly infant, and she was so exasperatingly vain about it I could have spanked her."

"You get the impression that it was genuinely a *fait accompli*? That"—Humbleby gestured vaguely—"that things had been signed?"

"Oh, certainly."

"She couldn't have been making it all up? Have been—um—anticipating the event?"

Judy shook her head. "She *could* have been—she was quite capable of counting her chickens before they were hatched—but in this case I'm almost sure she wasn't. The thing to do would be to go to the Legal Department and look for the contract."

"I'll do that, yes." Humbleby made a note. "Because if that contract *does* exist, it makes her suicide somewhat unaccountable."

"Exactly what I was thinking," said Judy. She got up and began to pace restlessly about the room. "From what I know of her, I shouldn't have imagined that *any* motive, however overwhelming, would have been sufficient to offset that contract."

"Though, of course"—and here Humbleby shifted uneasily in his chair—"there is the point that if this film were not to be put—um—on the floor for some time to come, the advance of her pregnancy might make it impossible for her to act in it."

"I haven't the least doubt," said Judy briefly, "that she intended to get rid of the child before it was born. Such things are done. And she wouldn't have been so cock-a-hoop about the part if she hadn't envisaged a way out of that difficulty."

"Um. Ah," said Humbleby, embarrassed. "Just so. Well, you've been very helpful, Miss Flecker. And from now on we must stand on our own feet." He got up and did this, presumably by way of illustration. "I think, perhaps, that——"

"Just one other thing," said Judy hesitantly. "How—how did it happen?"

Humbleby told her—while she stood with puckered brows, like one who swallows a disagreeable medicine, and the whining of a mechanical saw in the carpenters' shop provided a cheerlessly impersonal *obbligato* to the narrative. When it was over she nodded.

"That's very much the way I should have expected Gloria to do it, if she was going to do it at all. No premeditation—just a sudden appreciation of the means, and a sudden uncontrollable impulse. That's very like her.

And it's very like her, too"—Judy moved her shoulders as if to mitigate an access of *grue*—"to regret it the instant it was done. Her way of living was to do rash things and then regret them the instant they were done. . . ." Judy's voice dropped suddenly. "Oh, *Lord*," she said, and steadied herself against the desk.

For a moment they were all silent. Then the door opened and a middle-aged man, completely bald, looked in at them. With an effort Judy pulled herself together. "Hallo, Frank," she said.

"Hello, Judy. L.S.O. here?"

"Yes."

"Ireland here?"

"Not yet."

"What stage are we on?"

"Two."

"Ah." The man nodded and vanished; after a very brief interval he reappeared, said "Good morning" briskly to Humbleby and Fen, and vanished a second time before they had a chance to reply.

Judy called Johnny in. "Johnny, will you take these two gentlemen to Stage Five and find them a girl called Valerie Bryant? She's in the chorus."

"Oke," said Johnny inelegantly. "I know her. Leggy girl, dumb."

"And on the way," said Humbleby, "we'd better look in at your Legal Department."

"Can do," said Johnny.

Miss Flecker shook hands with Humbleby and Fen. And Fen, whose attentiveness had latterly alternated with an absence of mind which made him appear slightly half-witted, said: "Just one other thing. What was the attitude of the Crane family to Gloria Scott?"

"The Crane family?" Judy was a good deal surprised.

"Well, as to David, I don't think she knew him, or he her. Maurice I've told you about. I've no notion what Nicholas thought of her. And Madge—well, that's easy: she disliked Gloria very much."

"Why?"

"Because of Stuart North."

"Oh? Oh?" Fen raised his eyebrows. "A rivalry?"

"Madge is promiscuous, but she has her preferences, and Stuart North is the current one. Unfortunately his preference seemed to be for Gloria."

"And did Miss Crane relish the prospect of working with Gloria in *The Unfortunate Lady*, do you think?"

"That's a point," said Judy, interested. "I should imagine she was furious. In fact . . ."

"In fact what?"

"Oh, nothing. . . . But it might be worth your while to enquire just what Madge's reactions were."

"Yes," said Fen. "We'll do that, I expect." He moved towards the door. "Thanks very much, Miss Flecker. We'll leave you in peace now."

"Come and see me any time you feel inclined."

Fen smiled. "That would be too often to be convenient. But I'll let you know what, if anything, we find out."

"And, by the way," said Humbleby, "keep all this to yourself for the time being, will you?"

"Of course."

"Many thanks, then. And good-bye for the present."

5

It is only in idleness, Fen reflected as he was led away from the relatively humane atmosphere of the Music Department, that men are capable of impressing their personality on their dwelling-places; purposeful activity depersonalises even the best of buildings absolutely, making it seem as negative and meaningless as an empty egg-shell. And the studios were not, certainly, among the best of buildings. They represented, with all the detailed appositeness of a text-book illustration, that point at which the pursuit of the purely functional over-reaches itself and becomes absurd. Even in its primary intention of promoting efficiency, architecture like this was bound to fail, since the psychological effect of these blank, indistinguishable corridors, these vistas of fire-buckets, these monotonously unadorned stone staircases and metal balusters, must to the community moving among them be enervating and discouraging in the extreme. The persons to be encountered did not, it is true, seem visibly afflicted by their ghastly surroundings; but acquiescence in ugliness is even more devastating, spiritually, than the impotent enduring of it, and in an industry which was concerned with making pretty visual patterns, and in which the finer flowers of the imagination blossomed so sparsely, it was a pity that to the uncertain cultural level of its moving spirits should be superadded the additional disadvantage of a grotesquely depressing *mise-en-scène*. . . .

It became clear, as time went on, that the Legal Department was quite a considerable distance away. Led by Johnny—who, perhaps by way of encouragement, unintermittently whistled a personal redaction of *La Donna e Mobile*—Fen and Humbleby negotiated a long recession of halls and passages which in the upshot brought them, quite implausibly, to French windows giving on to a small, sinister, overgrown courtyard, tentatively Arabic in style and with a patently unworkable fountain at its centre; with its pitted walls it looked, Fen thought, like a place of execution left over from the Spanish Civil War. At its far side a flight of steps impelled them underground, and they traversed a short, dimly lit tunnel which inexplicably debouched, through a rickety wooden door, on to the roof of a box-like single-storey building; and from this, having achieved ground level by means of a spiral staircase, they emerged, disconcertingly enough, in front of a genuine greystone Victorian villa nestling amid laurestinus and rhododendrons. By this kaleidoscopic sequence of incongruities Humbleby was provoked to a muffled imprecation; and Johnny, who clearly took pride in the studios and who equally clearly interpreted this noise as a deprecatory comment on the relic confronting them, desisted from whistling for long enough to explain apologetically that the villa was already there when the studios were built and that in consequence it had been permitted to remain—on sufferance, like a sort of Red Indian Reservation—amid the modernistic splendours put up by the Leiper organisation.

"And it's only the Legal Department that uses it," he added—much, Fen thought, as a man might justify his possession of a cheap cotton handkerchief by saying that he kept it only to blow his nose on. "There's the door."

With this unnecessary information—apparently he feared that left to their own devices Fen and Humbleby would never succeed in making an entry—he beckoned them forward and into the presence, inside the villa, of another youth, with a pencil behind his ear, who greeted them mistrustfully and on learning Humbleby's identity retired, with enhanced suspicion, to consult with some person of more consequence than himself. Presently he returned—faintly complacent, like one who has contrived in the face of great odds to introduce a mountain into the presence of a prophet—with an exhausted-looking, grey-haired man; and with this individual Humbleby went into conference on the subject of Gloria Scott's contract for *The Unfortunate Lady*, learning that it did, in fact, exist, that it had been signed nine days previously, and that the remuneration and conditions were normal for that type of agreement.

"Responsibility for assigning the part?" the grey-haired man said in answer to a question. "Oh, that rests with the producer, though of course there are other people he consults about it."

"Ah," said Humbleby. "I think that's all I want to know, then. Thank you very much."

They retrieved Johnny, who by now had exchanged *La Donna e Mobile* for *O Star of Eve*, and set off in search of Valerie Bryant. The box-like building, the underground tunnel and the Arabic courtyard marked the stages of their return to the main body of the studios, but thereafter they struck out into hitherto unexplored territory, and it was only after a lengthy and bewildering journey that they came at last to the barn-like vastness of Stage Five. The end at which they entered it was in virtual darkness (there were, of course, no windows), but in the middle distance a moderate degree of activity was discernible, and across the tangle of ropes and cables on the floor they plodded cautiously towards this. The façade of a London public-house—of the rococo type distinguished by Mr. Osbert Lancaster as Public-house Classic—met their gaze; opposite it, on a frame covered with black cloth, the rudiments of shops were sketched in white chalk; in front of it was a pavement; inside it, and partly visible through the painted-glass windows, a number of extras in Victorian costume stood about waiting for something to happen. On the pavement were two young women in bustles and bonnets. A camera confronted them, with a microphone suspended above it on a boom like a carrot in front of a donkey, and a man in shirt-sleeves was measuring with a tape-measure the distance between its lens and their noses. Periodically other men would climb on to the camera, peer through its view-finder, and go silently away again. Overhead, on platforms hanging by chains from the high and invisible roof, electricians pottered with numbered spotlights, while on the floor their overseer, an irascible man with a cigarette adhering precariously to his lower lip, shouted at them: "Kill ten and twenty-three, Bert," or "You can save your number nine, Bill," or, more simply: "What the bloody hell do you think you're up to now?" The continuity girl clattered assiduously away at a typewriter; the director, a gentlemanly person of some thirty years, sat slumped in a canvas chair fingering a tattered script and gloomily contemplating the scene; a wind-machine, painted a minatory pillar-box red, crouched in the offing like some gigantic insect; and all about, people drifted aimlessly to and fro, muttered together in corners, or merely stood gaping. Scattered among them were a few scantily clad girls, and Johnny, having briefly interviewed one of these, returned to inform Fen and Humbleby that they were in luck, since the film was behind schedule and the chorus, dutifully present and changed, would not be required for an hour or two.

"Hang on," he said, "and I'll find the Bryant girl for you."

They hung on obediently, and after about two minutes of this the director, tiring abruptly of preparatory measures, called for a take. At once all was agitation: lights flashed on and off, technicians ran hither and thither, the camera crew coalesced round its machine, fresh powder was dabbed on the already thickly coated faces of the two young women on the pavement, the continuity girl gave over typing and rushed with a notebook to the director's side, and Fen, who had wandered round behind the pub's façade and was waving at Humbleby from a window, was unceremoniously removed to a safe place. A hush fell.

"Yes," said the director, wearily surveying the results of all this. "Yes, O.K."

"Absolute quiet, please," called someone.

"Roll it," said someone else, and a clapper-boy self-consciously clapped his instrument together in front of the lens.

"Background action," said the director, and the extras inside the pub swayed about in tipsy animation.

"Action," he said, and the two young women came along the pavement and halted at the pub door, where one of them, nudging the other, said: " 'Ow about a quick one, Gert?"

"Cut," said the director.

The tension dissolved. "That's fine," the director said. "Very, very good indeed. Miss Morris, I think I'd like a fraction longer pause before you give us your line, just a fraction. All right, everybody. We'll do another take straight away."

Fen, prowling restlessly, had come to the wind-machine, and was regarding it with dawning interest. He had already stretched out a hand to it when fortunately he was distracted by the return of Johnny, who was propelling in front of him, with a finger in the small of her back, a tall, dazed-looking blonde. She wore black, high-heeled shoes, black stockings with garters and a black-and-white frilly corset affair which permitted—not to say encouraged—an ample display of bosom and thigh. Her face, made up, was like a mask; her liberal expanse of bare flesh was painted a golden brown; and the total effect was peculiarly anaphrodisiac. Before this pseudo-ninetyish apparition Fen and Humbleby somewhat abruptly converged.

"Ah, Miss Bryant," said Humbleby cordially. "I'm glad they were able to find you. If you can spare a few minutes I should like to have a talk with you."

Miss Byrant put out her tongue at him. It was plain to everyone that she had extruded it in order to lick her lips and at the last moment had recollected their lacquered and unlickable condition, but the effect was none the less discomposing; and particularly, it seemed, to the girl herself, for tears started into her eyes and she began to tremble at the knees. Humbleby, unused to such adverse reactions to his mild and reassuring presence, said: "Come, come, Miss Byrant, there's nothing to be afraid of." Fen said: "My name is Gervase Fen." And Johnny, smacking her heartily on her lightly clad bottom, said: "Don't be so daft, girl." Of these various prophylactics it was the last which proved most efficacious. Miss Bryant seemed, indeed, to be almost cheered by it—perhaps because it belonged to an order of things with which she was more or less at home. She rubbed herself unselfconsciously and in a timorous little Cockney voice said: "I'm all right, thank you, sir."

"Good, good," said Humbleby expansively. Diffident, sensitive chorus-girls were obviously outside his experience, and he appeared to be at a loss what to say next. This problem, however, was solved for him by the cry of "*Absolute* quiet, please" which heralded the second take, and since it was evident that if they wanted to talk they must go elsewhere, he signalled to the others to follow him and tip-toed towards the door. Once outside, he demanded to be shown to a vacant room; and Johnny, after one false attempt which tactlessly disrupted the embraces of a canteen waitress and a sound engineer, soon found one for him—a square, under-furnished, unimaginative place whose windows, commanding a part of the estate, displayed a group of workmen with wheelbarrows lethargically digging a small hole in the ground.

"Anything else?" Johnny asked. "Because if there isn't

I ought to be getting back. . . . Mind you behave yourself, Miss Sex Appeal," he said to Valerie Bryant, "or they'll put you in the lock-up. I'll say cheerio, then. John Wilberforce Mornington signing off, at your service now as always." With this, mercifully, he went. And Humbleby, clearing his throat in an embarrassed fashion, said: "Do please sit down, Miss Bryant."

Miss Bryant sat down—with extreme caution, on the edge of a chair—and gazed upon them out of wide, pathetic eyes. "I 'as to be careful," she ventured, "not to get the make-up rubbed on me legs and arms."

"Yes," said Humbleby. "Yes, I'm sure you do."

Miss Bryant evidently did not find this ready acquiescence at all consoling, for she began to tremble again, though less violently than before. "I—is it true, sir," she stammered, "that you're from the p'lice?"

"Yes, it's true enough," said Humbleby, "but you've absolutely no cause to be alarmed, Miss Bryant. All I want is to ask you a few questions about Gloria Scott."

"Gloria?" Miss Bryant was startled. "She ain't in no trouble, sir, is she?"

Humbleby shook his head soberly. "I'm sorry to have to tell you, Miss Bryant, that she has—um—committed suicide."

Miss Bryant sat very still. After a moment two large tears ran down her cheeks, leaving shining tracks in the powder. Both Fen and Humbleby were afraid she was going to break down, but the impact of Humbleby's intelligence had numbed her, and she made no movement except to brush the tears away with the back of her hand. Presently she whispered:

"Gloria always said she would."

"Would kill herself?"

Miss Bryant nodded slowly. "An' I didn't believe 'er,

'cos they say it's never the ones 'oo talk about it as actually does it." Then she sat up abruptly as something occurred to her. "But she couldn't 'a' done, sir! Not after she got 'erself that big part in the 'istorical film. She was that pleased about it you wouldn't believe, and——"

"Yes," Humbleby interposed. "We've heard about that, Miss Bryant, and that's why we're trying to discover some other reason—some reason sufficiently compelling to outweigh the contract for *The Unfortunate Lady*—why Miss Scott should have—um—made away with herself. Perhaps you can help us to do so."

But with a surprising firmness Miss Bryant indicated dissent.

"She wouldn't 'a' done it, sir," she said. "I swear she wouldn't, I swear it!" And they glimpsed something like hysteria welling up towards the surface. "She was made away with, that's what must 'ave 'appened." Her voice rose sharply. "Some filthy devil——"

"Rubbish, girl," said Fen brusquely. "There were witnesses to the whole affair, and there's not the slightest possibility that she was murdered. Put that out of your mind once and for all, and talk sensibly."

Then, seeing that the headlong gallop towards a nervestorm was for the time being arrested, he added more gently: "It's distressing and horrible, I know, but there's nothing you or any of us can do about it." And half to himself he murmured: "We owe God a death."

The girl looked up at him. "That's a funny way of putting it." Like others on other occasions, she was discovering that Fen, simply as a presence and a personality, was strangely reassuring to be with. He smiled at her, inspiritingly and without sentimentality, and said: "Rather a good way, don't you think?"

Humbleby, meanwhile, had produced his notebook.

"Don't worry about this," he said. "I'm only going to take notes because I'm naturally forgetful." And at this solemn assurance the mercurial spirits of youth healthily obliterated immediate grief, and Miss Bryant giggled.

" 'S all right," she said, for the first time tolerably self-confident. "I know they say as 'ow I'm not much better than the Dumb Blonde in the *Pic.*, but you don't 'ave to treat me as if I was *mental.*" And she giggled again.

"No, of course not." Humbleby was much relieved at having the interview thus transferred to a less emotional level. "Let's start at the beginning, then." He poised his pencil. "Your name's Valerie Bryant."

"Valerie Rose Bryant. Only Rose is a *common* name, I always say, so it's not everyone I tells it to." And with this naïve access of coquetry Miss Bryant wriggled her bosom to a more comfortable position in the precarious grasp of her garment. "Ma always says——"

Maternal *obiter dicta*, however, were not what Humbleby wanted, and he cut them short by saying: "And your age?"

"Seventeen, sir."

"Seventeen?" Humbleby echoed weakly; this tall, beautifully poised girl looked at least twenty-five. "Seventeen, did you say?"

"Yes, sir, seventeen."

"Oh. Ah. Right you are, then. And how long have you known Gloria Scott?"

Miss Bryant wrinkled her pencilled brows and did a sum on her fingers. "Nearly a year now, sir. She was an extra at first, and we got chatting in the canteen one lunch-time."

"And you got to be close friends?"

Once more a tear trickled destructively down Miss Bryant's brownish-gold cheek. "She was lovely, sir," she said—and her tone of voice conveyed so simple and uncritical an act of homage that Fen was almost startled.

"And wonderfully clever, reelly she was. She was a reel actress—not just chorus like me, but a reel actress. I used to wonder what she saw in me, reelly I did."

And given that encomium, Fen thought, it was not difficult to envisage what the relationship between the two girls had been: on the one hand Gloria Scott, idolised and very much liking it, on the other this simple-minded child, as helplessly enslaved by high-falutin talk as was Desdemona by the narrated campaignings of Othello. The picture thus conjured up was, it occurred to Fen, a rather displeasing one, and the vague sympathy for Gloria Scott which Judy Flecker had implanted in him abated as he contemplated it.

Some reflection of a similar sort had apparently struck Humbleby, too, for he frowned slightly before going on to say: "And 'Gloria Scott' wasn't, I understand, her real name."

"No, sir, it wasn't. She used to say 'er family was very well known and so she changed 'er name so as people wouldn't be influenced in giving 'er jobs by knowing 'oo she was."

Yes, Fen thought, that's exactly what she would say; as a clue it was valueless. And a curiosity as to the extent to which the girl confronting him had been in thrall to Gloria Scott impelled him to ask:

"And was that true, do you think?"

"I don't know, sir." Beneath her make-up Miss Bryant flushed, made wretched by her own disloyalty. "I wondered sometimes if p'r'aps she changed it just 'cos 'er own name wasn't pretty enough for an actress."

"Her own name being?"

Miss Bryant shook her head dumbly.

"You don't know what it was?"

"No, sir."

Humbleby sighed. "Did she ever talk to you about any relatives? Or to your knowledge meet any relatives?"

"No, sir, I never 'eard about anything like that. She seemed"—Miss Bryant's voice trembled—"she seemed awfully alone, like, without anyone to turn to. She said once as 'ow 'er family wouldn't approve if they knew she was in the films, so she wasn't going to tell them till she'd made a name for 'erself."

"Then you got the impression that she'd run away from home?"

"Yes, sir, that's about it. Though she was always frightfully mysterious whenever I asked 'er outright, like."

"Being mysterious," said Fen with deliberation, "is an easy way to make an impression, isn't it?"

She was quick to grasp the intention of the remark.

"I know I was a fool about 'er, sir," she said humbly. "Only no one like that 'ad ever wanted to be friends with me before and—and now she's dead—and——"

"And no longer needs an admiring audience," said Fen. "You deserve a certain amount of admiration yourself, you know. Did she ever give it you?"

She stared at him wonderingly. "Me, sir?"

"You're a modest and good-hearted young woman with a very pretty face and a figure in a million."

Miss Bryant surveyed herself doubtfully.

"I know I got good legs," she admitted, "but—but—I don't see——"

"Don't you?" Fen smiled at her, inwardly reflecting that the advancing years were evoking in him emotions of a discouragingly paternal and moralising sort. "If you think about it you will. It sounds to me as if what you had was a tyrant, not a friend. Isn't that so?"

And to his relief—for he was well aware that amateur

therapies of the kind in which he had been indulging were perilously double-edged—she slowly nodded.

"Yes, sir, I s'pose you could say it was a bit like that. Still, I got to stick by 'er, 'aven't I?"

"Yes," said Fen gravely, "you must do that."

Though mildly amused by, and not unsympathetic to, this elementary display of spiritual healing, Humbleby was beginning to feel that the time had come to get back to business. He said:

"And that being settled, there are one or two other things you can tell us. For instance, did Miss Scott have any particular friends apart from yourself?"

"Not that I know of, sir. Girl-friends, that's to say. As to men——" She hesitated.

"Yes, I was going to ask you about that. Go on."

"Well, she was very beautiful, sir," said Miss Bryant rather desperately after a fractional pause, "so you'd expect 'er—well, to run around a bit, wouldn't you?"

"She was going to have a baby."

"Yes, sir," said Miss Bryant in a very small voice. "She did tell me that. . . . Almost"—her eyes were the eyes of a hurt child—"almost proud of it, she seemed." She glanced at Fen, who nodded.

"Very cool and worldly about it, I expect," he commented. "And were you impressed?"

"No, sir, I wasn't. I—I thought it was awful." Again tormented by the sense of her disloyalty, Valerie Bryant lowered her mascara-coated eyelashes; but when she looked up again it was to repeat, more loudly and clearly than before:

"I thought it was beastly."

"And I didn't put it in quite the right words, did I?" said Humbleby. "She wasn't going to *have* the baby. She was going to get rid of it before it was born."

"Yes, sir." And now, as if some perplexing issue were at last resolved, Valerie Bryant's manner was resolute. "She was going to 'ave an abortion. She wouldn't 'a' bin able to take that part in the 'istorical picture else."

"Quite so. Who was the father?"

"She didn't tell me that, sir. Just 'inted it was someone important." Again the glance towards Fen, signalling disenchantment and the willingness to face it squarely; in response to it he sympathetically smiled. "But of course I 'ad me suspicions."

"Of whom?"

She looked apprehensively about her, and Humbleby, interpreting the movement, said:

"Don't worry. What you say won't go any farther."

"Well, sir, in that case. . . . I thought it must 'a' bin either Mr. North—that's Stuart North, the star—or Mr. Maurice Crane."

"Yes, that fits in with what we know already. Where was Gloria Scott last Christmas?"

"Was that when it 'appened, sir? She was staying with the Cranes, so I s'pose——"

"Yes. Anyway, we'll look into it. Miss Scott didn't, I suppose, give you the impression that she was likely to get married?"

"Because of the baby, sir?"

"Not necessarily. Anytime—for any reason—to anyone."

"Well, she did use to just 'int now and again that there was someone as was really seriously interested in 'er, but that may 'a' bin only talk. I don't know, I'm sure, sir."

"Can you think of *any* reason why she should have killed herself?"

Valerie Bryant reflected long and earnestly. "No, sir," she said at last. "I can't—honestly I can't."

"When did you see her last?"

"It was the day before yesterday, sir. She dropped in to 'ave lunch at the canteen."

"And did she seem quite normal?"

"Oh, yes, sir. Very cheerful she was. Though I . . ."

"Yes?"

"I—I got the notion she wouldn't be wanting to see so much of me in the future." Valerie moved her golden-brown shoulders unhappily. "Of course, she 'ad 'er way to make, so it wasn't surprising, not reelly."

"In my official capacity," said Humbleby dispassionately, "I'm not supposed to make comments. But I don't mind telling you that this girl sounds to me like a bitch of the first water. . . . Did she say what she expected to be doing that evening?"

"Yes, sir, she did."

"Ah." Humbleby abandoned contumely and became business-like. "What, then?"

"She'd been invited to a party, sir. At Mr. Nicholas Crane's flat."

"Now we're getting somewhere." In the intensity of his satisfaction Humbleby positively snorted. "And after that you didn't see her again?"

"No, sir."

"Right." Humbleby snapped his notebook shut and imprisoned it in a large rubber band. "Oh—just a couple more questions. Where did Gloria Scott live?"

"In Kensington, sir. Number 22, Renfrew Gardens. . . . Oh, but"—Valerie remembered something—"she was going to move, I don't know where to. . . ."

"That's all right; we do. And the other question is this: Where was she, and what was she doing, before she started to work here a year ago?"

"Oh, that's easy, sir. She was acting in a repertory theatre at Menenford."

"Good." Humbleby stood up. "Then that's all, I think. For the time being, don't say anything to anybody about this, please."

Valerie, too, got to her feet. "No, sir, I won't. I—I—— Could you please tell me 'ow it 'appened, sir?"

"Certainly," said Humbleby, and briefly complied. She listened apathetically—too dazed, perhaps, by the central fact to assimilate much of the detail.

"And the funeral, sir?" she asked when he had finished. "I should like to go to that."

"It depends on what we're able to find out about her family," Humbleby explained. "But one way or another I'll try to let you know when it's to be. . . . And now we must go, and you must get back to your work."

She moved to the door, which Fen opened for her. The business man's dream, he reflected: it was not difficult to predict, in general outline, what would become of her. . . . She paused for a second and smiled diffidently at him; then, quickening her steps, went away down the passage, her shoulders trembling a little as she wept. . . . So one person, at least, unfeignedly mourned for Gloria Scott.

6

Fen and Humbleby stood irresolute as they watched her go.

"You ought to set up as a psychiatrist," said Humbleby sardonically. "*Spécialité de la maison*, the sublimating of unhealthy adolescent crushes. You seem to be a great deal more serious than I remembered."

Fen's brown hair, ineffectually plastered down with water, stood up in disaffected spikes at the crown of his head; his lean, ruddy, clean-shaven face was thoughtful.

"As I get older," he explained, "I get less resilient and more predictable. It depresses me sometimes." He sighed and looked at his watch. "Five to eleven. I must find my conference. What are your plans?"

"Maurice and Nicholas Crane are my plans."

"I shall be seeing them, you know: they're both involved in this film. Come along with me."

"Thanks, but I must telephone Charles first, and in any case I can't very well disrupt your conference with my—um—inquisitions. How long will it last?"

"Heaven knows. Not very long, I imagine, since Leiper isn't going to be there."

"Well, will you tell Maurice and Nicholas that I want to see them as soon as it's over?"

Fen looked dubious. "I'll tell them," he said. "I'll *tell* them all right. But people of that sort haven't the instinct of obedience, even where the police are concerned, and they'll probably drift away pretending to have forgotten about it. You'd better come yourself and try to put the fear of God into them."

"But surely they'd not be so irresponsible as to——"

"The films are a religion," Fen interrupted. "Even Government departments—Petroleum Boards, Tax Inspectors and so forth—kow-tow to them to some extent. And that fact induces in the more important film people a sense of immunity—not altogether an illusory sense, either. If you want to talk to the brothers Crane you ought to tackle them about it in person."

To this proposition Humbleby, after some further argument, agreed, and they set off for room CC, discovering it, somewhat to their surprise, only a short distance away. Though larger, it bore a disheartening resemblance to the room they had just left. Its parquet flooring was coming apart, with the result that there were treacherous projecting edges on which people tripped. The green paint was peeling from its radiators. Someone—possibly reacting after the manner of Martin Luther to an apparition of the Devil—had apparently hurled a bottle of ink at the wall. A table at the centre was provisioned, as for a board meeting, with ash-trays, scribbling paper and ink-pots, and had chairs of padded red leather and chromium tubing set about it. There were, however, two more or less humane influences present—one of them a framed photograph of the 1937 Studio Hockey Team, and the other a trolley with rubber wheels which contained cups of steaming coffee.

To this Fen addressed himself immediately on arrival—having previously, however, identified for Humbleby the brothers Crane. No official proceedings, he noted, had as yet begun. The company stood about sipping coffee and talking desultorily—a various assembly representing, as Fen knew, the personal enthusiasms, in a number of different spheres, of Giles Leiper. For the most part they were not people who in the ordinary way would have elected to work together, but in the present instance circumstances had been altogether too strong for them, and they had achieved a compromise solution of their social problem by coagulating into uneasy cliques. The atmosphere was not improved by the fact that at least half of them could be of no possible service on such an occasion as this, and were there only because Giles Leiper, who conceived films to be Corporate Works of Art, had insisted that all of the artists chiefly concerned should contribute to the planning of this one. Leiper was not—as Stuart North had prognosticated—himself present, but his influence impended over the gathering like a malediction in a fairy-tale, and an aura of gloom inevitably resulted. . . . But perhaps (Fen told himself) the mood of this particular conference—its mistrustful mutterings and its air of obscure apprehension—had some more potent and immediate cause than the whims of Leiper; persons eminent in the film industry do not, in pursuing their avocations, commonly exhibit any very marked symptoms of gaiety—but at the moment the sullenness of such of them as were present seemed extreme, and it was reasonable to suppose that there lay behind it some undivulged issue of a gravity sufficient to enhance even a melancholy so pervasive as that engendered by *The Unfortunate Lady*: the death, perhaps, of Gloria Scott. . . . Out of the corner of his eye Fen watched Maurice and Nicholas Crane while Humbleby spoke to them, and received the impression that both of them were discomposed by his request for an interview—and more specially (which was odd) Nicholas. . . .

His furtive scrutiny was interrupted by Gresson, a diminutive, futile Cambridge don whose task it was to advise on the history and sociological background of Pope's period. In an access of nervousness Gresson had failed, at the first script conference, to be able to recollect the date of Queen Anne's death, and this had so lowered him in the general esteem that he had scarcely been consulted since. He was not, however, much cast down by this unlucky circumstance, since his motive in accepting the post of historical adviser had been less a desire to ensure the accuracy of the film under consideration than a dream of fair women. Like Humbleby—though in Gresson's case to a degree so extreme as to border on actual hallucination—he conceived the studios to be a sort of stalking-ground or game reservation for the male devotees of the pandemic Venus, where young and beautiful girls, intent upon fame and fortune, were to be found in immense numbers lining up for the purpose of surrendering their bodies to whomever of the opposite sex they supposed capable of obtaining a screen test for them. With any man less immitigably ensnared by lubricious fancies than

Gresson, this preposterous notion would not have stood the test of observation for a single day. He, however, clung to it even yet, and it was in a satyr-like tone of voice that he said to Fen, after the conventional greetings had been perfunctorily accomplished:

"Those girls—they're wearing engagement rings."

Fen was aware of Gresson's delusion and could not summon up much interest in it. He followed his gaze to where two indistinguishable blonde secretaries, belonging to Jocelyn Stafford and to Nicholas Crane, sat murmuring together, their notebooks balanced on their thighs, while they waited for the conference to begin.

"Yes," he agreed. "So they are."

"Now, do you think," Gresson pursued, "that they really *are* engaged? Or do they just wear the rings as—as a protection?"

"The rings are nothing but camouflage," Fen replied firmly. He disliked Gresson and had just remembered that the *fiancé* of one of the girls was a heavyweight boxing champion. "As far as that's concerned, I should say that either of them was yours for the taking. And in particular, perhaps, the one on the left."

Gresson laughed nervously; he was not altogether pleased at having the impulses which underlay his question thus ruthlessly illuminated.

"Oh, come," he said, "I wasn't thinking of anything like *that*. I was just curious, that's all. . . . I suppose," he went on casually, "that a girl like that would be very keen to break into films, wouldn't she? I mean, a lot of them take these secretarial jobs just for the sake of a foothold in the studios, don't they?"

"You've only got to talk to them to find out how keen they are," said Fen with malice. "I believe some of them would willingly murder their own mothers for the sake of a test."

"Ah. You really think so?"

"There's not a doubt about it."

Gresson drew a deep, contented breath. "Well, well," he said. "Human nature's a queer thing, isn't it?"

"Very queer."

"I think"—Gresson put a finger judicially to his lip—"I think I'll just go and ask them about trains back to London. That's the sort of thing they'd know, I expect."

"Be careful," said Fen waggishly, "that you don't get yourself seduced."

"Aha!" At this delightful suggestion Gresson's *idée fixe* came leaping uncontrollably to the surface, like a salmon in a weir. "Seduced! Well, it mightn't be so very unpleasant, at that. Which of them would you say had the better legs, now?" The penultimate word emerged as a libidinous gurgle. "Which would you say——"

"The one on the left," Fen answered rather shortly; being volatile in temperament, he was by now tired both of the topic and of Gresson. "You have a good look at their legs while you ask them about the trains, and then come back and tell me if you agree."

"Unmannerly," said Gresson. "I'm afraid that might be unmannerly." His nervousness was reasserting itself, and since it was clear that he would never, however complaisant the girl to whom he addressed himself, get in practice even to first base, Fen abandoned him, immured to all eternity in the priapean imaginings of his own mind, and went to intercept Humbleby, who had disengaged himself from the Cranes and was making his way towards the door.

"All settled," said Humbleby in an undertone. "They're meeting me in what they call the Club here, at midday or shortly after."

"Did you tell them what it was about?"

"Yes. Will you be coming along?"

"Since I have no official standing," said Fen, "they may not want me there. But I may as well make the attempt; and if I'm shooed off I can arrange to meet you for lunch. You don't mind my hanging about?"

"My dear fellow!"

"I'll see you later, then."

In the doorway Humbleby almost collided with Madge Crane. He stood aside to let her pass, and she thanked him brightly and unaffectedly. Her lack of affectation had been much publicised in the newspapers, and when strangers were about she lived up to it very resolutely. Fen had just time to note that as a consequence of his exchange with Humbleby the brothers Crane were eyeing him warily before Jocelyn Stafford, the producer, raised his voice to suggest that the conference should begin. Abandoning coffee-cups, it settled itself obediently at the table.

Fen found himself between Gresson on the one hand and Aubrey Medesco on the other. Medesco, an elderly man of formidable height and displacement, was the scenic designer, and like everyone else there he had a particular grudge against *The Unfortunate Lady* and everything to do with it. On hearing that he was to be employed on a film about Pope he had not unnaturally jumped to the conclusion that the villa at Twickenham, with its grotto, would be amply represented in it, and to the successful accomplishing of this *mise-en-scène* he had devoted, prior to the first script conference, a great deal of careful thought. Unluckily, however, the date chosen for the film's occurrences had been 1716, when Pope was still living at Binfield; and the discovery that Twickenham did not, therefore, come into the picture at all had so soured Medesco that even in the face of Leiper his co-operation had thenceforth been non-existent. Now, as on previous occasions, he was sitting with an air of massive disapproval, rapidly though with delicacy conveying the fragments of a two-ounce bar of milk chocolate from the table in front of him to his mouth. And the only person who had so far been able to elicit any cordiality from him was Fenn, whose capacity for unobtrusive slumber had early on awoken in him a connoisseur's interest and devotion.

With grace and efficiency the indistinguishable blondes went about placing a copy of the revised script in front of each person present—a massive typewritten affair, this, neatly bound in green pasteboard and red ribbon. Some at once rummaged in it with an appearance of curiosity and good will, while others, Fen and Medesco among them, ignored it. The blondes thereupon settled down with pencils and notebooks at the ready, and under the chairmanship of Jocelyn Stafford the conference went cumbrously into action.

Stafford was a well-covered man of middle age, with diminishing brown hair and slightly protruding eyes. Fingering the revised script, he paid it a number of very civil compliments. And to these its author, on his right, somewhat wanly responded. The wanness, Fen thought, was on the whole to be expected. Evan George, a successful popular novelist who had made his name with a succession of those solid, comfortable books about ordinary-people-like-you-and-me to which the female middle classes are so unswervingly loyal, had reacted to his first film job (thrust upon him by Leiper) very much as was to be expected: first with a tempered enthusiasm and confidence; then—since in spite of the lavish praise accorded to his initial draft of the script a great deal of it apparently needed to be altered—with misgiving; and finally, as he surveyed the poor flinders which were all that remained of his original cherished conception, with despair. He was a small, wiry man of some fifty years, with a creased brown face, clothes which looked as if he had contracted the habit of sleeping in them, and a tendency to dyspepsia which he tried to alleviate by the frequent swallowing of magnesium trisilicate in capsules. At his right hand Stuart North monotonously coughed and spluttered, while Madge Crane watched him with a concern which she clearly intended him to observe. Beside her, and eyeing this by-play with sardonic amusement, sat Caroline Cecil, an actress noted in pathetic roles who was destined for the part of Mrs. Weston. And beside *her* was Griswold's second in command at the Music Department, surreptitiously reading a novel.

But of all these people it was the Cranes who were receiving most of Fen's attention: Madge, black-haired, smooth-complexioned, unconvincingly helpful and bright; Nicholas, reserved, quiet, thirtyish, an assistant director on leaving his public school, a camera-man at twenty-three, a director at twenty-seven: and Maurice, raffish, narrow-eyed, complacent and looking—it occurred to Fen—rather unwell. There was little of family resemblance between them, unless perhaps in the impeccable shape of the nose; but they were united, it seemed, in an uneasiness which betrayed itself by an occasional wordless message delivered from eye to eye. And the reason for that, Fen thought, was scarcely obscure: the motive for Gloria Scott's suicide had suggested itself to him some time ago, and he was tolerably certain his guess was correct.

The Cranes, if he were right, did well to be apprehensive, since unless the scandal of the suicide and its motive could be stifled—and it was unlikely that Humbleby would abet this—it might not inconceivably put a full stop to all their careers. . . .

The conference dragged on. Fen was summoned out of his brooding to put a date to *The Rape of the Lock*; the young man from the Music Department, required to specify music for a ballroom scene, suggested the *Berenice* Minuet, and fell into an unexpected fit of rage when told that the piece was too hackneyed; and Gresson—with one eye on the indistinguishable blondes, whom patently he hoped to impress—delivered himself of a dreary lecture, needlessly long, about the drinking customs of Pope's age. But it was clear that the end was in sight: suggestions for changes in the script were few and trivial, and the discussions arising out of them wholly lacking in fervour. By a quarter to midday the conference had reached a stasis for want of matter, and it must have been at about this point that Maurice Crane got up abruptly and left the room. It seems curious that Fen, in view of the nature of his thoughts, did not pay more attention to this significant departure, but in fact he hardly noticed it. A monstrous premonition held him in trance. Someone had tried to obliterate Gloria Scott's identity. Well—why? And there came to him, like the first stirring—"*Lass' mich schlafen*"—of the dragon in *Siegfried*, a couplet from Pope's ode which clamoured at his intelligence like a rune or an incantation: "*On all the line a sudden vengeance waits, And frequent hearses shall besiege your gates. . . .*"

Maurice Crane was not away for long. He came back just as Stafford, amid universal relief, was pronouncing the meeting over. His face was white and beaded with sweat: he breathed stertorously, irregularly, painfully. His lips moved once, as he attempted to speak. Then he staggered, caught vainly at the doorpost, and fell. A single violent convulsion gripped him as he lay. When that had passed there was no further movement, and they saw that he was dead.

CHAPTER II

I

"You may be justified in making all this fuss," said Humbleby. "Maurice Crane *may* have been poisoned—as you seem to imagine. But really, you ought at least to explain what it is that's made you suspicious. The position at present is distressingly complicated and—um—irregular."

He looked for support to Superintendent Capstick, who responded with bemused signals of assent. In the twenty minutes since his arrival at the studios Superintendent Capstick had achieved a condition of bewilderment so complete and far-reaching that it had altogether bereft him of speech. By the antiphonal narrative of Fen and Humbleby his intellect had been utterly fogged, and for the moment, and in spite of the fact that theoretically he was in charge, he was capable of nothing more constructive than sitting and staring, with his mouth ajar. It must not, however, be thought that Capstick was a stupid man. He possessed, as a matter of fact, a very fair share of natural intelligence. But he had been haled away from the Gisford Police-station with his mind full of a cherished project for reforming the town's traffic arrangements, and this preoccupation, combined with Fen and Humbleby's allusive habit of speech, had disastrously limited his mental reach. He had not, so far, succeeded in grasping who Gloria Scott was, why she had committed suicide, what connection she had with Maurice Crane, what Fen was doing at the studios, or why it should have been suggested that in the manner of Maurice Crane's death there was anything at all sinister; and being slightly awed by Humbleby, and much more awed by his surroundings (for he was an assiduous film-goer), he had not cared to press for a more lucid explanation of these matters than he had received so far. At Humbleby's demand to Fen, therefore, he leaned forward hopefully in his chair: one point at least, he told himself, was going to be cleared up.

But to his chagrin it was not. Fen grew testy at being pinned down, and spoke annoyingly of premonitions. The doctor, he said, had agreed that it might have been poison that had killed Maurice Crane; and on its being pointed out to him that the doctor had also agreed that it might not, he countered by reminding Humbleby that both Madge and Nicholas had testified to their brother's unexceptionally good health.

"All the same, natural deaths do occur now and then," said Humbleby rather nastily. "Just once in a while someone pops off for some reason other than malice aforethought. And the mere fact that Maurice Crane *hadn't* been ill isn't evidence. Everyone has to make a start with illness sooner or later."

"He was sick." Capstick, who was becoming unnerved at his own inanition, plunged headlong in with what appeared to be one of the few incontrovertible features of the affair. "That was why he went out of the room. To be sick."

Both Fen and Humbleby ignored this—not because they wished to be rude but because it was so negative as to defy answering. And Capstick, brought once again to a stand, slumped back in his chair and wiped a large handkerchief across his mottled, sweating brow.

"No, my point is this," Humbleby went on. "Unless Crane's death has some significant relation to the suicide of Gloria Scott, I'm trespassing on officially forbidden territory, and I must get off it, quick. But when I ask you to *establish* a significant relation, it turns out that all you can do is mutter about some reasonless foreboding or other. . . ."

"Damn it," said Fen, nettled, "Crane was a material witness in the Gloria Scott affair, wasn't he? You shouldn't fret so much about red tape, Humbleby: it's not as if there were any question of your taking *charge* of the case. All you're doing is asking Capstick for his co-operation in dealing with a matter which may possibly be connected with it. Isn't that so, Capstick?"

"Ah," said Capstick hurriedly. "Ah."

"All right," said Humbleby, with the air of one compelled against his will to abandon all responsibility. "All *right*. But for heaven's sake, why murder?"

"Because someone tried to prevent you from finding out who Gloria Scott really was."

"Now, that's an interesting thing," said Capstick. "I remember once when we were rounding up a gang of race-course touts——"

"I fail altogether," said Humbleby, "to see the connection."

Capstick was abashed. "I only thought," he said submissively, "that it might be interesting for you to hear how——"

"No, no. I mean the connection between the obliteration of Gloria Scott's identity and the notion that Maurice Crane was murdered."

"Really, Humbleby, you're unenviably dense." And Fen stared at that officer in some suspicion. "You'd agree, I suppose, that the motive of the person who ransacked the girl's rooms wasn't to conceal her identity *as 'Gloria Scott'*?"

"I'll grant you that, yes. Since she's been in a film or two, that was bound to come to light pretty rapidly."

"The idea, then, was to conceal her *real* identity."

"Yes."

"And since the motive for her suicide was almost certainly something recent—that's to say, something that had happened to her while she was calling herself Gloria Scott—then *X*'s purpose in turning her rooms upside down can't very well have been to hide that motive."

"You mean," Capstick interposed cautiously, "that if some chap was introduced to her as Gloria Scott and did her a mischief, and she killed herself because of it, then he couldn't hope to avoid being tied up with the business just by cutting the laundry-marks out of her clothes and so forth?"

"Exactly. You see, Humbleby, how readily Capstick has grasped the essentials of the situation." And upon this unwitting irony Fen paused for breath. "Therefore *X*'s purpose in visiting her rooms was something quite different."

"There are a lot of loopholes in this exposition," Humbleby complained. "Not to say—um—paralogisms. But go on. What was *X*'s purpose?"

"As far as I can see, we're bound to assume that his purpose was to keep secret a connection between himself and her *which existed before she took the name of Gloria Scott and which ceased to exist—so far as anyone could know—as soon as she took that name.*"

"Not bad," Humbleby conceded. "Not bad at all. . . . And we can trace her back for about two years in the identity of Gloria Scott. . . ."

"Can you?"

"Yes. I've rung up Charles again, and in the last hour or two he's had a good many telephone calls from people who've seen the photograph, including two from Menenford, one from the producer at the repertory theatre and one from a woman who keeps a boarding-house where the girl lived while she was working there. It seems that no one at Menenford realised that her name *wasn't* Gloria Scott. In fact, no one we've heard from knew her under any other name."

"Perhaps," said Capstick warily, "that actually *was* her *real name*."

"We've no definite proof that it wasn't," Humbleby agreed. "But on the other hand, no one so far has admitted to knowing her prior to two years ago, when she turned up as 'Gloria Scott' at Menenford."

"That's a paralogism, if you like," said Fen; and was on the point of explaining why when Capstick, in hungry pursuit of his momentary advantage, forestalled him.

"But it's her *face* you've asked people to identify," said Capstick. "And even if she changed her name, she can't have changed her *face*. The fact that no one's come forward who knew her earlier than two years ago probably means that up to two years ago she just wasn't in England."

"Just so," said Fen.

"Ah, yes. Stupid of me," said Humbleby with aggravating cheerfulness. "I ought to have seen that. So perhaps her real name *was* Gloria Scott. She may simply have said it wasn't in order to make an impression by being mysterious."

But Fen shook his head. "In that case the destruction in her rooms becomes *totally* inexplicable."

"Oh, yes, so it does," said Capstick after a moment's cogitation; and thereupon he retired from the field—though not, he felt, wholly without honour—and reverted to mopping his brow.

And Humbleby gestured assent. "So getting back to *X*'s purpose in trying to conceal an at least two-year-old connection with the girl . . ." He hesitated, considering. "I grant that it wouldn't be reasonable to look as far back as that for a motive for her suicide—though now I come to think of it"—and here he unexpectedly changed his tack—"I suppose it's not inconceivable that something or someone cropping up out of her past drove her to it. Blackmail, for instance."

"I think, you know," said Fen, "that we shall probably find the motive for her suicide very much nearer at hand. And if that's so—if it's something which concerns Gloria Scott and not Aggie Thistleton, or whatever her real name was—then as far as I can see there's only one explanation of *X*'s invading her rooms and doing what he did."

"And that is?"

"Vengeance," said Fen.

The word has ordinarily a distinct flavour of melodrama about it; but at its use in this context neither Humbleby nor Capstick felt much inclined to smile. Perhaps this was because the proximity of Maurice Crane's body, lying covered with a dust-sheet where it had fallen, had a sobering effect even on men professionally inured to death. Apart from it, and from themselves, the room was now empty. The scattered scribbling paper on the table, the loaded ash-trays and the jettisoned scripts of *The Unfortunate Lady* bore mute witness to the conference which an hour ago had been so catastrophically broken up. The trolley stood loaded with half-empty coffee-cups, their contents cold, grey and unappetising, and other cups had been put down in other places about the room. The hand of the electric clock above the door jolted forward audibly in the silence; beyond the windows the breeze was freshening in the trees, tossing the buds like a juggler's balls, so that their tender green glistened in the sunlight. And Humbleby, very pensive, said:

" '*On all the line a sudden vengeance waits* . . .' Is that what you have in mind?"

"It was that which first suggested the possibility."

"A sudden vengeance waits," said Capstick bemusedly. "A sudden——" With an effort he pulled himself together. "What are you talking about *now*?" he demanded.

They explained what they were talking about and failed to impress him with it.

"But that's nothing but a poem," he said rather indignantly. "Poems haven't got anything to do with what happens in real life. I tell you frankly, I don't at all see what you're getting at."

"What I'm getting at is this," said Fen. "If a man wanted to revenge Gloria Scott's suicide by killing the people who drove her to it, and if that man was known to be connected with her only under her real identity, then effacing that identity would be a step towards ensuring his own safety. Suppose that you're her brother, Capstick. She's run away from home and you haven't seen her or heard of her for three years. Then one evening, quite accidentally, you meet her somewhere in London. She explains that she is in great trouble and tells you who is responsible. She kills herself, and you, witnessing the suicide or hearing of it, decide to take vengeance. But you know that the police will visit her rooms and will find, pretty certainly, evidence that her name is really Jane Capstick. And that means that as soon as the people who wronged her start dying off, the police are going to start investigating you with some care. But if you can hide the fact that your sister was called Capstick, then you've got a much better chance of getting away with your murders undetected, since the police won't know in what direction to look. So you go to her rooms and obliterate that name from all her belongings. And then you make a start on your victim or victims."

"It's a very fine fantasy," said Humbleby. "But nothing more than that."

"It's at least a possible hypothesis," said Fen defensively. "And if Maurice Crane proves to have been poisoned I shall consider it a probable one. He has good qualifications for the role of First Victim, you know, since it's tolerably certain that he got the girl with child."

"Well, I grant you all that, sir." Capstick's weak spasm of annoyance was subsiding as the issues became more comprehensible to him. "But the question is, Does your hypothesis justify me in treating this business"—he nodded towards the body on the floor—"as murder, and all these folk we've got shut up in the next room as suspects?"

"There are some things," said Humbleby, "which you can do without treading on anybody's toes. For example, you can impound these coffee-cups and have their contents analysed, and you can take a sample of what was—um—egested. Also, you can try to find out which of the cups was Maurice Crane's, though this room's in such a muddle that I'm afraid it'll be difficult."

"And what about searching people?" Fen asked.

Capstick was shocked. "Search *them*, sir?"

"Why not? Just because they're in the film industry that doesn't mean they're vested with—with Benefit of Clergy or any such privilege."

"I doubt if it'd be wise." Capstick spoke glumly. "They're influential people with a lot of money, and you have to watch yourself when you're dealing with that type. As it is, we've kept them shut up a sight longer than we ought." He sighed nostalgically, remembering the comfortable impersonality of parking regulations and one-way streets. "I don't want to *neglect* anything, of course, but . . ."

He paused and looked appealingly at Humbleby, who to his relief said:

"Anyway, I can't imagine that searching them would

do much good. If there *is* a poisoner among them, he'll obviously be prepared for that. But we must interview them, of course, even if it means keeping them here another half-hour or so. I hope it won't disrupt half the business of the studios."

"This is a Saturday," said Fen, "and work here stops at mid-day on Saturdays. You may upset their week-ends, but I can't say the thought of that distresses me very much."

Capstick looked again at Humbleby. "Well, would you be prepared to do the talking, Inspector? I know you've got questions of your own to ask about the girl, and one way and another," said Capstick with some pathos, "I should say that for the moment you're rather more in the picture than I am."

"If you want me to, of course I will," said Humbleby. "You'd better keep quiet, Fen," he added as an afterthought. "They'll definitely resent it if you start putting on a Torquemada act, and that might make trouble for the Superintendent."

"You seem to have no faith at all in my discretion," Fen grumbled as he got to his feet, "and I don't know what I've done to deserve it, I'm sure. If I'm to be gagged, you must ask my question for me."

"And that is?"

"Ask Madge and Nicholas Crane if they know of any reason, other than Maurice's salacity, why Gloria Scott should have killed herself. They'll say they don't, but go on asking just the same."

"Have you got information that you're keeping from me?" said Humbleby suspiciously.

"No, it's another premonition." And Fen nodded affably. "I'm very fertile in premonitions today. Give me time and I'll dream up the winner of the three-thirty for you. . . . Shall we go?"

2

In the adjacent room some restiveness was apparent. Had Leiper been present, the *Unfortunate Lady* conference would have gone on till one o'clock or later, but this reflection in no way palliated the prevailing sense of injury at being still confined to the studios. In one corner Madge Crane was displaying quiet grief, and but for the fact that her immediate reactions to her brother's death had not been of quite that order, might have been supposed to have been actually experiencing the emotion. Stuart North, impelled by some obscure sense of duty, was sneezing fitful consolation at her, while Caroline Cecil, as the only other woman present, gravely abetted his efforts. Medesco sat alone, defiantly sketching grottoes, while the young man from the Music Department stared out of the window and whistled the *Berenice* Minuet through his teeth. Evan George, resolutely though discreetly cheerful, was talking to Nicholas Crane; Jocelyn Stafford prowled up and down, scowling; and Gresson, in an undertone, was regaling the blonde stenographers with what he conceived to be light badinage. They all looked up as Fen, Capstick and Humbleby entered, and Fen at least they eyed with distinct mistrust; it was disconcerting, no doubt, and obscurely suggestive of betrayal, to find an erstwhile collaborator suddenly transferred to the opposite side of the fence.

Humbleby got down to business without delay.

"We're extremely sorry to have kept you so long," he said ingratiatingly, "and particularly in such distressing circumstances." He bowed to Madge Crane, who summoned up, in response, an effectively lachrymose little smile. "Our trouble has been that Mr. Crane's death was so very sudden and unexpected."

Medesco grunted. "Who are you?" he demanded.

Humbleby contemplated him with disfavour. "I am a Detective-Inspector from Scotland Yard," he said. " And I'm here on business which may in some way be linked up with Mr. Crane's death. . . . Sudden and unexpected, I was saying; and unfortunately the doctor hasn't been able to give us any information as to what caused it."

"So you're thinking he may have poisoned himself," said Medesco brusquely, "or that someone did him in."

At this, Madge Crane gave vent to a little cry of dismay. Such things need careful practice if they are to come off, and the effect of this essay suggested not so much spiritual anguish as the callous insertion of a pin. Nicholas Crane, sensible, perhaps, that she was a little over-playing the part, frowned slightly and said:

"Really, Aubrey, I don't think that's in the best of taste."

"It is not," said Humbleby—and he uttered the reproof with a gravity so overwhelming that Jocelyn Stafford stopped pacing in order to regard him with a startled and speculative eye; film people are always on the look-out for fresh acting talent, or anyway delude themselves that they are. "We are not," Humbleby continued mendaciously, "entertaining any such suspicions as those which you—um—adumbrate. But naturally there's bound to be an inquest, and we're obliged, therefore, to investigate all possible contingencies, however remote and unlikely they may seem. Now, if I may have your cooperation for a few minutes . . ."

They gave it—in a few cases with truculence, but for the most part readily enough. It revealed nothing whatever that was to the purpose. No one could remember where Maurice Crane had put his cup when he had finished with it, and no one, up to the moment of his leaving the room, had observed anything unusual in his behaviour or in anyone else's.

"Thank you," said Humbleby when this parade of nescience was at last over. "And now we come to the matter with which I'm more directly concerned. The matter of Gloria Scott."

There was a sudden pregnant hush, in which Madge Crane's face hardened and she glanced swiftly at her brother. Of all the people there, only Gresson and the young man from the Music Department seemed unaffected by the name. The two stenographers, their poise momentarily in abeyance, looked at one another meaningly. And Stuart North was so surprised that he simply gaped.

"Gloria Scott?" he said. "What the hell . . .?"

"I take it you haven't seen this morning's papers, Mr. North."

"No, I have not. My eyes are so rheumy I shouldn't be able to read them."

"In the majority of them," said Humbleby, "there's a picture of Miss Scott. Some of you others may have seen it." Madge, Nicholas, Medesco and Jocelyn Stafford all nodded. "The picture has been published thanks to the fact that during the night before last Miss Scott committed suicide."

Something like horror appeared in Stuart North's brown, creased face.

"M-my God," he stammered. "You—you can't m-*mean* that."

"It's true, I'm afraid."

North stared dazedly at the damp handkerchief crumpled in his hand. "That sweet, silly child," he said vehemently. "It's incredible. . . . Why, she——"

And then, recollecting something, he checked himself

and looked down at Madge Crane where she sat beside him in grey and olive-green. Everyone there was displaying some degree of astonishment—everyone, that is, except Nicholas Crane, who remained impassive, his hands thrust deep into the pockets of his over-elegant sports jacket. To Fen it seemed probable that he was deliberately avoiding his sister's eye. There was little that Humbleby missed, and he, too, must have observed this, but he made no comment, and his voice was non-committal as he said:

"We have reason to believe that 'Gloria Scott' was merely a stage name. Does anyone know what this girl's real name was?"

Silence.

"Was anyone here acquainted with her before she came to the studios a year ago?"

Again silence.

"Can any of you suggest a reason why she should have killed herself?"

And now there was restless, uneasy movement. Heads were turned, feet shuffled, eye met eye in dumb interrogation. But still no one spoke.

"It may be," said Humbleby, "that one of you has an answer to that question, but doesn't want to blurt it out in public. If that's so, either the Superintendent"—he indicated Capstick, who was hovering self-consciously at his elbow—"or myself will be available in private after we disperse or at any time."

Evan George, small, harassed and untidy, opened his mouth as if to speak and then hurriedly shut it again. There was no other response.

"Very well," said Humbleby. "Now, there's just one other matter. . . . Mr. Crane, I believe you gave a party the evening before last—Thursday evening, that is."

Almost imperceptibly Nicholas Crane stiffened. Then,

relaxing again, he produced a gold case from an inside pocket, took a flat cigarette from it, and put it with deliberation into the corner of his mouth. His grey eyes were intent beneath heavy lids; his corn-coloured hair, with its displeasing suggestion of an artificial wave at the front, gleamed where the sun caught it; his body, the body of an athlete run to seed, seemed to droop from his shoulders like a coat on a hanger. His left cheek twitched with what could be the beginnings of a *tic douleureux*, and when, lighting the cigarette, he curled back his full lips, you could glimpse strong, yellow, irregular teeth.

He inhaled and blew out smoke before replying.

"Yes," he said indifferently. "I gave a party all right. What about it?"

"And Miss Scott was one of the guests?"

"Certainly."

"May I ask, please, why you invited her?"

Nicholas's eyes widened. "I liked her," he said mildly—and there was something about the statement which compelled belief. "She was a nice kid. Unaffected."

It occurred to Fen that with persons as important as Nicholas she would, of course, necessarily be that: only professional inferiors such as Valerie Bryant would see the less prepossessing side of her character. Fen stirred where he stood, and Humbleby, noting the movement and apparently fearing that he was on the point of breaking his vows of silence, hastened to say:

"And was anyone else here at your party?"

Nicholas glanced round the room. He took his time about it, though he was not so leisurely as to be uncivil.

"Madge was," he said. "And Aubrey—Mr. Medesco. And Mr. Evan George. And Mr. Stuart North. And Miss Caroline Cecil." He seemed to take an ironic relish in this formal mode of speech. "There were others, too—my brother David, for instance. I can give you a complete list if you need it."

"And Mr. Maurice Crane?"

"He wasn't able to come."

"I see." Humbleby devoted a moment to ingesting this information. "That seems clear enough. . . . I should like the people who were at that party to remain for just a few minutes longer. The rest, I think, can go, unless——" He turned interrogatively to Capstick, who, caught off-balance, made a hurried, evasive noise in his nose. "Right you are, then. Remember, please, that the Superintendent and myself are at your disposal if you should feel you have anything important to tell us about Miss Scott or Mr. Maurice Crane. . . . Thank you all very much."

In an unnatural silence, with downcast gaze and stepping warily, like mourners at a funeral, Gresson, Stafford, the two stenographers and the young man from the Music Department took their departure. As soon as their rear-guard had closed the door, a babble of pent-up talk penetrated through it, and presently diminished along the corridor outside.

Nicholas Crane, who had settled himself on the edge of a table and was swinging an impeccably trousered leg, raised his eyebrows quizzically.

"Gossip and scandal-mongering," he said. "We're going to get a lot of that for the next week or two. . . . Would it be in order, Inspector, for me to ask what my party has to do with this wretched girl's death?"

Madge lifted to Stuart North a face whose tear-stains she did not seem in any hurry to remove.

"Poor darling Maurice," she murmured. "And now—and now poor sweet little Gloria. . . ." She turned to Humbleby. "I know it's awful about Gloria," she pleaded, with a catch in her voice, "but Maurice was *nearer* to me, and somehow—oh, I don't want to be brutal, but somehow it seems so awful to be talking calmly about *her* when darling Maurice is next door, lying—l-lying——"

"Lying dead." It was Medesco, cold, massive and immovable, who contributed this unfeeling gloss—and as he spoke, Madge's pretty face grew suddenly mean and spiteful.

"You mind what you're saying," she told him, her voice sharp and purposive, "or I'll see to it that you never get another——"

She stopped abruptly, belatedly aware that this would not do. In another moment, and with an aplomb which Fen could not but admire, she was quietly sobbing, the heel of one slim and delicate hand pressed shamefastly against her brow.

"Oh God, I'm getting hysterical," she whispered. "I'm getting overwrought. Stuart . . . Darling . . ."

Stuart North somewhat ineptly patted her shoulder, uttering condolences which would have been more effective if they had not coincided with a prolonged fit of coughing. And Nicholas, who had been contemplating his sister without any very evident sympathy, took the opportunity of repeating his question to Humbleby.

"Oh, that." Humbleby had abandoned his official manner and seemed friendly and confiding. "That's easy. We don't understand why Miss Scott killed herself, and as we're professional busybodies we want to find out. We know she was cheerful and normal at lunch-time that day; we also know that at two a.m. that night she committed suicide. So you see, it's a question of trying to discover what upset her, and your party is a possible line of approach." Humbleby raised his voice to address the company at large. "Listen, please, everybody. I want to know all you can tell me about what Gloria Scott said and did at Thursday evening's party, what sort of mood she was in, and so forth. . . . Was there any special reason for the party, by the way?"

Nicholas grinned, not unattractively. "It was my birthday."

"Congratulations," said Humbleby politely. "A very good pretext for a party, I always think. . . . And now, about Gloria Scott . . ."

She had been almost the last to arrive, he learned, and the time of her arrival was agreed to have been roughly ten o'clock. She had been cheerful enough. And the only odd thing was that in the first minute or two something had apparently startled her. It was Nicholas and Caroline Cecil who were the witnesses to this; the others, Humbleby gathered, had not noticed it.

"Startled?" he said. "In what way startled?"

"Oh . . . Rather as if she'd seen a ghost," said Caroline Cecil. She was an agreeable, black-haired girl who in private life compensated for her screen roles with an unflagging amiability. "It didn't last long—she got over it almost at once. I asked her what was the matter, and she embarked on some tale about imagining the elastic of her knickers had given way." Miss Cecil chuckled earthily. "I admit that sort of thing does give you a turn—but just the same, I didn't believe a word of it: it was obviously a smoke-screen."

"But a smoke-screen for what?"

Miss Cecil shook her head. "There you've got me. And as I say, it didn't last."

"Apart from that she was cheerful, was she?"

"We-ell." Miss Cecil pursed her lips dubiously. "She was *thoughtful*, I'd say. Not gloomy. Just thoughtful. As though there were a problem she had to work out—not a distressing problem, but a difficult one."

"Not, in fact, the sort of problem that would drive her to suicide?"

"Good Lord, no. She'd forget about it for minutes at a time, and be just as riotous as the rest of us. Then she'd remember it again and go all *distrait.*"

"Was she watching any particular person there?"

"Well," said Miss Cecil, "I did get the impression that she was *avoiding* watching some particular person. But that may have been just a romantic fancy of mine—and which of the gang it was I can't tell you."

"Who did she talk to?"

"Everyone, I should say. The party was getting pretty lively when she arrived, and people were shifting about a lot. She got landed with me to start with, but that wasn't for long, and I honestly can't remember how she made out later. By midnight," said Miss Cecil, pleased, "the males had got their sexual steam up, and us girls were being bounced from hand to hand like a lot of beach-balls. . . . So we none of us had much time to watch what the others were doing. It really was a lovely party," she concluded in heartfelt tones.

And this seemed to be the general opinion; people had been so busy enjoying themselves that they had had no attention to spare for Gloria Scott, and although it was agreed that she had not seemed at all in a suicidal frame of mind, there emerged nothing more substantial concerning her than the information Caroline Cecil had already given. Had she run amok with a bread-knife—thought Humbleby gloomily—the occurrence might have been noted and remembered; but any *nuance* of behaviour subtler than that had been doomed by the circumstances to be swept permanently out of recollection the instant after it happened.

"And when did she leave?" he asked.

She had been the last to go, Nicholas Crane said. A small diehard contingent which included Medesco, Caroline Cecil and Evan George had made their farewells and clattered downstairs into the street, and Gloria Scott had remained behind for a minute or two, alone in the flat, with her host.

"Why was that?" said Humbleby.

"She wanted to talk about her part in *The Unfortunate Lady*. Getting it had rather gone to her head. I shooed her away as soon as I possibly could. Films are just work as far as I'm concerned, and when I'm not actually doing that work I like to forget about it."

"And you didn't upset her in any way?"

"Good heavens, no. She went off quite happily to join the others, who were still hanging about chatting on the pavement. That was about two in the morning, I fancy."

"And you others—did *you* find her cheerful when she came out of the flat and joined you?"

Medesco sniffed. "We didn't have time to notice, my dear man," he growled. "She picked up Evan George in a single comprehensive movement and trotted away with him towards Piccadilly. . . . 'You'll take me home, won't you, Mr. George?' " Medesco mimicked. "And pouf!—they'd gone."

Humbleby turned to that novelist, who was slightly flushed with embarrassment. "Did you know her well, then, sir?"

"I never set eyes on her before the party," said George hurriedly. "It's quite true—you can ask anyone." He looked round for support. "She'd—well, she'd been making up to me a bit during the evening. I don't know why, I'm sure," he said apologetically, "because there were plenty of younger men about. . . . Anyway, it's true that she asked me to take her home. We went off to try and find a taxi."

"And what did you talk about while you were finding it?"

George looked blank as he struggled to remember. "Oh, anything and everything," he said at last with exacerbating vagueness. "The party. The film—I told her a bit about what had been going on at script conferences. Oh, and just people. The trouble is," he said uncomfortably, "that I was a bit under the weather. . . . But she didn't look to me as if she was going to commit suicide, and I'm sure I can't have said anything to upset her. Damn it, I scarely *knew* the girl."

"And in the end you didn't take her home?"

"No, I didn't. I was quite liking the prospect, I tell you that frankly, but when we got to the Piccadilly end of Half Moon Street she suddenly flared up at something I said."

"What was that?"

"Well, it was about Miss Crane." George cleared his throat uneasily and flushed again. "I just happened to mention how much I admired her looks." Miss Crane, at this, smiled a little smile which combined in very masterly fashion diffidence, gratitude and overweening sadness at her brother's death. "Obviously that was a mistake, because Miss Scott said something like: 'Oh, for God's sake, must you talk about other women when you're with me?' and there was a cab coming along and she hailed it and ran and got into it without saying good night or anything, and just drove off leaving me standing there."

"It doesn't sound to me," said Medesco, "as if she was in a very well-balanced state of mind. And my own recollection is that you'd reached such an advanced stage of alcoholic stupor that you wouldn't have noticed if she'd stopped in her tracks and stripped herself naked."

"I've already admitted," said George with an attempt at dignity which his size, and the ravaged condition of his clothes, somewhat nullified, "that I was a bit under the weather." He paused. "Come to think of it, though, she was rather *silent*. I seemed to be doing most of the talking." He scratched his head. "I wish I could remember more about it—I'm afraid I'm not being a very good witness."

"None of this is helpful," said Humbleby with candour. "Mr. Crane, was there any opportunity for Miss Scott to talk to anyone, or make a 'phone call or read a letter, between the time she left you and the time she joined the group on the pavement?"

Fen had been watching Nicholas, and had been interested to observe in him, as Evan George's narrative proceeded, an appearance of growing relief. By now he appeared to be positively light-hearted.

"None whatever, Inspector," he said. "I took her down to the door myself and saw her join the others before I closed it."

Humbleby flicked his fingers in uncontrollable irritation; the evidence was nebulous to a degree, and an explanation of the motive for Gloria Scott's suicide apparently as far off as ever. Something had startled her—no one knew what. And something, at some stage in the proceedings, had been said to her which had caused her to brood and brood more and more dementedly, until on Waterloo Bridge the thread of reason had snapped and an insane impulse had scourged her with horrible pain into eternity. . . . But why? And as Humbleby, recalling the question he had been told to press, glanced at Fen, he saw that Fen was very slightly shaking his head. It was likely, the gesture said, that Nicholas Crane could not be induced to change his story, and any effort expended in that direction would certainly be effort wasted. Humbleby went on, accordingly, to the last questions which he had to ask.

"Just who," he demanded, "was responsible for giving

Miss Scott the part of Martha Blount in *The Unfortunate Lady*? Mr. Stafford, was it?"

Nicholas looked surprised. "The final decision was his, of course. He's producing."

"And did he select the girl on his own initiative?"

"No," said Nicholas. "I put him up to it."

"You did?" It was Humbleby's turn to be surprised. "Not your brother Maurice?"

"Not my brother Maurice," said Nicholas gravely.

"May I be told your reasons?"

"Certainly. She wasn't at all a bad actress—she had a cameo part in *Visa for Heaven*, which I directed, so I knew what she could do—and in appearance and physique she fitted the part. And besides that, I liked her, and wanted to give her a leg-up. Fortunately, the casting of Martha Blount was one of the few things in the film that Mr. Leiper didn't have preconceived ideas about, and Jocelyn had an open mind on the subject, so he accepted my recommendation quite readily."

"And you, Miss Crane," said Humbleby with deceptive mildness. "Did you think it was a good selection?"

Without thinking, she burst out: "I thought it was a——" But then, as she became conscious of Stuart North's regard, her tone altered. "Why, yes, of course. Gloria needed training and experience, but one day she was going to be a very, *very* good actress. I was looking forward to working with her."

"Were you, dear?" Caroline Cecil spoke with tempered malice. "I did get the impression that you were a *little* bit doubtful about it."

"Oh no, darling," Madge answered sweetly. "Or if I was, it was only because I was afraid that Gloria might damage her chances by not being *quite* up to standard. You see, Inspector, you have to be so *awfully* careful in the film business; because if you fail just *once* you're *never* forgiven."

"And you didn't"—Humbleby's tones flattered like an unguent—"you didn't at all resent Mr. North's attentions to her?"

For a fraction of a second there was hatred in Madge's eyes; then, as though a lantern-slide had been whisked from a screen and another substituted for it, she was all amazement.

"But why should I? I didn't even know that Stuart was interested in her." She looked up at him. "Were you, darling?"

Mr. North vociferously sneezed.

"I don't quite know how you'd define 'interested'," he said peevishly. "I took her out once or twice, if that's what you mean, but there was nothing serious about it.... How the hell have we got on to this dreary topic, anyway? What does it matter?"

He looked at Capstick, who nodded haplessly—and then, resipiscently and with equal ambiguity, shook his head.

"Anyway, it provides us with a *sequitur*"—Humbleby was unperturbed—"to my final questions: which concern the relationship between Miss Scott and Mr. Maurice Crane."

"Final," echoed Medesco. "Let's hope they are. I want my lunch."

"I believe"—once more Humbleby was addressing himself to Nicholas—"I believe that last Christmas Miss Scott was staying in your household. Is that right?"

"She stayed at my mother's house."

"You yourself don't live there?"

"No. Nor Madge. Maurice and David do."

"I should like to know who invited her."

"Maurice did."

"Were you there at the time of this visit?"

"No. David and I were away sailing in Bermuda."

"And in that case your brother Maurice would be the only man in the house—unless your father——"

"My father died years ago. . . . Yes, Maurice would have been the only man in the house. Was Gloria going to have a baby?"

"She was, yes. . . . And now, Mr. Crane, if you'll just let me have a complete list of the guests at your party. . . ."

It was done; and presently the assembly dispersed. Nicholas, Madge and Stuart North were the last to leave the room, and Nicholas nodded to Fen as he went.

"This is very much your element, isn't it?" he said in passing.

"Perhaps," said Fen non-committally. "May I give you a word of advice?"

"Please do."

"For a few days," said Fen, "don't eat or drink anything that other people aren't eating and drinking. That goes for your sister, too. . . . And suppose you wanted to break an actress's contract without getting into legal trouble—how would you set about it?"

Nicholas's eyes narrowed. "Well, well," he murmured. "There's a law of slander, Professor Fen. If you should think of making any rash accusations, I'm sure it could be brought into service against you. So be careful, there's a good man. . . . And good-bye for now. We shall meet again, I hope." With a quick smile he went.

3

An hour later, after a hurried ale-and-sandwich lunch at "The Bear", Fen was on his way back to Oxford. He gave little thought to the morning's events, for he realised that without more data speculation would yield nothing new. Instead, he fell to conceiving and casting a film about Wordsworth and Annette, and this, combined with occasional sanitary draughts of Jamesian hyperbole, kept his mind occupied until he arrived home.

On the morning of the following day—which was the Sunday—he was removing his gown in his rooms in College after attending Matins when the telephone rang, and with a civility begotten probably of awe the operator announced a Personal Call from New Scotland Yard.

"Gervase Fen speaking," said Fen.

"Mr. *Gervase* Fen?"

"Speaking."

"One moment, please, Mr. Fen." The diaphragm of the receiver crackled morosely at Fen's ear. "You're through now. I say, you're through now, Mr. Fen."

"Yes, very well."

"Are you there?"

"Gervase Fen speaking now."

"Here is your call, sir."

The line immediately went dead—but presently, as the consequence of a series of reverberating clicks, it was possible to make out a murmur of background noises: a typewriter, crockery, conversation, someone whistling. Fen put the instrument down in order to light a cigarette. After about half a minute the mistrustful hallo-ing of Humbleby, issuing from it like the voice of an incarcerated elf, caused him to pick it up again.

"Are you there?" Humbleby was saying. "Is anyone there at all?"

"Calm yourself," said Fen, "and tell me what has happened."

"Oh, there you are at last. . . . Well, they've done the autopsy on Maurice Crane, and it's as you said: he was poisoned."

"What with?"

"Colchicine."

Fen frowned. "Colchicine ? Well, well. It's a pity we bothered about the coffee-cups, then."

"Oh, so you know all about colchicine, do you? I'm damned if I did: poisoners aren't usually so—um—esoteric in their choice."

"How was it administered?"

"In a bottle of some tonic he was taking. Bagley routed it out when he went to the house late last night."

"And when?"

"It could have been almost any time. The house is one of those big, rambling affairs where you can easily sneak in and out. I can't pin it down at all."

"Well, obviously Crane drank the stuff before leaving for the studios yesterday morning—so that must be the *terminus ad quem.*"

"Yes. But it's the *terminus a quo* that's the trouble. The bottle says twice daily after meals, but people often forget to take medicine—or else just can't be bothered."

"M'm. How do you stand?"

"I'm officially in charge now. Capstick persuaded his Chief Constable to call in the Yard, and I persuaded the A.C. to let me postpone my holiday and take the case on."

"And what have you discovered so far?"

"Nothing."

"I see. Who gets Maurice Crane's money?"

"Ah, that's a point. His mother does, and there's quite a lot of it. The father was a well-to-do manufacturer of flea-powders and laxatives and things, and he left fifty thousand to each of his children. Only they can't touch it till they're thirty-five, and if they die *before* they're thirty-five, it reverts to the mother. . . . It's a motive, you know."

"Thank you, I can see that. What about Gloria Scott?"

"Poor Charles has been inundated. Half of England seems to have recognised that photograph. But no one claims to have known her under any other name, or earlier than two years ago. There's been a lot of routine investigation going on, but the upshot of it all is that we *still* don't know anything more about her than we knew yesterday morning."

"And in the cold light of a new day you're afflicted with considerable doubts as to whether Maurice Crane's death has anything to do with her at all."

"Yes, I don't mind saying I am. . . . You know what I think?"

"What?"

"I think you're detecting things that aren't there."

"Indeed."

"I think that the coincidence about the film and that ode has thrown you a bit off balance."

"You think my mind is softening."

"Since you insist on it, yes."

"I don't insist on it at all. In fact I deny it. But you people simply *won't be told*. . . . What are your plans?"

"We're going through the motions prescribed for cases of murder. Something will turn up."

"Good heavens. Micawber Humbleby, the Demon of the Yard. Are you going to keep me posted?"

"Yes, I see no objection to doing that. In the meantime, have you any *suggestions*?"

"Yes. Steamship companies. Circulate Gloria Scott's photograph to the stewardesses of passenger boats which arrived in England during the month before she turned up at Menenford. Once you find out who she was, you'll have a line on Maurice Crane's murderer."

" 'That strain again'."

"Well, if you won't, you won't. But don't blame me if anything happens to the other Cranes."

Fen rang off. *Colchicine*, he thought. Whatever the ultimate issue of the case, it would certainly become a toxicological classic. His text-books on poisons were all at his North Oxford home, but he found that he was able, without too much difficulty, to recall the chief characteristics of this particular toxin. It constituted, he remembered, one of the two active principles in the bulbs and seeds of the autumn crocus or meadow saffron, and a powerful decoction of the stuff could be obtained from those two sources without very great trouble. Its symptoms were vomiting, salivation and stomach pains, and death resulted from failure of the respiratory centre. And in one respect it was almost unique among poisons: it had no effect at all on the victim for several hours after ingestion. Fen could think of no instance in which it had ever before been used homicidally. . . .

And in the meantime, what was to be done? As far as he was concerned, he felt, the answer would have to be Nothing. Crimes calling for routine investigation were not at all in his line, and from what he knew already the last dram of enlightenment had been squeezed—without, however, giving him the smallest clue as to who Maurice Crane's murderer might be. Something further would have to be discovered, or to happen, before speculation could usefully be resumed. Accordingly, he went home and spent the remainder of the day eating, sleeping, reading, vilifying his children and practising desultorily on the French horn. From his viewpoint the case was becalmed; and it was not until the appearance, towards teatime on the following day, of the four-o'clock edition of *The Evening Mercury*, that the winds began to blow again and the ship to veer towards new shallows, new reefs.

4

Fen was apt to say subsequently that he had never known a case in which the murderer was so inexorably hemmed in by mere unforeseeable circumstance. At every turn of the way Chance lay in ambush, plotting his progress as on a map, sketching in his face feature by feature, in the upshot announcing quite plainly and incontrovertibly his identity and name. And in hastening that final revelation nothing that Fen or Humbleby could do was of any avail; until such time as the Norns condescended to supply the final link which gave coherence to the whole chain of events, they were obliged to kick their heels in ignominious passivity. Although the crime presented a problem whose solution required deduction and hard thinking, the data required for that deduction and that thinking remained throughout inexorably the prerogative of blind destiny. . . .

And on the Monday morning destiny wove the first strand of the net.

Her instrument was named Bartholomew Snerd, and by profession Mr. Snerd was a private enquiry agent. Private enquiry agents are commonly persons of integrity, but to a dishonest man their business offers certain violent temptations, and to all of these Mr. Snerd had at one time or another wittingly succumbed. He had, indeed, so often and so narrowly escaped prison that he had come half to believe that there hovered at his elbow a personal deity unremittingly sequacious of his interests; and this sense of supernatural protection had brought him, at the time of the events to be described, to a condition in which the balance between rapacity and caution was being only very precariously maintained. Mr. Snerd was aware, certainly, of the dangers of over-confidence; but the capacity of men for deluding themselves is virtually infinite, and the warnings of Mr. Snerd's more circumspect instincts, though increasing daily in vehemence and number, were paradoxically less and less heeded by that part of him which took decisions and which acted. And it was this dangerous psychological condition, presumably, which involved him in the perilous enterprise of robbing Madge Crane's flat.

Mr. Snerd was a personable man, well built (though tending unobtrusively to fat) and with an agreeably candid physiognomy. Though he was nearing forty he looked at least ten years younger, and the care with which he performed his toilet and chose his clothes helped to make a very presentable figure of him. In the grades and varieties of courtship he was widely experienced, and his flair for suiting his approach to his victim had proved to be one of his most valuable business assets, as well as a source of much more or less innocent pleasure to himself. He always went for the women; with men, despite his bluff and comradely manner, he was somewhat ill at ease. And going for the women had this advantage in the way of business, that it frequently opened up lucrative opportunities for a little quiet blackmail—and in blackmail Mr. Snerd was an artist. It was a rigid law with him never to make an excessive demand and never to make more than one, and it was doubtless this wise and temperate plan which kept him immune from retribution. Indeed, it had developed, as time went on, into something very like a principle of ethics; *unfair*, or *ungentlemanly*, were the terms with which Mr. Snerd would have stigmatised any attempt to take the pitcher a second time to a previously plundered well; and his attitude to his victims, once they had acceded to his demands, was a kindly, paternal tolerance. In many ways, and in spite of encountering so much of life's seamy side, Mr. Snerd had a very simple and unsullied mind; the fornications, perversions and trivial betrayals with which it was necessarily stocked made no more profound impression on it than if they had been the multiplication table; and this ingenuousness, when at last and inevitably his sins found him out, was so clearly unfeigned that if the evidence against him had not been overwhelming, his tutelary spirit—the magistrate being an impressionable man—might well have salvaged him once again.

Among his more legitimate activities the pursuit and detection of marital infidelity easily preponderated, and his neat and tasteful office off Long Acre had witnessed many distressing confessions of conjugal mistrust. It is one of the advantages enjoyed by private enquiry agents that, since the middle and upper classes resort to them only furtively, they are ranged in no universally recognised heirarchy of reliability and competence such as exists among tradesmen and even, to some extent, among lawyers, doctors and other professional persons who do not have to be consulted under the rose; and the consequence of this is that, as the clients of private enquiry agents are obliged to select them at random, the plums of the profession are not reserved to the more sober and experienced firms, but fall with reasonable frequency into the laps of quite lowly practitioners. It thus came about that there appeared one day in Mr. Snerd's office the wife of an eminent film magnate who had, it transpired, reason to suspect her husband of adulterous inclinations and practices, and who for reasons into which Mr. Snerd did not enquire was anxious to have proof of these goings-on; and one of the considerable list of supposititious *inamorate* with which she assaulted Mr. Snerd's ear was Madge Crane.

The progress of Mr. Snerd's investigation—which was

interesting as well as profitable—need not be related here. It is sufficient to say that although a fair proportion of the film magnate's wife's guesses turned out to be well founded, that relating to Madge Crane was, so far as Mr. Snerd could ascertain, wholly unjustified. And there the matter might well have ended, but for the fact that Mr. Snerd's examination of Miss Crane's private life had involved his making acquaintance with Miss Crane's personal maid, an attractive brunette called Felicity Flanders. Miss Flanders, thanks to the fame of her mistress, was a supercilious young woman, not to say cagey, and even for one as practised as Mr. Snerd the process of gaining her affections (and thereby such confidential information about Miss Crane as she might possess) had been a long and arduous one. Once gained, however, those affections were revealed as being of so passionate a sort that Mr. Snerd began to fear he would never again be able to disentangle himself from them. Miss Flanders was, he perceived, the sort of girl whom it is not politic to jettison too abruptly. And so, long after his original motive for establishing the relationship had ceased to be operative, long after the film magnate's wife had paid him off and departed with the ammunition against her luckless husband which he had provided, Mr. Snerd continued to pay his attentions to Miss Flanders. When all was said and done it could hardly be described as a penitential exercise, for Miss Flanders was good-looking, complaisant and not, apparently, at all zealous to regularise the granting of her favours with bell and book. At the time of Maurice Crane's death, therefore, Mr. Snerd was still able to regard the association as an agreeable one; and when Felicity, informing him that her mistress was away for the week-end, for the first time invited him to the luxurious little Westminster flat, Mr. Snerd cancelled his other plans and accepted the invitation with genuine pleasure.

That was on the Sunday, the day following those events at the Long Fulton studios which have already been described. At nine o'clock that evening Mr. Snerd met Felicity for a sandwich supper and a drink or two at "The Queen's Head" in Great Peter Street, and heard from her such details of yesterday's catastrophe as she had succeeded in picking up.

"Not that Madge was all that upset," she said; behind Miss Crane's back Felicity always referred to her by her baptismal name, since she liked to be thought of as a confidante of that famous young woman rather than as a servant. "There wasn't any love lost between her and Maurice, if you ask me. And I don't wonder at it, either, not with him being the sort of man he was."

"Ropy type, eh?" Mr. Snerd, though he had ingeniously evaded conscription in the late war, was prolific of Service slang.

"No better than a—than a satyr, he was. The way he used to behave to me!"

"Ah, I know the sort." Mr. Snerd nodded sagely. "Can't keep their hands off a girl's ins and outs." He winked. "Not that I really blame him, darling, where *you're* concerned."

Felicity giggled. "Oh, go on with you, Peter," she said (Mr. Snerd had not thought fit to entrust her with his own name; or with his vocation, since she supposed him to be in the motor business). "You're *awful*, really you are."

"Well, how's about shutting out the horrid sight with another of the same?"

"D'you think I could have a gin this time?"

"Better stick to beer, ducks." Mr. Snerd was careful with his money. "Upsets the old tum-jack to mix 'em." He ordered another round. "Look here, you're sure it's safe for me to come up to the flat? I don't want you to get into trouble if she was to come back unexpectedly."

"She won't come back, don't you fret. She spent last night with her mother and today she's gone on to her cottage."

"Where's that?"

"Doon Island. Near Portsmouth."

"I'd have thought she'd have needed you with her wherever she was."

"Said it was time for me to have an 'oliday." Felicity considered retrieving the truant "h", and decided that this would only draw attention to its absence. "Quite true, at that. So I'm me own mistress till she comes back on Wednesday."

"And what about the secretary?"

"Lord, Pete, you aren't half *nervy*."

"I'm not nervy," Mr. Snerd asserted stoutly. "Not me, ducks. It's you I'm thinking of."

Being of the more percipient sex, Felicity thought this profession unlikely; but she accepted the fact that men habitually lied as a part of the order of things, and so made no attempt to argue the matter.

"Secretary's gone with her," she said. "She's well out of the way, never you fear."

"Just as well to be sure about these things," said Mr. Snerd cheerfully. "I remember when I was in the Raf we had a flight-sergeant who . . ."

He drifted off into fictitious war anecdotes.

At closing time they finished their drinks and left. Madge Crane's apartments, near the Westminster Hospital, were in a small, expensive block of service flats of the sort which in these latter days are within the reach only of the exceptionally well-to-do. Mr. Snerd knew what things cost, and the sight of its furnishings and fittings impressed him mightily, though he took care to conceal this fact beneath the casual air of one inured from birth to such opulence. From a sideboard in the dining-room Felicity fetched gin and orange squash; and having liberally sampled this they retired about midnight to bed.

Mr. Snerd was awakened at seven o'clock by the Monday morning traffic. Felicity was still soundly asleep, and it occurred to Mr. Snerd that here would be a suitable opportunity to have a look round the flat. It is doubtful if he intended to steal anything much, for such larcenies as he was accustomed to commit concerned objects so little valuable as to make it seem likely, when their owners discovered the loss, that they had been merely mislaid. It is even more doubtful if he had blackmail in mind; he had never yet selected a victim who was eminent or notorious, being aware that, even in this democratic day and age, wealth and influence are still liable to get round behind a man and deal him shrewd knocks. No; his motive, so far as it can be ascertained at all, seems to have been mere curiosity—or, if you prefer it, a natural love of surreptitious doings even when they served no useful purpose. His reasons are not, in any event, important to this chronicle. It is his actions that count—for those actions were destined to be largely instrumental in cornering a particularly subtle and ruthless murderer.

As he climbed cautiously out of the bed, perfunctorily covered his nakedness and slipped barefooted from the room, Mr. Snerd was not at all conscious of the portentousness of what he did: he was conscious, rather, of that exhilaration which comes to a man when his actions are unlawful without being specially perilous. Outside in the passage he paused for a moment, and then made his way silently to the sitting-room, where the previous evening he had noticed a small rosewood desk which would probably repay attention. With ears alert for the slightest sound of movement from Felicity he began to investigate it, replacing everything, once examined, with scrupulous accuracy in the position in which he had found it. However, little that was noteworthy rewarded his efforts, and presently he was reduced to a speculative contemplation of the desk's only locked drawer. His proceedings were disinterested, and he knew that there was absolutely no necessity for him to see what was inside it; having absented himself from Felicity a sufficient while, he might at this point quite easily have returned to her and left it at that. But his habit of inquisitiveness pricked him like a goad, and there came a crucial moment when he was no longer capable of denying it. He crept back to the bedroom.

Felicity lay as he had left her, the damp flush of exhausted slumber on her brow. Pausing only to assure himself that she really was asleep, Mr. Snerd took his gloves from the dressing-table and put them on (since he was wearing nothing else but pants, this gave his appearance a decided quality of the bizarre), extracted a bunch of skeleton keys from his trousers pocket and again slipped from the room.

The drawer's contents might be confidential, but they were not, he found, at all numerous. To start with, there was a packet of treasury notes; over these Mr. Snerd lingered wistfully, but in the end he virtuously replaced them untouched. Next came a privately printed volume, with curious illustrations, entitled *A Whip for Veronica*, and this, after a little thought, Mr. Snerd determined to appropriate for his own use and enjoyment. Finding it gone, Miss Crane would probably imagine that she had left it lying about and that a servant, perhaps Felicity, had picked it up; but she would scarcely be in a position to enquire about it, and although relations between mistress and maid would undoubtedly deteriorate as a consequence, that (Mr. Snerd felt) was Felicity's look-out. . . .

Finally, there was a letter.

It was written on good-quality notepaper in a sprawling, slightly childish hand. And as Mr. Snerd read it, his knees grew weak with excitement, and in order to avoid tottering and perhaps falling he was obliged hurriedly to sit down. The cause of this excess of emotion was as follows:

"Thursday night, 2 a.m.

"My dear Madge:

It's done, and now I'm wishing like hell it weren't. I've just told Gloria—asked her to wait behind after the others had gone—and I was afraid she was going to faint or be sick or go for my throat. I've never seen anyone in such a state—getting that part meant absolutely everything to her. I warned her she'd find herself facing a slander action if she said anything about being tricked into breaking her contract, and for reasons you know, Jedd won't talk. But it's a devil of a risk. If anything comes out I'm finished in films—and I don't mind saying I'll see to it that you are, too. For God's sake burn this letter and never breathe a word about it to a living soul.

"She certainly won't wait for the studios to sue her for breach of contract—couldn't possibly afford to fight the action. I said I'd do what I could for her in the future, but of course she didn't believe that for a single moment—thinks she's completely washed up in films. She knows damn well you're at the back of it all, too, with your ridiculous jealousy. I should watch out for yourself. She hardly seemed sane when she left here.

"I feel very bad about it all. As you know, I like the kid—not in Maurice's way, either. Don't try to talk about it when we meet on Saturday morning."

"NICHOLAS."

Mr. Snerd did some quick thinking. An enterprising Press had nosed out the fact that there was an element of mystery in Gloria Scott's suicide, and the Sunday papers had reported it at length, touching discreetly on Nicholas Crane's party and stating that the police had been unable so far to uncover any motive for the act. Mr. Snerd was therefore familiar with the general outlines of the affair: he had, he realised, chanced on a particularly revealing document connected with it—and one, moreover, which disgracefully implicated two notabilities of the film world; and as he sat there, grotesquely arrayed and clutching the letter in his gloved hand, he asked himself, with as much detachment as he could muster, what would be the most profitable thing to do about it.

And presently, after much strenuous cerebral effort, Mr. Snerd determined to take the letter and purvey it to *The Evening Mercury*.

Now in this decision, that softening of the intellect in which Mr. Snerd's ever-growing confidence had resulted is very clearly exemplified. He realised, of course, that once the letter was published there would no longer be any discretionary bar to Miss Crane's reporting its theft to the police; he realised that Felicity would know him for the culprit. But he was foolish enough to suppose that for fear of losing her job Felicity would not denounce him; and even if she did, he fondly imagined that providing he never saw her again his pseudonym would protect him. With the money obtained—which should be a very tolerable sum—he would shut up his office and go away on a holiday; and by the time he returned the whole business would have blown over.

Thus did Mr. Snerd plot and plan, while unobtrusively his guardian angel abandoned ship. As we shall see, he badly under-estimated both Felicity and the resources of the Metropolitan Constabulary. But for the time being his scheming seemed to him good, and he proceeded immediately to put it into action.

In the bedroom Felicity slept on. Mr. Snerd gathered up his garments and donned them elsewhere. Nicholas Crane's letter he enclosed in the pages of *A Whip for Veronica*, and *A Whip for Veronica* he placed in the pocket of his raincoat. Subsequently, having closed and relocked the rifled drawer, he prowled about the flat, wiping his finger-prints off everything he could remember having touched. If by some mischance any remained, that could not be helped; his prints were not in the police files, and any that were found would therefore remain inexplicable. He considered forcing a window, so as to make it appear that the flat had been broken into, but decided, on further reflection, that it would be difficult to make this look at all plausible; moreover, it would involve noise, and noise would waken Felicity. For her he scribbled a note, explaining that his work called him away early and arranging to meet her at "The Queen's Head" that evening—a *rendezvous* at which, needless to say, he had no intention of turning up. And having deposited this on the dressing-table, he waved a regretful but determined last farewell at her unconscious form and let himself quietly out of the flat.

It was a grey morning, promising rain. Out on the pavement with his spoils in his pocket, Mr. Snerd at first hesitated as to what direction to take. But presently, his mind made up, he boarded an 88 bus, which took him up Whitehall to Charing Cross. Alighting there, he headed for St. Martin's Lane. And the clocks were striking eight-thirty when he pushed open the ornate bar door of "The Scissors".

Being in the neighbourhood of Covent Garden, where

they work all night and require a drink early in the morning, "The Scissors" was enabled by special dispensation of the Licensing Laws to trade at this hour; and consequently, confirmed alcoholics, as well as the market porters, were regularly to be found there. It was for a person of this former class that Mr. Snerd was looking—a person named Rouncey who reported for the *Mercury*. Mr. Rouncey and Mr. Snerd were old cronies; in this and other bars they had over a period of several years cemented that companionship in shadiness which served them for friendship; and so far as either of them was capable of trusting anyone, they trusted one another. It was by the agency of Mr. Rouncey, then, that Mr. Snerd proposed to convey Nicholas Crane's letter to the *Mercury*—and he had little doubt that the *Mercury* would pay well for it. For the *Mercury*, almost alone among English newspapers, was a scandal-sheet of the worst and most unscrupulous sort. Its sales were founded on vilification and near-pornography, the latter type of pabulum being justified by the adoption of hypocritical moral attitudes ("*Such a state of affairs, we believe, will not be tolerated by the British people. . . .*" "*It is our view that we are performing a public service in revealing the practices of this depraved and vicious section of the community . . .*" and so forth); its myrmidons paraded monotonously in and out of the civil and criminal courts and were frequently gaoled; and yearly it disbursed huge sums by way of damages for libel, regarding these, apparently, as no different in kind from any other overhead expenses. Its policy earned it very large dividends and the execration of all who were intelligent enough to see through its pretensions to high-mindedness; and since it professed an unwavering abhorrence of the rich ("*Whatever happens, it will not be Lord X who will suffer; it will be the decent, ordinary folk—the miners and railwaymen and steel-workers and their wives and children . . .*"), the *Mercury* was a very popular paper indeed.

Mr. Snerd soon saw that he had come to the right tavern, for Mr. Rouncey was established in his usual corner of the bar, with whisky in his hand, a Woodbine in his mouth and a battered felt hat on the back of his head. He was an elderly, shifty man, whose peculiarity it was that alcohol invariably made him cry. This reaction was wholly physical and not related in any way to his mood, which though commonly gloomy was hardly ever lachrymose, and on strangers it was apt to have a disconcerting effect. Mr. Snerd, however, was accustomed to it and had long since ceased to think of it as out of the way. Undeterred by Mr. Rouncey's smeared cheeks and overflowing eyes, Mr. Snerd advanced on him with affability.

"Morning, old man," he said. "What's yours?"

Without replying, or even looking up, Mr. Rouncey emptied his glass, pushed it across the bar and waited in silence while it was replenished at Mr. Snerd's expense. Such demonstrations of incivility, which were habitual with him, had persuaded Mr. Snerd that he was a "character", and so Mr. Snerd was not offended by his lack of response, but settled down at his side, drank manfully, fought off a sudden attack of queasiness and presently tapped his companion confidentially on the knee.

"Got something for you," said Mr. Snerd. "Something hot."

Mr. Rouncey turned a welling eye on him and removed the sodden cigarette from his mouth.

"And what'd that be?" he said without perceptible interest.

"Soon show you." After glancing round to make sure that they were not overlooked, Mr. Snerd produced Nicholas Crane's letter. "Just you take a gander at that."

Having wiped his eyes and wearily adjusted in front of them a pair of bifocal steel-rimmed spectacles, Mr. Rouncey obeyed. When he had read the letter, without any change of expression, he handed it back and swallowed his drink at a gulp.

"How about another?" he said.

"Your round, old man."

"Is it?"

"You know bloody well it is." Mr. Snerd spoke without rancour; attempts to avoid paying for rounds were part of his conception of Mr. Rouncey as a "character". "I'll have the same again."

Mr. Rouncey resignedly gave the order.

"Well?" said Mr. Snerd.

"Yes, it's hot stuff all right," said Mr. Rouncey. "Too bloody hot, if you ask me."

"Don't tell me that. You can use it."

"How do I know it isn't a fake?"

"You've got my word for it," said Mr. Snerd with dignity.

"Oh, yes. Sure I have. But my News Editor doesn't know you, Bart boy, not like I do. It's him that's got to be persuaded."

"Get a sample of Crane's writing. Have 'em compared."

"Where the hell do you think I can . . . Wait, though." Mr. Rouncey, in a formidable burst of energy, contrived to snap his fingers. "He wrote a letter to the paper, not more than a week ago, and I've an idea it was written, not typed. There's a chance there."

"Go for it, old man."

"It'll have to be carefully written up," said Mr. Rouncey meditatively. "Full of *allegeds* and *we make no comment.* Whatever happens it'll mean a libel action, but we might get away with that on the Public Interest tack.... Where'd you get the letter?"

Mr. Snerd winked. "Blew out of a window. So of course I had to look at it to see whose it was, and there weren't any surnames or addresses, so I brought it along to you thinking you might be able to help, and——"

"Stow all that, Bart boy," said Mr. Rouncey amiably. "It won't do for the paper. I think our line'll be that it came anonymously through the post, from someone who wanted to See Justice Done. Of course, we don't like anonymous letters, not when we're holding forth to the ruddy public anyway, but we thought it was our duty as citizens to get the handwriting experts on to it and then turn it over to the police. . . . Yes, that's our line, I'd say: just reporting what we've done. We Make No Comment And Shall Be More Delighted Than Anyone If The Name of These Fine Artists Can Be Cleared." Exhausted by his performance, Mr. Rouncey paused and groped for his drink. "Here, let's have another look at the thing."

Mr. Snerd handed the letter over, and Mr. Rouncey, shaking away the tears which blurred his vision, read it again.

"Jedd," he murmured. "We'll have to rout him out before we print anything."

"Who is Jedd, anyway?"

"Theatrical manager. *Lover's Luck*, at the Curtain." Mr. Rouncey's eyes widened suddenly. "That'd be it, Bart boy."

"What'd be what?"

"This Scott girl stood in for Marcia Bloom at Tuesday's performances. I remember hearing Sark—that's our theatre stooge—talking about it."

"So what, old man?"

"Easy. When you sign up with the films you guarantee

not to appear in any shows without permission. So it looks as if Crane tricked the Scott girl into thinking she'd got the studios' permission to play in *Lover's Luck* when actually she hadn't. And that meant Crane could blackmail her into cancelling the contract by threatening a suit for breach."

Mr. Snerd was genuinely indignant at this disclosure. "Dirty trick," he said.

"Show business, that's all." Mr. Rouncey, Mr. Snerd felt, was sneering at his ingenuousness. "Well, we'll have to see what can be done." He got unsteadily to his feet. "How much do you want?"

"A clear one-fifty."

"You won't get that much, Bart boy."

"That's my price," said Mr. Snerd easily. "It's up to you to get it. I'll collect in 'The Feathers' at opening time tonight." He caught Mr. Rouncey by the elbow as he turned to go. "And you won't forget I know about that business at Brighton, will you, old man? I shouldn't like you to get into any trouble over that."

"Ruddy blackmailer," said Mr. Rouncey.

"Now, that's no way to talk," said Mr. Snerd eupeptically. "We're good pals, aren't we? You do your best for me, and I'll do my best for you. Can't say fairer than that, can I?"

Mr. Rouncey was pocketing the letter.

"Bart boy, I can't promise anything," he said earnestly. "This ruddy letter's dynamite, see? If I can sell it 'em at all, you'll get your money. And that's the most I can say." He moved towards the door. "Remember, boy, it's ten to one they just won't touch it at all, scoop or no."

But Mr. Rouncey's prognosis was altogether too flattering to his employers' sense of decency. They touched it all right.

CHAPTER III

I

As its custom was, the four-o'clock edition of *The Evening Mercury* appeared on the streets of London at about three.

It was not a paper which Humbleby read, except when his business compelled him to or when, for masochistic or argumentative reasons, he felt the need to convince himself of the imminent collapse of all moral and cultural values. But on this fateful Monday it was on his desk by five past three, carried there by a sergeant with the air of those heralds in Greek tragedy who convey calamitous and often barely credible news to choruses of aghast and wondering citizens.

Humbleby had twice refused promotion, since he was not anxious for the increase in purely administrative work which it would certainly involve; but in spite of this (or perhaps even because of it) he was a person of some consequence at Scotland Yard, and his rage—the more impressive because it was so rare—spread through that elaborate hierarchy like an etheric wave. Indeed, the oily young man from the *Mercury* who brought him the original of Nicholas Crane's letter received from him such summary and shattering treatment that on emerging from the building he had to go to the park and sit down in order to recover himself.

The story had been written up very much on the lines contemplated by Mr. Rouncey. Its insinuations disported themselves beneath banner headlines, and the letter itself was reproduced in facsimile. Humbleby gazed upon it and fluently cursed; in spite of what he had said over the telephone, he was keeping Fen's theory of the case well in mind, and if that theory were correct, the *Mercury* had gratuitously performed a valuable service for the murderer in telling him where next to direct his energies.

As to the genuineness of the letter Humbleby was not in much doubt, but he passed it on to the Yard handwriting experts for their opinion. And having done that he set off, compassed about with a cloud of subordinates, to investigate its history.

The editor of *The Evening Mercury* received him with ill-concealed apprehension: Humbleby's mood made him appear disconcertingly like an agent of the Eumenides. Yes, said the editor, the letter had been sent anonymously through the post. To him personally? Well, no; actually to one of his reporters. . . .

Mr. Rouncey, far advanced in liquor and weeping copiously, was produced. With Mr. Snerd's knowledge of the Brighton affair vivid in his mind, he corroborated with unshakable obstinacy his editor's account of the letter's provenance. In the end Humbleby was obliged to leave them, unenlightened; but he thought it in the highest degree unlikely that Madge Crane would have left the letter lying about for anyone to pick up, and that must mean that it had been stolen. He drove on, accordingly, to her flat, where he found Felicity, a regular reader of the *Mercury*, in a very shaken and pensive frame of mind.

Judge's Rules went overboard in the interview that followed; Humbleby thought it improbable that Felicity had stolen the letter herself, since its publication was bound to bring her instantly under suspicion, but his examination was none the less completely ruthless. And Felicity, perceiving that her future as an employee of Miss Crane was now in any event dubious to a degree, did not fence with him for very long. She, too, saw that the letter must have been feloniously taken, and she had no doubt in her mind as to who had taken it. Thus it was that the whole story came out.

Long ago, she told Humbleby, she had suspected that "Peter Williams" was not what he represented himself to be. She had not specially resented his attempt at camouflage, but she had felt it necessary in her own interests to find out who he really was, and had therefore, one midday after they had said good-bye, followed him unobtrusively back to his office in Long Acre, and there acquainted herself with his true identity. He had spent the night with her at the flat, she said, and had left before she was awake. She was sure it was him as had done the thieving, the rotten dirty sneak, and left her to take the blame.

Where would Miss Crane have been likely to hide the letter? Well, there was a locked drawer in the desk in the sitting-room. . . .

Humbleby, finding the desk suspiciously innocent of all finger-prints, was much inclined to concur in Felicity's view of the matter. He haled her away with him to Long Acre in his car.

And there, sure enough, they came upon Mr. Snerd in his office, humming tunefully to himself and tidying up in readiness for his projected vacation. Confronted simultaneously by Felicity and the police, he was at first all injured innocence. But Humbleby had a shrewd notion that Mr. Snerd had handed the letter direct to Mr. Rouncey, and he stated, simply and firmly, that Mr. Rouncey had admitted this.

Thereupon Mr. Snerd lost his head, and fell to regaling them alternately with admissions of his own guilt and denunciations of Mr. Rouncey's supposititious treachery. Mr. Snerd was determined that if he were going to sink, Mr. Rouncey should sink with him, and he waxed orotund over the details of the Brighton affair. It concerned, apparently, the deliberate suppression for a bribe's sake of evidence important to the elucidation of a racecourse affray two years previously—but this was not Humbleby's business and he did not pay any very earnest attention to it. Leaving it to the cloud of subordinates to see to the arrests of both Mr. Snerd and Mr. Rouncey, he drove back alone to New Scotland Yard, conscious of having done a very satisfactory two hours' work.

The next step, obviously, was to see Nicholas Crane. Humbleby telephoned his flat in Mayfair, but there was no reply. Application to his mother's house had better results: he had driven there, it seemed, as soon as he had seen *The Evening Mercury*.

Humbleby collected certain chemicals and apparatus from the Yard's laboratories—a consequence, this precaution, of his unwilling respect for Fen's intelligence—and at six-thirty set out for Aylesbury.

2

He came to Lanthorn House, the residence of Mrs. Crane, as the last light was dropping over the western horizon. The house lay embowered in a cup-like confluence of low hills—so deeply embowered, indeed, that from the road it was not visible at all. Humbleby drove through dimly discerned heraldic gates, with adjacent stone-built lodges, and was at once among the trees of a large and unkempt estate. The carriage-way ran gradually and inexorably downwards; a gardener, trudging homewards in the company of an unattractive little girl, stopped and stared at Humbleby as he passed; massive rhododendron bushes loomed up on either side. And now, having at last achieved the floor of the hollow, Humbleby turned sharp left round a clutter of outhouses, and the featureless bulk of the house was in front of him. Between a phalanx of Corinthian pillars and a pedimented front door he brought the car to a halt and climbed out.

On the railway line which skirted the far side of the grounds a goods train whistled sardonically and clanked with deliberation out of earshot. Humbleby pressed the bell. Above his head the light of a caged electric bulb waxed and waned in rhythm with the pulsing of a heavy-oil engine which had become audible as soon as the car's ignition was switched off. He waited, and presently, becoming irritable at the delay in admitting him, pressed the bell again; and he was about to supplement this by plying the ornate brass knocker when the door was opened to him by an old, improvident-looking butler.

"No Press," said the butler promptly. "Be off with you, now, and quick about it."

"I am the police," said Humbleby coldly. "Please take me immediately to Mr. Nicholas Crane."

The butler peered at him with suspicion.

"You're not the one," he said, "as came and took away Mr. Maurice's medicine bottle. Don't you try any tricks on me, now."

"Stop arguing and let me in. It was one of my subordinates who was here before."

"A nice character you are to 'ave subordinates," said the butler resentfully. "I'll bet they love you like a father. . . . Well, I'll 'ave to admit you, I s'pose. Come on in and don't keep me standing 'ere 'alf the night."

Thus graciously inducted, Humbleby climbed the three shallow treads to the threshold and stepped inside. A mass of gleaming white statuary confronted him; the room, large and high as a gymnasium, was disposed about it like a frame. Faraday, the statuary might be; or Samuel Rogers; or just conceivably Palmerstone. Seated, it stared apprehensively at the door, as though anticipating the arrival of duns or bailiffs. Its base pinned a large though inferior Turkey carpet to the parquet floor. Portraits in ponderous gilt frames conversed wordlessly, and with the effect of administering a decisive snub, across the top of its head. A number of well-polished but clearly functionless tables—of the sort described as "occasional", but whose occasion somehow never arises—were ranged about the room's periphery like sitters-out at a ball. And the only other furniture consisted of two immense Victorian hat and umbrella stands which, flanking the door, flourished a multiplicity of knob-crowned arms, Vishnu-like, at the ceiling.

"You just wait 'ere," said the butler brusquely, "and I'll go and find out what's to be done about you."

He departed, and Humbleby resigned himself patiently to waiting; his profession had long since inured him to kicking his heels in ante-rooms at the pleasure of householders a great deal less cultivated and estimable than himself—and one usually, he reflected, got one's own back on them in the end. Comforted by this inexplicit prospect of retribution, Humbleby glanced idly up at the ceiling, where a number of ethereally graceful gods and goddesses were rioting about in one of those complicated and implausible intrigues which were apparently the main preoccupation of Olympus' waking hours. Angelica Kaufmann, perhaps; it was quite good enough for that. And to judge from this hallway, the rest of Lanthorn House would probably exhibit a very similar mingling of the æsthetically desirable and the æsthetically null. . . . It did not belong to Mrs. Crane, of course: she had rented it six months ago from Lord Boscoign, latest and probably last holder of an irremediably obscure barony, whose grandfather had refurnished it in its present style by dint of selling the near-by village, and who was now living precariously on its rent in a Harrogate boarding-house. A place as large as this, Humbleby reflected, must cost a good deal to run these days. So also must racehorses—and he had learned that these were Mrs. Crane's chief interest in life. So a windfall of fifty thousand pounds would very likely come in useful, and . . .

But at this point Humbleby's meditations were interrupted by the reappearance of the butler.

"They'll see you," said the butler, with the air of one whose good news is much against his inclination. "They'll see you now." He observed that Humbleby was removing his hat and coat. "Chuck those down anywhere. And get a move on, will you? I've got other things than you to attend to."

"Until I choose to be ready, you most certainly haven't," said Humbleby.

"Bossy, aren't you?" the aged creature snarled. "You just wait till the revolution, that's all. That'll finish you and your sort."

"There is not going to be any revolution."

"No, I don't think so either," said the butler unexpectedly. "And more's the pity. . . . Don't you go trying to make a complaint about me," he warned. "They won't listen to you, because if they sacked me they'd never get another like me."

"And thankful," said Humbleby.

The butler considered this, and when he spoke again his tone was confiding.

"No, you're wrong there," he said. "They're snobs, see? They'd rather have a stinking rotten butler like me," he said with candour, "than none at all."

"Yes, well, stop talking and take me to see them."

"All right, cock." The advance of old age had apparently induced in the butler that volatility of temperament most commonly associated with youth, and by now he was quite affable. "Keep your wool on. I'll look after you, never fear. This way, this way. And watch out for the mats, or you'll trip and do yourself a mischief." He tottered cheerfully away, and Humbleby followed.

The reception-room into which he was conducted was about the size and shape of an average cinema. The gallery of a mezzanine floor encircled it on three sides. There were more pictures in gilt frames—one of a horse, one of a blurred, crepuscular landscape, one of an eighteenth-century actor, more than twice life-size, starting up in exaggerated terror from a satin-covered couch. These, presumably, represented the taste of the present Lord Boscoign's grandfather. But there was also, withdrawn in a corner as if attempting to dissociate itself from the general decorative scheme, what looked very much like a Veronese. And there was more statuary—though here it was on an altogether discreeter and less forbidding scale than the nineteenth-century notability who so remorselessly scrutinised the inside of the front door. Faded, indifferent tapestry covered such of the wall-space as the paintings had been able to spare; an eight-foot settee and a variety of chairs stood in front of the fireplace; and in the fireplace itself—at whose sides two nude figures of surprisingly indeterminate sex struggled courageously to sustain, on the napes of their necks, an elaborate overmantel—there was a small log fire which hissed and flared sulkily.

Inside the door the butler halted, made a feeble attempt to look imposing, and after a little thought said:

"'Ere 'e is. This is 'im."

This task performed, he retired, inadvertently slamming the door behind him; and across broad acres of carpet Humbleby advanced on the group of people who stood or sat by the fire.

3

Nicholas Crane, sprawled on the long settee, looked up as he approached.

"Hallo, Inspector," he said. "Come and join the conference. And have some sherry."

"I won't for the moment, thank you, sir." Humbleby had not intended to speak stiffly, but after the *Mercury's* revelations he could feel no enthusiasm for Nicholas, and the words sounded unfriendly despite himself. "Not for the moment," he reiterated in more mollifying tones.

"Well, anyway, sit down."

Humbleby sat down and surveyed the gathering. Apart from Nicholas, Medesco was the only person present whom he knew—and he was slightly surprised to find Medesco on such intimate terms with the family that he could be admitted to an assembly whose purpose was clearly to discuss the *Mercury's* thunderbolt. Medesco sat with his great height and bulk overflowing a small chair, and with a cigar in the corner of his mouth; his small saurian eyes, framed between the formidable brow and the smooth, fat cheeks, gazed on Humbleby coldly and unblinkingly.

"Well, Inspector," he said. "We're in the thick of it, as you'll have guessed. You shall sit by and pick up the crumbs."

Nicholas nodded.

"I'm sorry we're not able to help you by having Madge here as well," he said. "If she was here, all the dirty linen could be washed at one go. But she hasn't got in touch with us, and there's no reply from the Doon Island number. Probably she hasn't even seen the blasted paper."

A little bald man, who was hovering at his side, gave a monitory cough.

"Now, now, Mr. Crane," he interposed. "We must be

careful what we say, mustn't we? Very, *very* careful indeed."

Nicholas sighed.

"This is my lawyer," he said to Humbleby. "Mr. Cloud. He's quite a nice chap in the normal way, but at the moment he's just a quivering mass of legal circumspection."

"In your own interests, Mr. Crane!" Mr. Cloud burst out. "In your own *interests*! If we are going to sue this newspaper——"

"We're not," said Nicholas briefly.

"But this is absurd! An action would lie. I can assure you that an action would lie. The greater the truth, the greater the libel. This is to say that——"

Mr. Cloud checked himself, belatedly conscious that in the present context his utterance of this forensic saw had been scarcely tactful. And Nicholas laughed.

"You don't spare my feelings, do you, Cloud?" he said. "But never mind. The *Mercury's* imputation is true, and for that reason——"

"Mr. Crane, I beg of you——"

"—for that reason, I shan't attempt to contest it." Nicholas smiled wryly. "This scandal is no more than I deserve. . . . Do you believe in atonement, Inspector?"

"As a Christian of sorts," said Humbleby cautiously, "I must."

"Well, putting up with this will be my atonement for that wretched girl's death. Not a very adequate one, I'm afraid, but thoroughly deserved."

"You think the scandal will affect your career?" Humbleby asked.

"It will finish my career," said Nicholas simply. "There are a great many very decent people in film business, and they'd no more work with me after this than they'd work with a leper."

Humbleby looked at him curiously. His reaction was unexpected but inspiriting; it seemed that he was by no means lost to all decent feeling. And Nicholas, perhaps sensing the trend of Humbleby's thought, shifted and reddened uncomfortably.

"Not that I want to make a great thing about it," he added. "But you must understand quite clearly, Cloud"—his voice sharpened—"that I'm *not* going to bring an action for libel. That's definite. If you try to argue about it, you'll simply be wasting your efforts."

His mother, who was standing in front of the fire and watching him thoughtfully, for the first time spoke.

"Madge will probably sue," she said in a naturally husky voice. "And what will happen then?"

Eleanor Crane was a tall woman—as tall, almost, as Medesco, but slim and stately. She had a lean, greyish face, untidy hair in which streaks of white mingled with the dull gold, and pale green eyes with a certain glint of humour in them. Humbleby had expected her to be in mourning for her son Maurice, but in fact she wore a coat and skirt of purplish-brown tweed, with rough wool stockings and brogue shoes.

"No, I'm not in black, Inspector." She had rightly interpreted his appraising glance. "Maurice was only my step-son, and I had no great liking for him, I'm afraid. He was a rake, and stupid."

"You agreed," said Humbleby, "to his bringing Miss Scott to stay here at Christmas."

"Certainly. But as soon as she arrived I took her aside and warned her directly of what she could expect if she didn't look out for herself. I told her of Maurice's habits, and I told her that if she gave in to him she needn't look forward to either marriage or advancement in films as a reward. She took," said Eleanor Crane coolly, "very great offence at my suggestions. And I understand that she paid no attention to my warnings. But if she wanted an ally against Maurice's intentions, she knew where to come, so I don't consider I shirked my obligations at all. . . . Where apparently I have shirked them is in my children's upbringing. They're all deplorable in one way or another —except, of course, David, who is merely dim."

David Crane was the only person there who had not yet opened his mouth. He was a young, thick-set man, going prematurely bald, of a type that emanates social uncertainty like ectoplasm.

"Oh, l-look here, m-mother," he protested.

"But let's get back to the point," said Eleanor Crane tranquilly; she was more immediately prepossessing, Humbleby thought, than any other member of the family he had encountered so far. "The point is, as I've said, that Madge will probably sue. And that means that if you, Nicholas dear, are going to persist in your very creditable policy of self-sacrifice, you'll have to go into the witness-box against her. It will make a very depressing spectacle, and one which I think ought to be avoided if possible. Mr. Cloud, what line would my daughter's lawyer be likely to take in a libel action against *The Evening Mercury*?"

Mr. Cloud, gratified at being appealed to, puffed himself up importantly.

"The publication of this letter," he said, "is calculated to bring Miss Crane into hatred, ridicule and contempt. So much is obvious, there would be no difficulty in proving it, and for that reason the action might possibly succeed. I refer, of course, to a civil action only. Alternatively, or in addition, Miss Crane might apply to a police court for a summons for criminal libel. If she does that, then the defendants will not have to prove that the letter is true—since in criminal libel that matter is largely irrelevant—and it is conceivable that Mr. Crane here would not be involved at all. On the other hand——"

"Quite so, Mr. Cloud." With some address, Eleanor Crane nipped this nascent homilectic in the bud. "But what I'm trying to ascertain is whether a civil action brought by my daughter would be likely to succeed. You say it 'might possibly'. What could prevent it from succeeding?"

"Proof," Mr. Cloud answered gloomily, "that the letter was true."

"Well, you're acquainted with the circumstances of the affair. Could such proof in fact be produced?"

"Yes, I rather think it could," said Mr. Cloud even more gloomily. "So long as Mr. Crane persists in asserting the letter's veracity, that is. Now, if he were to *join* Miss Crane in bringing the action——"

"I am not," said Nicholas firmly, "going to do anything of the sort."

"And in that case," said his mother, "my daughter's action would probably fail?"

Mr. Cloud nodded. "I'm afraid that that is so, yes."

"Well, if you think that, no doubt her lawyer will think it also. And I believe she has just sufficient sense to take his advice. The remaining problem is, will she apply for a summons for criminal libel?"

"As an act of vengeance, perhaps," said Mr. Cloud somewhat histrionically. "She could not, of course, by that method obtain monetary restitution, and I doubt if it would help to salvage her reputation."

"Then the position is clear at last." Eleanor Crane took her sherry from a niche in the overmantel and sipped it. "Nicholas is intent on immolation and will not take any sort of action. And Madge cannot succeed in a civil suit without his co-operation, and a summons for criminal libel would do her no earthly good. I think that since that's so she'll cut her losses and keep quiet—don't you, Aubrey?"

Medesco grunted. "The girl's a conceited, over-sexed little ass," he opined dispassionately, "and the power she wields over everyone in film business has gone to her head. In my view she's perfectly capable of cutting off her nose to spite her face. But I suggest that the thing to do is to stop theorising about it and wait until we can get in touch with her."

"And in the meantime?" Nicholas asked.

"In the meantime," said Humbleby, "I think you should take certain precautions, Mr. Crane."

"Precautions . . .? Oh, ah. Yes, I see what you mean. Your Professor Fen made the same suggestion on Saturday. Your idea is that in view of what the *Mercury* has published I'm likely to be the poisoner's next victim—or possibly Madge."

"There is that possibility," said Humbleby seriously, "and it would be silly to neglect it." He frowned. "In fact, your failure to get through to Miss Crane at Doon Island is worrying me slightly. If you'll be so good as to take me to a telephone I think I'll ring up the Doon Island police and ask them to pay her a visit—simply as a precaution."

It was Nicholas who led him to the telephone. Humbleby returned, having done what was necessary, in five minutes, and found them silent and embarrassed—a consequence, perhaps, of something that had been discussed while he was away.

"So you still have no notion, Inspector," said Eleanor Crane, "as to who killed Maurice?"

"I'm afraid not, Mrs. Crane. We're doing everything that can be done."

"Vengeance." Almost imperceptibly she shivered. "Is that your theory about the motive?"

"It's an idea I'm keeping in mind," said Humbleby reservedly as he sat down again.

Eleanor Crane laughed, suddenly and harshly, but not without amusement.

"Another," she said, "being that I get control of Maurice's money. You knew that, didn't you? Yes, of course you did. I told that pleasant young man you sent here on Saturday afternoon."

Humbleby remained impassive and said nothing. But:

"Oh, l-look here, m-mother, that's absurd," said David Crane. "It's s-silly to put ideas into p-people's heads. I know you n-never p-pay any attention to what I say, b-but . . ."

"David dear, your loyalty does you credit but not, I'm afraid, your intelligence. . . . And I may as well admit, Inspector, that I need that money. I've had heavy losses recently on the tracks, and I was beginning to wonder if I'd ever be able to meet my obligations."

"Indeed, ma'am." The investigations of his subordinates had made Humbleby acquainted with this fact twenty-four hours ago, and the admission did not interest him. What did interest him was the presence here of Aubrey Medesco, and he went on to say casually: "I was a little surprised to find this gentleman with you."

"There is absolutely no limit," said Medesco, "to the things that surprise the police. Their capacity for amazement makes Candide look like the most degenerate of urban sophisticates."

"Mr. Medesco," said Eleanor pleasantly, "is an old friend of the family, Inspector."

"W-well, n-not an *old* friend, m-mother." David seemed anxious to be helpful. "B-because when I c-came back from U.S.A. t-two years ago we didn't know him, and I remember w-when you said you w-were going to m-marry him I s-said to m-myself . . ."

"David!" said Eleanor in good-humoured exasperation. "I thought I told you that my engagement to Mr. Medesco was to remain a secret for the present."

"Oh, s-sorry, m-mother. I only thought . . ."

"No, dear. You only failed to think." There was a hint of real annoyance underlying Eleanor Crane's tolerant smile. "Well, that's one cat out of the bag, Inspector."

"My congratulations, sir," said Humbleby gravely. "And to you, ma'am, every happiness." He was not surprised that they had wanted to keep the engagement a secret, for a *mariage de convenance* is always apt to arouse the world's scorn, and particularly if it is between elderly people; but he was also not surprised that in this instance it had been arranged, since he had sensed from the first—little though they had spoken to one another—a very definite sympathy between Medesco and Mrs. Crane. Whether this posture of affairs would prove to have any importance in the case he did not know; there was the point, of course, that——

And Mrs. Crane caught up his train of thought at precisely the stage where she interrupted it.

"So there is the point," she said, "that Aubrey, too, had a motive for killing Maurice—since presumably he would prefer to marry a wife who was *not* impecunious."

Medesco looked up at her, and it was the first time Humbleby had seen him smile.

"My dear girl," he said, "I'd marry you if you were a barmaid."

Eleanor Crane had crossed to the table on which the sherry decanter stood, and was refilling her glass.

"Apposite," she commented. "Perfect timing. Are you

sure you won't have a drink, Inspector? If you don't like sherry our insufferable butler could be made to produce something else. Or is it a regulation that you mustn't drink when you're on duty?"

Having assured her that no such regulation existed, Humbleby accepted sherry and pledged her very courteously in it.

"And now," she said, "we've been holding you up for too long with chatter about our personal affairs. Tell us why you came."

"To investigate in detail, I'm afraid, this whole affair of Miss Scott's contract." Humbleby turned to Nicholas. "If you'd prefer to talk about it in private, sir . . ."

"No, no," said Nicholas wearily. "We may as well drag the whole squalid business out into the open, and be done with it."

At this, Mr. Cloud became vastly agitated.

"I have to advise you, Mr. Crane," he said perturbedly, "that you are not under any obligation to answer the Inspector's questions. And indeed, in your own interests——"

"Hush, Cloud." Nicholas wagged a finger at him. "I appreciate your efforts, but they're misplaced. Your job is to protect me from the Press. . . . And by the way, where *is* the Press? They're being remarkably discreet. I expected hordes of reporters, and not a single one has turned up so far—though they have rung me up to ask for a statement."

"They are obliged to go carefully," said Mr. Cloud. "The situation is delicate, and they are obliged to go very, *very* carefully indeed. We might take a hint from them, eh, Mr. Crane?"

Nicholas groaned. "Sit down, Cloud," he said. "Stop fidgeting about. Drink your sherry."

"Very well, sir." Mr. Cloud was clearly offended. "But if you will not be ruled by me I can take no responsibility, none whatever." He sat down heavily and mopped his brow. "Please understand that this statement is not made with my approval."

"*Mea maxima culpa,*" said Nicholas. "You shall have a signed exoneration, Cloud, signed and witnessed. . . . And now, Inspector, let's get on with it."

4

An expectant silence fell upon the group. Eleanor Crane had her shoulder against the mantelpiece, and was staring absently at the Veronese in the corner. Medesco remained immobile, his small eyes almost closed. Mr. Cloud, deflated, sipped his sherry as though it were unspeakably distasteful to him. And only David Crane seemed unaffected by the atmosphere: he had picked up an illustrated magazine and was turning its pages attentively, as if, cat-like, he had for the time being completely forgotten what was going forward.

"I'm sorry to have to probe this matter, sir," said Humbleby. "But for one thing, it's obviously bound up with Miss Scott's suicide, and for another, there's Mr. Maurice Crane's death to consider. You see——"

"Yes, yes, Inspector," Nicholas interrupted. "There's no need to apologise. I don't suspect you of having come down here out of mere idle curiosity." He paused to light a cigarette, inhaled deeply, and went on:

"This is what happened.

"Madge was at the bottom of it all—I don't say that to excuse myself, but the fact remains that she was the prime mover. She hated poor Gloria; and the reason for that, of course, was Stuart North.

"Stuart and Gloria were both in *Visa for Heaven*, which

I directed. Gloria only had a tiny part, but her scene in the film involved Stuart as well, and that was how they met. Stuart fell for her, in a mild way. I don't know whether she was genuinely interested in him, but anyway, it flattered her to be touted about by a star."

"Yes, and that raises a point I don't quite understand," said Eleanor Crane. "What on earth made her go after Maurice as well? Did she seriously imagine she could run both of them simultaneously?"

"Well, I don't *know*, but I've an idea she left Stuart for Maurice as soon as she found out how much Stuart detested films. Specifically a film career was what she was after, and from that point of view Maurice was a more promising ally than Stuart, who wanted to get away from films as soon as he possibly could. But where all that's concerned your guess is as good as mine.

"We finished *Visa for Heaven* at the end of November, and it was about then that Stuart met Madge for the first time. I don't pretend to be able to interpret my precious sister's motives, but anyway, she made a dead set at Stuart. And unluckily for her, Gloria had got in first.

"That, no doubt, made her keener than ever. She's got a nice technique of persuasion, has Madge. You see, apart from Leiper himself, she's easily the most important person at the studios, and no one who doesn't want to risk losing his job dares offend her. Even Leiper has to handle her carefully, because she's a fabulous money-maker, and if he lost her to Rank or Korda his profits 'd drop like an express lift.

"But the trouble about Stuart, from her point of view, was that she couldn't put this technique into action against him, for the simple reason that he'd much rather be on the stage than in films. So if Madge wanted him for an *inamorato*, she'd have to rely on her unaided charms. And with Gloria about, they didn't seem to work very well."

Outside the two high windows that flanked the fireplace it was almost completely dark, and the rising wind blew a spatter of raindrops against the panes. The huge room—surely, in origin, a ballroom—was dimly lighted; only round the fire was there a circle of greater radiance, and this waxed and waned perceptibly with the pulse of the engine that supplied it. The fire was burning low, and Nicholas got up to throw another log on to it before going on.

"Well, that was the situation," he said. "Until *The Unfortunate Lady*, my sweet sister couldn't do anything nasty to Gloria, for the simple reason that Gloria didn't have a job. Then the question of casting Martha Blount came up, and I recommended Gloria for the part. Jocelyn—Jocelyn Stafford, that is—is a bit other-worldly where studio scandal is concerned; he had no idea there was any antagonism between Madge and Gloria, and I didn't go out of my way to tell him. So he interviewed the girl and signed her up. I thought that when Madge heard about it she'd just resign herself to making the best of a bad job. I was wrong. I honestly hadn't a notion how much she loathed Gloria. If I had had, I certainly wouldn't have suggested Gloria for that part. She deserved to get it, mind you—but my encouragement of young actresses normally stops short if it seems likely to create a first-class, flaming row.

"And that's just what it did create. When Madge heard what had happened, she cornered me and issued an ultimatum. If Gloria's contract wasn't revoked, she said, she'd go to Leiper and tell him that if I didn't leave his organisation she would. And we were both well aware which of us he'd choose to keep. I wasn't signed up for anything after *The Unfortunate Lady*, and if I'd ignored Madge's orders I should have been out on my neck."

"My dear boy," said his mother, "surely with your reputation, Rank——"

But Nicholas shook his head.

"Unlikely," he interrupted. "The industry's at a low ebb at the moment, and the other companies have got many more directors on tap than they can use. I'd quite definitely have been out of a job—and that possibility didn't please me a bit."

He looked at them wryly.

"Cowardice, you think? Yes, I admit it was. But I couldn't possibly have foreseen that Gloria would *kill* herself, could I? And I swear to you"—he leaned forward and spoke very earnestly—"I swear to you that I meant to make it up to Gloria afterwards in some way Madge *couldn't* interfere with.

"The plan was Madge's. Even for her sake Leiper probably wouldn't have gone back on that contract once it was signed—and in any case, she wasn't at all anxious to have it known that she was doing Gloria down. The basic idea, of course, was to leave the dirty work to me. And the circumstances were all in favour. Marcia Bloom was playing the lead in *Lover's Luck*. Her father had died, and she wanted to go to Ireland for the funeral, and that meant a stand-in for last Tuesday evening's performance, and just as it happened, her understudy had been taken off to hospital with appendicitis or something. And Jedd—*Lover's Luck* is his show—is a man I know fairly well. It all fitted very nicely.

"You know what the idea was. People who have contracts with a film company have to have permission from the company to appear on the stage or the radio. It's nearly always given, so really the thing's little more than a formality. Still, if you don't observe that formality you've broken your contract, and you're capable of being sued.

"In their own interests theatrical managers generally see to it that that permission has been given." Here Nicholas grew perceptibly uneasy. "But as Jedd knew me, he was prepared to take my word for it and didn't ask for any other evidence."

"In your letter," Humbleby interposed mildly, "there is a sentence which suggests that——"

"Mr. Crane!" Cloud, who had been following the narrative with an air of hypnotised gloom, now sat upright so abruptly that he upset his sherry on to his knee. "It would be undesirable for us to enter into detail at this point. Very, *very* undesirable. We don't want to give the Inspector the idea that we're an accessory after a fact, do we now? We don't want——"

"Calm yourself, Cloud," said Nicholas. "And wipe your trousers. There's no question of my being an accessory after a fact. Where Jedd's concerned, there isn't a fact. To my knowledge, he's never done anything in the least criminal."

"Then," Humbleby prompted, "the reason why you assured Miss Crane that he would not give the—um—conspiracy away was——"

"Was to do with his private life. A matter of marital infidelity."

Cloud gave vent to a loud moan. "Mr. Crane, Mr. Crane! We must not lay ourselves open to any imputation of blackmail. We must not——"

"Once and for all, Cloud," said Nicholas in exasperation, "will you be *quiet*. . . . I merely told Jedd that I should like Gloria to have the opportunity of standing in for Marcia Bloom, and after he'd talked to her he agreed to give her the chance."

Eleanor Crane raised her eyebrows.

"Theatrical managers," she observed dryly, "are obviously more trusting nowadays than they used to be."

Her son brushed this sarcasm peremptorily aside. "None the less, that is what happened. And you'll understand that Gloria herself wasn't at all averse to the idea when I put it up to her. . . . I was contemptible enough," said Nicholas steadily, "to tell her she'd be doing me a favour by standing in for Marcia; and God help me, she was very anxious to do me any favour she could. . . .

"Well, it was all arranged. I told Gloria—not in front of witnesses—that I'd see to getting the company's permission for her to appear, that she could leave all that side of it to me. Of course she trusted me." Nicholas gave a short, toneless laugh. "Why shouldn't she? I liked her and I'd always done what I could for her."

Eleanor Crane made a movement of impatience.

"These self-tormentings may be all very well, Nicholas," she said, "but a public exhibition of them strikes me as being in poorish taste. You've assured us several times how badly you feel about it all, and we quite believe you. So for the moment just confine yourself to the facts."

Nicholas looked at her queerly.

"Very well, mother," he answered in a dull, uninflected voice. "I'll confine myself to the facts. . . .

"The next fact is that Gloria slaved for four days to get the part up. I'm told she was very good in it, though I didn't see her myself.

"And then, of course, I had to tell her what she'd let herself in for.

"That was really why I asked her to my party. When everyone else had gone, I kept her behind to talk to her.

"There's no need to tell you in detail what I said. I should have liked to have put the blame on Madge, but I didn't dare. And anyway, by that time I was quite as culpable as she was.

"But the really horrible thing is that what I said to Gloria was almost pure bluff. It wasn't that she'd been tricked into an impossible position; it was that I deceived her into *imagining* she had. In other words, I was trading on her relative ignorance of film business. My line, you see, was that she'd broken her contract by appearing in *Lover's Luck*; and that if she didn't want to be sued for breach she'd better let me arrange for the contract to be cancelled—a thing I could quite easily do. But the point is that if she'd just dug her heels in and said 'Let them sue', I was foxed, because I knew damn well how unlikely it was that they would."

Grimacing, Medesco threw the butt of his cigar into the fire.

"And she realised, no doubt," he observed, "that if she fought your obvious intention of gerrymandering her out of her contract, you'd see to it that she never got another. So whether she believed you or whether she thought you were bluffing, it all came to the same thing from her point of view: she was finished in films."

"Oh, God, I hadn't thought of that." Nicholas closed his eyes and with his thumb and forefinger massaged their lids, like a man in the last stages of physical exhaustion. "Well, anyway, you know how it worked out," he went on after a moment's pause. "I—I knew she'd be upset, naturally. But I never dreamed she'd take it as badly as she did. Her reaction was so violent and horrible that I could scarcely believe she wasn't just acting. But her face went grey, it looked pinched and frightful, and you can't act that sort of thing. When I'd finished she didn't say anything—anything at all. She just turned and ran out of the flat.

"And then . . .

"Well, then she went away and killed herself."

5

For a long half-minute there was complete silence.

Nicholas' final words had sounded thin and bloodless in that huge room, and the shadows which on three sides beleaguered the group by the fire seemed now to be darker and more pervasive. Draughts fingered the worn tapestries on the walls, and the effect of the ebb and flow of the light had become mesmeric. You could hear that now it was raining in real earnest; though you could not see it, because the window-panes were as dull and black as if they had been coated with creosote. The balustrade of the mezzanine gallery was ghostly in the upper darkness.

And the drowned girl, it seemed to Humbleby, stood among them as vividly as an actual phantom. Except perhaps for David, everyone there had her in his mind's eye. A tag from Voltaire drifted irrelevantly into Humbleby's mind: "*Make love like fools when you are young, and work like devils when you are old: it is the only way to live*". And that, it occurred to him, enabled one to diagnose accurately enough what had been the defect in Gloria Scott: while still in her teens she had been an uncompromising *arriviste*, and about such a figure there is something inevitably pathetic and incongruous. First and foremost the young should always concern themselves simply with living, with experiencing. Let them be ambitious, yes; but what is precious—Humbleby had a sentimental liking for this poem of Spender's which Fen might not have approved—what is precious is never to forget the delight of the blood drawn from ageless springs breaking through rocks in worlds before our earth. And *arrivisme* is always and everywhere a denial of that. . . .

Humbleby pulled himself together. Nebulous, amateurish excursions into mysticism might be all very well, but this was not the moment for them.

"Thank you, Mr. Crane," he said; and as if the words had been a signal, the group round the fire shifted and broke. David threw aside his magazine. Medesco heaved himself out of his chair and moved his great bulk, not without a certain feline grace, to a position in front of the hearth, where he stood with his hands clasped behind his back. Eleanor, glancing at her watch, excused herself briefly and left the room on some domestic errand. Nicholas got to his feet, replenished his glass with sherry, drank it at a gulp, and filled again. Only Cloud, subdued by what he had heard, and ruminating, perhaps, some opposition between his professional advantage and his personal sense of moral fitness—only Cloud remained motionless.

"Well, that's that," Nicholas said with an attempt at levity. "The confessional is now closed for the night, and the repentant sinner will direct three Government documentaries by way of expiation. . . . Is that funny? No, I suppose in the circumstances it isn't."

Humbleby was regarding him speculatively.

"I think," he said, "that I must have missed Professor Fen's warning to you."

"Warning?" Nicholas echoed vaguely.

"You said earlier on that on Saturday he advised you to take certain precautions."

"Oh, that. . . . Yes, he did. He said he thought it'd be a good thing if Madge and I didn't eat or drink anything except what other people were eating and drinking."

"And have you been taking his advice?"

"I have, yes. He's got something of a reputation as a criminologist, I understand, so I thought that probably he had reason for the warning. And besides that, he said another thing which made me decide that he must be rather a perceptive sort of person."

"What was that?"

"A plain hint that he'd guessed there was hanky-panky about Gloria's contract. It can't possibly have been anything *except* a guess, but it was an uncomfortably accurate one."

"And did you pass on his warning to your sister?"

"I did. But I doubt if she's been paying any attention to it. She's probably reached that stage of megalomania at which you begin to fancy you're immortal. And in any case," Nicholas added, dropping to a more prosaic level, "she's one of those people who quite automatically do the opposite of what they're advised to do. If I wanted her to go to Iceland for a holiday, I should tell her that the sunshine of Italy was what she needed, and the next thing I knew she'd be at Reykjavik or the North Pole, chucking soap into geysers for the benefit of the newsreel cameras."

"I see. . . . What precautions have you yourself taken?"

"Well, I've been having all my meals and drinks out, at restaurants and bars, that's really what it amounts to. And even before you found out that Maurice's tonic had been poisoned, I gave up taking my own medicine. . . . Look here, Inspector, was Maurice's death an act of revenge?"

"I can't say more than I said before, sir, and that is that there's a fifty-fifty chance it was."

Nicholas considered this. "Then let's suppose that thanks to the *Mercury* the poisoner wants to get at me as well. He can't put his stuff in the drinks at my flat without breaking open the sideboard, because the woman who cleans for me is slightly dipso. and I have to keep them locked up. He *can* put it in the odds and ends of food and drink I keep there, and he *can* put it in my medicine—provided, of course, that he can get into the flat. . . . As a matter of fact, I've got the medicine with me. . . . No, no, I'm not intending to *take* it, my dear chap. But I've got a chemist friend in Aylesbury and it occurred to me to ask him to test it for me. One does like to know where one stands. I forgot to take it to him on the way down here, but I can drop it in tomorrow morning."

"If you care to let me have it, sir, I can test it for colchicine straight away."

"Test it for *what*?"

"Colchicine. That's what killed your brother."

"Damned if I've ever heard of it."

"It's rare, certainly. And even if your medicine has been poisoned, that particular toxin may not have been used—though poisoners usually tend to stick to their formula."

"It's like a dream, isn't it?" said Nicholas a little dazedly. "Dispassionate, civilised chat about whether someone is trying to kill one or not. . . Well, I'll get you the medicine. When you say you can test it straight away do you mean here and now?"

"If you can give me a room to work in."

"Yes, of course we can. I'll consult Mamma about it. . . . Oh, here she is now. Mother, the Inspector wants a room to do chemical experiments in."

"Good heavens." Eleanor Crane's astonishment was pleasantly artificial. "Not trying to isolate bloodstains, surely?"

Nicholas explained the position to her and she nodded. "Yes," she said, "that can certainly be managed. There's a sort of box-room that might do, with a table and a chair and a wash-basin and a gas fire that works. You must have a look at it, Inspector, and see if it suits you."

"I'll fetch the stuff and bring it back here," said Nicholas, and departed.

"But first, how about dinner?" said Eleanor. "We usually dine at eight, and it's after nine, and our cook pretends to take pride in the food she serves up, revolting though it generally is, and she's muttering about giving notice. Inspector, you'll dine with us, I hope?"

"Thank you, ma'am," said Humbleby urbanely. "It's kind of you to ask me, but I'd rather go ahead with this job. Perhaps, if it wouldn't be too much trouble, a sandwich. . . ."

"By all means. Mr. Cloud, you'll stay, of course?"

The lawyer stood up slowly. His face had a strained, vacant look.

"Thank you, Mrs. Crane, but I should prefer not to," he said. "In the usual way I don't allow my personal feelings to intrude upon my business, but in this instance—in this case . . ."

The little man's struggle to express himself at once honestly and tactfully was not without dignity. After a fractional hesitation he went on:

"I'm sorry to say that after what I've heard I shall never again be able to devote myself wholeheartedly to Mr. Crane's affairs. And I think, therefore, that it would be best for him to have some other legal adviser. I—if you will pardon me, I'll leave now, and write to him about it in the morning."

"I can see your point of view, Mr. Cloud," said Eleanor gravely, "and I quite sympathise with it."

"You're very kind, Mrs. Crane. Very kind. . . . No, please don't ring. I can let myself out. Good evening, Mrs. Crane. Good evening to you all. . . ."

He bowed himself through the door. And by the time Nicholas returned, David, too, had left—in order, as he was at pains to inform them, to wash his hands in readiness for the impending meal. The medicine proved to be a milky fluid in the usual graded bottle; about a third of it had been used.

"What is it prescribed for?" Humbleby asked.

Nicholas grinned. "What they call nervous dyspepsia—though when I look at poor old Evan George, with all his bellyaches, I feel quite ashamed of making a fuss about it. . . . I imagine it's mostly bicarbonate. That's what it tastes like, anyway."

"Ah. Well, I'll get my bag out of my car, and then, if you'd be so kind as to show me to this room . . ."

Ten minutes later he was alone there. It was small, bare and inhospitable, high up among the attics, but quite suitable for his purpose. Beyond its uncurtained windows, in a darkness unrelieved by moon or stars, the tops of tall trees sighed and whispered in the steady downpour. The aged but mercurial butler brought him substantial quantities of sandwiches and beer.

"Some scandal, eh?" he said affably. "Driving poor honest working girls to suicide. But that's the boss class all over."

"Miss Scott worked only spasmodically," said Humbleby, "and there is no evidence that she was honest."

The butler ignored this. "But Mr. Maurice, 'e got what was coming to 'im," he observed. "Seduced 'er, 'e did. Droy de saygnur, that's what they called it in the bad old days of laysez-feer.—I dare say you don't know French, so I'll translate that for you. It means working girls being forced by law to go to bed with the upper classes, see?"

"You know what you're like?" said Humbleby. "You're like some ghastly relic left over from the earliest origins of the Fabian Movement."

The butler ignored this, too.

"So I can tell what you're saying to yourself," he pursued. "You're saying to yourself: 'Now, 'ow does it come about that a straightforward chap like old Syd Primrose *works* for a lot of degenerate capitalists like the Cranes?' You're saying to yourself——"

"I'm saying to myself that I shouldn't be surprised to find you licking the boots of people who torture little children for the fun of it."

The butler took this observation in very bad part. His face became suffused with senile fury.

"You shut yer trap," he snarled, transported. "*And* keep it shut. Don't think you can malinger me," he shouted, "and get away with it. Just you wait till we 'ave the revolution. Just you——"

"You said earlier," Humbleby pointed out, "that we weren't going to have a revolution."

"Never you mind what I said, Mr. Bossy. Castin' a man's words in 'is teeth. Spittin' in a poor old chap's eye. Why——"

"I'll boot a poor old chap hard in the backside," said Humbleby, "if he doesn't get out of here and leave me alone. For God's sake, go away and read *The New Statesman* or something. I'm busy."

The ancient Primrose summoned up his energies for an annihilating blast of invective. None, however, came. It was not that he had thought better of it; rather it was as if he had suddenly lost all recollection of what was being talked about. His face smoothed itself out, and he nodded agreeably.

"So that's settled, then," he remarked inconsequently. "Got all you want, 'ave you? You've only got to ring if you need anything." He made for the door and paused there. "About torturing children," he said earnestly. "I don't 'old with it." He adopted a lecture-room posture, one finger upraised. "Now——"

"Get," said Humbleby, "out."

Primrose went.

Thereupon Humbleby settled down to work. He enjoyed playing with chemicals, and applied himself single-mindedly to the task in hand. From his case he took test-tubes, nitric acid, sulphuric acid and caustic potash, and for ten minutes was pleasantly occupied with them. Then he sat back and pensively considered the results.

To both the tests he had applied the reaction had been positive. One needed a control experiment, of course, using medicine that was known to be unadulterated; but it was very unlikely that a prescription for dyspepsia would contain any substance capable of provoking the same chemical reactions as colchicine—unlikely, indeed, that any such substance existed. Zeisel's reaction (which was rather too complicated for Humbleby to perform at the moment) would clinch the matter, but even without that there was no doubt in his mind that Nicholas Crane's medicine contained colchicine.

It looked, then, as if Fen's original reading of the case—his interpretation of it as an act of vengeance—might well be correct. But there were two other possibilities—the first, that a murderer unconnected with Gloria Scott had reason for killing Nicholas as well as Maurice; and the second, that Nicholas had killed Maurice from a motive yet to be discovered, and was now attempting to disarm suspicion by simulating a scheme for murdering himself. Neither of these alternatives, however, struck Humbleby as being particularly convincing, since neither accounted for the obliteration of Gloria Scott's true identity by the ransacking of her rooms in Stamford Street. The girl's motive for committing suicide was now plain; on no conceivable hypothesis could the invasion of her rooms have helped to keep that motive secret; therefore the Stamford Street affair—unless it were wholly irrelevant and accidental, which Humbleby simply refused to believe—must be connected with the murders. And the only connection which Humbleby could imagine was precisely that which Fen had adumbrated in the first instance—the theory of an avenging murderer, associated with Gloria Scott at the time when she was using her proper name, and anxious (naturally enough) to occlude that connection before initiating his ghastly vendetta.

Thus Humbleby meditated, while he munched sandwiches and gulped beer. And the urgent problem, he saw, was how far-reaching this vendetta was likely to be. Since it included Nicholas, thanks to the *Mercury's* informative ways, it would presumably be bound to include Madge as well. And further than that? Well, it might prove to be a vendetta in the strict sense of the word—an indiscriminate attack on the entire family, regardless of whether they had harmed Gloria Scott or no. In that case, Humbleby reflected, it was going to be very difficult to deal with indeed. Better, on the whole, assume that the poisoner's malevolence was directed against specific people until events proved otherwise. . . . And upon this callous decision—since the "events" he contemplated would almost certainly be homicidal—Humbleby finished his viands, pushed the tray aside, and began repacking his chemicals and apparatus. The next step, anyway, was clear: he must find out what opportunity there had been for poisoning Nicholas' medicine.

6

In the event, however, this enterprise was slightly delayed. Humbleby met Nicholas coming up the stairs to report a telephone call from the police at Doon Island.

"Ah, yes, I asked them to ring me back as soon as they'd made sure Miss Crane was all right," said Humbleby.

Nicholas turned and they went down to the hall together.

"You've completed your tests?" Nicholas enquired.

"Yes."

"And the result? Or mayn't I ask?"

"Of course you may. After all, it does concern you very intimately. . . . The bottle of medicine you gave me was in fact poisoned."

"With this colchicine muck?"

"Yes."

Nicholas whistled.

"Well, at least I know where I am now," he said wryly. "What happens next?"

"I must talk to you about opportunity for poisoning the medicine. Are you nearly at the end of dinner?"

"Yes. We've been gobbling away in an unsociable silence. I can be with you as soon as you've finished talking on the 'phone. We'll have some coffee in the boudoir—that's that door there."

Inspector Berkeley, on Doon Island, seemed disposed to be chatty.

"Yes, she's as safe as houses," he said in answer to Humbleby's first query. "I interviewed her personally—luscious bit of flesh, isn't she?"

Humbleby frowned at this familiarity; he did not, he said, want to waste time evaluating the merely aphrodisiac properties of the girl. What had happened at the interview?

"Well, I told her there was a possibility she was in danger," pursued Berkeley, chastened, "and to be short about it, she just laughed at me."

"Good heavens above, you can't have been very impressive with her, can you? Had she seen the *Mercury*?"

"Oh, yes. There was a copy there in the room. She

was pretty brazen about it all, but I could see she was on edge."

"With your discernment, you should have been a psychiatrist."

"Yes, but it's a useful gift when you're in the Force, too," said Berkeley, unaware of the irony. "She was on edge all right. And of course, when I say she laughed at me, I don't mean she actually *laughed.*"

"No. You just put that bit in to confuse me."

"She wasn't in a *jolly* mood, that's to say. And small wonder, if you ask me."

"Small wonder indeed," said Humbleby heavily, "with a libidinous flatfoot like you goggling at her."

"Hey!" said Berkeley indignantly. "That's a slander. . . ." A new thought struck him. "I tell you what, though. Her legs are a disappointment."

"With your imaginings, you'd probably find any real pair of legs a disappointment. . . . This is serious, man. *Did you manage to impress on her that she's got to look after herself?* Since I 'phoned you first, new evidence has come up which makes it even more urgent. She really is in very grave danger of being killed."

"Cripes," said Berkeley soberly. "Well, all I can say is that I did my best."

"You warned her about food and drink and medicines and that sort of thing?"

"Yes, I did that. I don't think that she's going to pay any attention, though."

"And even if she does, we can't just leave it at that. Our *X* may try a more direct approach. You must have a man stationed outside the house night and day."

"Right," said Berkeley briskly. "I'll deal with that at once. Anything else?"

"Let's see. . . . Is the house burglar-proof?"

"Far from it. It's only a little cottage."

"Well, try and see to it that she locks the doors and shuts the windows when she goes to bed. You can't force her to, of course, but with a little tact you may be able to manage it. . . . Oh, look here, I'd better telephone her myself."

"You can try, but I doubt if you'll get through. The thing rang three times while I was with her, and she didn't answer it once. Seems to be a policy."

"Blast the girl. Well, I can't spare the time to come down and argue with her, so you'll have to take complete responsibility. I'll get the A.C. to contact your Chief Constable so that you can have all the men and facilities you need."

"Oh, for God's sake don't do that," wailed Berkeley. "I don't want Sir Cyril hanging round the station all day. I can manage it easily on my own. It's a slack time here."

"All right, then. . . . Oh, now I come to think of it, you'd better have two men at the cottage: one to follow her—in a car, if necessary—whenever she goes out."

"She's not going to like that, you know. What do I do if she turns nasty?"

"Stick to your guns—but politely, of course. If she makes a fuss at a higher level, I'll shoulder the blame. . . . Is she alone?"

"No. Got her secretary with her. Grim, hatchet-faced female. As far as I can gather, the secretary's doing all the cooking and whatnot."

"M'm. Get her on your side if you can. And for the Lord's sake, Berkeley, don't trip up on the job. There's a murderer loose, and if he gets a chance at Madge Crane there'll be a national uproar."

And that, thought Humbleby as he replaced the receiver,

is about as much as I can do along those lines. Now for Nicholas.

Nicholas, it was obvious, had devoted the interregnum of Humbleby's telephoning to putting his evidence in order. After a brief, incurious enquiry as to his sister's safety he embarked on it.

"The first thing," he said, "is that my flat is practically impossible to break into. And up to the time I left it this afternoon it hadn't been broken into, I can assure you of that."

"Good. And then?"

"Well, as you know, Thursday was the night of the wretched party, so I suppose I'd better start from there. After Gloria had gone, I locked up the flat and went to bed. And early on Friday I came on here; when I get sick of my own company I sometimes do that, and stay a night or two, and I wasn't feeling at all fond of my own company after that ghastly business with Gloria."

"Let me get just one thing clear: you're not working at the moment?"

"Not apart from *The Unfortunate Lady* conferences, no. I'm between films."

"Just so. Go on, then."

"Well, the thing is, you see, that there are burglar alarms on the door and windows of the flat; they ring in the porter's office on the ground floor, and there's always a man there. The fellow who had the flat before me was a diamond merchant, and it was him had the alarms installed. I always switch them on when I go away from the flat for more than a few hours, because I've got one or two pictures —a Cézanne and a Picasso—that'd be quite worth stealing. . . . Anyway, what it all amounts to is that up to the time I went back to the flat—that's to say, Saturday afternoon, after Maurice's death—no one could possibly have got at that medicine. And *after* that, for reasons I needn't go into in detail, no one could have got at it till this morning."

"This morning, then: how was it accessible this morning?"

"I told you I've been having my meals out, didn't I? Yes. Well, this morning I got up early and strolled up to a sort of snack-bar place in North Row for breakfast. They do you delicious home-made sausages there, with little crisp bits of raw onion in them. . . . However.

"The point is that I didn't shut the front door of the flat properly. When I got back I found it was open—not wide open, mind you, but not latched. At first I imagined someone might have got hold of a duplicate key somehow, but then it struck me that if someone had, they'd certainly have been careful to close the door properly when leaving, so as not to suggest that the place had been entered; and besides, I remembered vaguely—the way one does—that the door hadn't clicked properly when I shut it on the way out."

"You mentioned duplicate keys. Are there any?"

"Only the one my servant has. And he's been away on holiday for the past week, and I got his key off him before he went. Here it is, with mine." Nicholas produced a key-ring, and displayed two elaborate, identical Yale keys. "As you can see, it's a very special sort of lock—that's the jewel merchant's doing again—and I think any other keys besides these two are out of the question. What's more, I can guarantee that these haven't been out of my possession for a single moment."

Humbleby nodded. "Good enough. When did you leave the flat for breakfast and how long were you away?"

"I can remember that. I left at almost exactly seven a.m. and I got back at almost exactly eight."

"And you looked round, no doubt, to see if anything had been disturbed?"

"I most certainly did. But there was nothing out of place that I could discover. And in any case my policy was not to eat or drink anything that was kept in the flat, so it was just a question of carrying on with that. There was no proof, of course, that anyone had entered the flat at all."

"Did you ask your porter about that?"

"Yes. But he was shut up in his room—they aren't expected to hang about the entrance hall all day—and wouldn't have seen or heard anyone go in or out. So that was no help."

Humbleby consumed his thimbleful of black coffee, asked for more, and, having received it, lit a cheroot.

"And then?"

"Well, after that our poisoner didn't get another chance till I arrived here."

"When was that?"

"About five this afternoon."

"And what sort of a chance did he have then?"

"I unpacked and dozed for a bit on the bed. Then about six I came downstairs. I should think it must have been about an hour later when it suddenly occurred to me that it wasn't very sensible to leave the medicine lying about in my bedroom for anyone to get at. So I went up and locked it away; and it stayed locked away till I got it out to give to you."

"Then what it all adds up to," said Humbleby slowly, "is this: colchicine could have been introduced into the medicine *either* before your party and Miss Scott's suicide, *or* between seven and eight this morning, *or* between six and seven this evening. Is that right?"

"Perfectly. And presumably number one can be ruled out."

"I think so, yes."

"And number two as well? The *Mercury* didn't appear till three this afternoon, and I take it the attempt to poison me was a result of the publication of that unfortunate letter."

Humbleby considered acquainting him with his theory of a literal vendetta, and decided against it; it was not a contingency which he liked to contemplate himself.

"That is probable," he agreed. "So by far our likeliest time is between six and seven this evening. Now, just what were *X*'s chances of getting at the medicine then and remaining unseen?"

They had been considerable, he elicited; and subsequent questioning of Eleanor, David, Medesco and the servants confirmed this. The overgrown condition of the estate made an unobtrusive approach to the house perfectly feasible; at any one of a dozen open doors and windows an outsider could have made his entry; and inside, there were innumerable places where he could have concealed himself in an emergency. A very vulnerable place, Humbleby reflected, with the vendetta theory nagging at the back of his mind; the only snag was how, without searching all the bedrooms (a perilous though not impossible course), *X* could have known where Nicholas was sleeping—for the Cranes had only occupied the house for a few months, and the location of Nicholas' room could not have been at all widely known, except to the family and domestic staff. However, an enterprising person could have solved that problem without excessive difficulty; and the strength of those who killed for vengeance rather than gain, as well as their weakness, was that commonly they were prepared to run abnormal risks. . . .

It was after eleven when at last Humbleby took his departure. Nicholas walked out with him to his car. The rain was temporarily holding off, and here and there a drowned star winked blearily through a gap in the clouds. The gravel was loud underfoot, and an accumulation of water gurgled and dripped in the gutters. Humbleby was by this time thoroughly exhausted—and so also, he guessed, was Nicholas, for the *tic* on his cheek had become more frequent and pronounced, and at each spasm his face screwed up with the pain.

"Well, that's that," he said. "And hope you're able to make sense of it, because I don't want to go in fear of sudden death for the rest of my days. . . . By the way, have you any idea how the *Mercury* got hold of that bloody letter?"

Humbleby told him.

"Why my idiot sister didn't burn the thing," he commented when the story was finished, "I simply cannot imagine. But women are like that. They can none of them ever bring themselves to destroy anything."

Humbleby opened the car door and climbed in. Through the window he said:

"And you're quite certain you don't want police protection? It can easily be arranged."

"No, I can look after myself, thanks. I've got my pistol, I shall sleep with my bedroom door locked, and from now on I'll do all my eating and drinking at pubs in Aylesbury."

"Then you're going to stay on here?"

"For a day or two, till I see how things turn out."

Humbleby grunted. "Well, be careful. For the Lord's sake, be careful."

"Don't worry," said Nicholas, laughing. "I've no intention of dying yet awhile. . . . Good night."

Humbleby drove off. Once, just before trees and bushes screened the carriageway finally from the house, he looked back. Beneath the wan, fluctuating bulb outside the pedimented front door Nicholas was standing alone and motionless, his hands thrust hard into the pockets of his obtrusively well-cut dinner jacket, staring blankly after the retreating car. . . .

And that was the last time Humbleby saw him alive.

CHAPTER IV

I

MOROSE AND MISTRUSTFUL, Tuesday's dawn loitered in from the east like a trade unionist contemplating a strike. From the bedroom window of her Bloomsbury flat Judy Flecker looked out at it, and at the damp prospects it revealed, and sleepily sighed. Then she stripped off her pyjamas, bathed, dressed, cooked and ate her breakfast, and by eight o'clock was in the street. A short walk brought her to a bus stop at which, while waiting, she was able unemotionally to contemplate the massive colonnades of the British Museum; and the bus took her to Marylebone, most restful and appealing of the London termini, where she embarked on a train for Long Fulton.

By ten o'clock of a day which was to be the most eventful—as also the most sheerly terrifying—of her life, Judy had cleared up such routine work as the Music Department could provide, and was in Sound Stage Number Two, listening while the Philharmonia Orchestra, under Griswold's direction, rehearsed and recorded the score for *Ticket for Hell*. Upon the screen in front of her two lovers, bereft of their sound-track, mouthed preposterously at each other; in the sound engineer's glass-fronted control-room, behind her, the composer sat complacently imbibing through a substantial loudspeaker the noises he had contrived. The ticker on the wall spelled out the seconds;

Griswold, with headphones adjusted and a cigarette in his mouth, glanced rapidly and continuously from the players to the score to the ticker to the screen; and music appropriate to its erotic context—susurration of strings, plangency of French horns, the oily sweetness of tubular bells and the aqueous ripple of harps—filled and overflowed the room. Not a bad score, Judy conceded: in his concert works Napier was a somewhat acrid modernist, but like most such composers he unbuttoned, becoming romantic and sentimental, when he was writing for the films.

Presently the take ended and the lights went up again. Someone came and sat down rather heavily in the canvas chair next to Judy's, but for the moment, since the film's Chief Editor had buttonholed her and was talking shop, she had no idea who it was. Only when the Chief Editor had taken himself off did she turn round to identify the newcomer.

It was David Crane.

His appearance there did not surprise Judy particularly, since in recent months he had developed the habit of drifting into her office at odd times of the day for a purpose which he seemed at a loss to isolate and define but which struck Judy as being in all probability fundamentally amorous. These irruptions were a nuisance, but with David Crane it was impossible ever to be seriously exasperated—and, moreover, his diffidence was such that it usually drove him away again, inchoately apologising, within five minutes of his arrival. Of all the Cranes, David, in spite of his intolerable *gaucherie*, was the one Judy liked best. The air of blank misgiving with which he habitually faced the world aroused her protective and maternal instincts. He got little sympathy, she suspected, from his fellow-workers in the Script Department, and was consequently obliged to forage abroad for that commodity.

"Hello," she said pleasantly. "How are things?"

"G-good morning, M-Miss Flecker." Despite the studio vice of always using Christian names, he had never addressed her in terms less formal than these. "I hope I'm n-not in your w-way."

Judy laughed. "Of course not. I'm slacking." She stretched her long legs out luxuriously, noting in amused but not scornful tribute to his solid conventionality that he was wearing black. "And you?"

"I b-beg your pardon?"

"I mean, has the Script Department given you an hour off?" Rather a condescending turn of phrase, Judy reflected: he wasn't, after all, an office-boy. But David, it seemed, had been born to be victimised, even by those who wished him well, and in his presence one's language seemed to mould itself automatically into shapes of unintended derogation. Fortunately, he seemed quite incapable of taking offence.

"There's n-not much d-doing this m-morning," he said; and suddenly smiled. "And anyway, they n-never let me handle anything i-important because they're afraid I should m-make a m-mess of it. So I can g-get away whenever I l-like, really."

"What nonsense!" said Judy, who was none the less admitting to herself, with regret, that if this were so they were probably very wise.

"I d-don't m-mind it, really. I'm quite happy just p-pottering about. No b-brains, that's my trouble."

Judy felt slightly embarrassed by this admission, which in candour it would have been difficult to gainsay. Rather awkwardly she changed the subject.

"And how is everybody at home?" she asked; in the circumstances—she realised as soon as the words were out—a fatuous and even slightly impertinent question. But again David seemed unconscious of the *blague*. He ran a hand through his scanty hair and applied himself to answering as earnestly and painstakingly as if some detailed piece of technical information had been required of him.

"M-mother's all right," he said. "B-but I c-can't imagine anything ever really ups-setting her. N-nick's a b-bit jumpy, as you can imagine. And we h-haven't h-heard from Madge at all." All at once he looked wretched. "It's h-horrible, isn't it? About that g-girl, I m-mean."

"Did you know her?"

"I m-met her for the f-first time at N-Nick's p-party. She s-stayed with mother at Ch-Christmas, but I was away with Nick in Bermuda."

"And I suppose you'd no idea what was going on?"

"No. N-none. They d-don't confide in me m-much. B-but it's a frightful d-disgrace. I c-could hardly b-bring myself to c-come here this m-morning. I f-felt I wanted to c-creep away and hide s-somewhere, like c-cats do when they're ill." Upon this zoological simile he paused; he was a man who rarely indulged in such advanced and literary tricks, and this present lapse must, Judy thought, be the issue of powerful emotions.

"No one," she hastened to reassure him, "could possibly blame *you*, David."

"No, I know, but you s-see, it's a f-family affair. A m-matter," he said simply, "of honour. Th-that's how I s-see it, anyhow, though I suppose it's v-very old-f-fashioned of me."

"I think it's a very proper feeling to have," said Judy. "But you mustn't," she added firmly, "let it g-get—damn! sorry—get you down."

He smiled. "It's f-funny how c-catching a stammer is."

"Anyway, it's not as bad as my lisp," said Judy repentantly. "I'm afraid that between us we must sound like the 'Before' section of an Elocution School advertisement."

"Oh n-no. I l-like your lisp." David flushed. "It's very attractive."

"Plebeian," Judy countered severely. "I've studied the subject, and I know. You hardly ever get it in the middle and upper classes."

David appeared to be uncertain about the proper response to this.

"Anyway," he said at last deprecatorily, "it's only v-very slight. . . . I say, though, it's awful ch-cheek of me to be t-talking about you l-like this. Rotten b-bad form."

Judy looked into his large spaniel eyes and was saddened by the feeling she glimpsed there, since she knew that she would never be able to reciprocate it. She was, however, a particularly feminine young woman, and consequently her mild dejection was mixed with a determination to make modest use of David's infatuation. She crossed her legs and looked shyly at her toes.

"Good lord," she said, "I should be a fool if I thought there was anything offensive about *that*. . . . I say, David, is your brother going to sue that loathsome paper?"

It had been decided that the last take was satisfactory, and Griswold was accordingly going on to deal with the next music section. "Roll the film, please," he said; and when it obediently appeared on the screen he conducted the score through, in silence, with one eye on his stop-watch, while the Philharmonia gossiped, did crossword puzzles or read detective stories. Napier came up, and before David could answer her question, Judy said:

"Good morning, Mr. Napier. It's a beautiful score."

"For heaven's sake," said Napier, visibly pleased, "don't judge me by this stuff."

"That's what all you composers say." Judy smiled.

"On the day one of you admits that his film score is the best thing he's ever done, the Music Department will take a week off and get plastered by way of celebration."

Napier chuckled and went off to pester Griswold. "Sorry, David," said Judy. "I interrupted you."

"N-not at all," he said, with conscientious civility. "Actually, N-Nick isn't going to s-sue." He wriggled and hunched his shoulders. "You s-see, he admits it's all t-true—about that g-girl and the c-contract, I mean."

"Oh," said Judy rather blankly. "But surely he must realise that if he doesn't, the studios——"

"They'll k-kick him out." When David, who was the soul of courtesy, descended to interruption, it was patent that he was strongly moved. "He knows that and he's ready to p-put up with it. Atonement, he s-said. Quite d-decent of old N-Nick, in a way. I m-mean," David added unhappily, "one'd think it was d-decent if he hadn't p-played such a rotten uns-sportsmanlike trick. And on a g-girl, too. That m-makes it m-much w-worse."

"And Madge? What will she do? If this story isn't disproved, then even the abysmal film-going public is likely to lose a lot of their enthusiasm for her. And that means that Leiper will be in a state about it, too."

"M-Madge is i-incommunicado." And David paused, slightly disconcerted, it was possible to surmise, at having dredged up so venturesome a word. "W-we c-can't," he interpreted, "c-contact her. I j-just d-don't know what she'll do." He glanced nervously about him and lowered his voice. "I s-say, d-did you hear that s-someone had tried to p-poison N-Nick?"

Judy sat up abruptly. "*What?*"

"It's quite t-true. S-someone put p-poison in his medicine."

"Lord, *Lord*. . . ." Mingling with Judy's very genuine

shock there was an impulse of unholy curiosity. "But this morning's papers——"

"No, the P-press hasn't been told about it yet," David explained gloomily, and there was a brief, painful silence before he went on. "It's like a n-nightmare, isn't it?"

"Oh, David, I'm so awfully sorry," said Judy in unfeigned sympathy. "It must be hell for you."

He shrugged. "Doesn't do to m-make a f-fuss about these things," he said rather shortly. "G-grin and b-bear 'em, that's the ticket." He turned towards her, once more diffident. "But I say, Judy—ah, M-Miss Flecker, I m-mean. . . ."

Here we go, thought Judy: this is the storm cone going up. And aloud she said: "Yes, David?"

"You—you w-wouldn't c-care to have d-dinner with me some t-time, w-would you? I d-don't expect you w-would," he added rescissorily, "b-but I thought I'd j-just ask. I just thought I'd——"

"But of course, David," said Judy. "It's sweet of you to invite me. I'd be charmed."

"You really w-would? You d-don't think it'd be b-bad form, with M-Maurice d-dead? We c-could g-go somewhere v-very quiet."

"No, of course I don't think it'd be bad form." Oh dear, Judy thought, how appallingly ingenuous this conversation must sound. . . . "Did you have any particular day in mind?"

"It's awfully d-decent of you." David's gratitude was so overwhelming as to be almost pitiful. "Just whenever you s-say, of course. . . . I s-suppose you w-wouldn't be f-free tonight?"

"Well, it's rather short notice, but——"

"P-please don't let me be a n-nuisance. I——"

"But as a matter of fact I *am* free tonight. What time,

and where?" said Judy somewhat brusquely; in order to stop David apologising and get to the point, it was necessary, she felt, to be forthcoming and unmaidenly. Moreover, there had occurred to her a scheme calculated to satisfy the rather unscrupulous inquisitiveness she was nourishing as to the Cranes' reactions to the scandal in which they had become so suddenly involved, and it would be desirable, in pursuance of this, to keep the conversational initiative—no very difficult job, admittedly, where David was concerned.

"W-well," he said, "where would you l-like? There's the S-screenwriters', or the S-savoy, or . . ."

"I've got an idea." Judy smiled a conscientiously winning smile. "Do you think we could perhaps dine at your house?"

David looked rather doubtful. "W-well," he began.

"I've never been there, you know, and I've often wanted to see it. But of course," Judy added wistfully, "if you'd really rather not. . . ."

The glance he gave her was disconcertingly shrewd.

"You want to s-see the house?" he enquired. And had Judy not been convinced that he was temperamentally incapable of being sardonic, she might well have suspected him of it now. As it was, she felt slightly uncomfortable.

"Yes, I should like to," she said a little breathlessly. "And also, of course, also"—she cast about in her mind for some more specific object of curiosity, and after a rather too lengthy pause found one—"oh, the Maze."

"The M-Maze?" David echoed; and again there was that in the way he spoke which evoked in Judy a fleeting uneasiness. "Well, I d-don't see any reason why you shouldn't s-see the M-Maze, if you're i-interested. I should quite l-like to have a l-look at it myself."

"You never have?" said Judy incredulously; she could

scarcely believe that there existed a person capable of having a maze on the estate and yet not exploring it at the first possible opportunity. Labyrinths are romantic and adventurous places, and beneath her surface urbanity Judy was a romantic and adventurous young woman. "You really never have?" she reiterated.

David made a fussed, apologetic gesture.

"Well, it's a l-long w-way from the house," he explained. "N-near where the old T-Tudor m-manor used to be. And it's v-very n-neglected and over-g-grown. But you can certainly have a l-look at it if you c-come before the l-light goes."

"David, what's at the centre?"

He stared, for the moment uncomprehending. "The c-centre?"

"Of the Maze, I mean. There's always *something* at the centre of a maze. A sundial, or——"

"A t-tomb."

"Well, perhaps, but that must be——" Abruptly Judy checked herself; her eyes widened; for an instant looked absurdly young. "You mean there *is* a tomb," she said excitedly, "at the centre of *your* Maze?"

"That's what I've been t-told," said David with indifference. "T-tomb of the chap who m-made the M-Maze, oh, hundreds of y-years ago. F-funny idea, if you ask me."

Judy drew a deep breath of pure pleasure.

"David, we *must* explore it. Promise you'll take me."

"Yes, all right." He was quite honestly uninterested. "I d-don't mind."

And at this point Judy remembered, rather belatedly, that her suggestion of dining at Lanthorn House had not been received with any great enthusiasm, and that she must not be so discourteous as to forget that it was still a *re infecta*.

"Oh, but look here," she said contritely, "it isn't really fair of me to intrude on your family when—well, with things as they are. Perhaps some other time . . ."

"N-no, please." David seemed preoccupied with some species of inward calculation. "It'll be quite all right. M-mother'll be d-delighted to m-meet you. And p-perhaps it'd be as well if I w-wasn't s-seen d-dining out. L-looks callous, you know." He emerged from his abstraction and smiled. "G-good idea of yours, really."

"Well, if you're really sure . . ."

"Oh, yes. You see, I w-want M-Mother to m-meet you. I'm sure you'll t-take to each other."

Like a serialised Victorian novel, Judy reflected: the son, of good family, introduces to his termagant Mamma the poor but honest girl whom he loves and hopes to marry. Will she turn up in a frightful hat? Will she drop her aitches and eat peas with a knife? Will he be threatened with disinheritance if he persists in his suit? And which will prevail in him—his passion for that quite impossible She or his sense of class solidarity? (No, that wasn't right: *unsullied family traditions.*) Read what happens in the next quarter's issue of *Household Words*. . . .

Poor David, thought Judy, as she abandoned this fantasy, it's a shame to take advantage of him when one's feeling for him is so irremediably temperate. . . . But such penitence as she felt was unfortunately quite inadequate to restrain her from taking advantage, and she therefore said:

"Yes, I'm sure we shall. I look forward to it."

"I'll d-drive you there, shall I? I b-borrowed Nick's B-Bentley to c-come here this morning."

"That sounds lovely. But what time are you likely to finish work? I may have to stay a bit later than usual."

"Oh, I c-can w-wait for you."

"No, don't hang about." Judy's considerateness was partly conditioned by the fear that he might elect to do his waiting in her office. "You go on home as soon as you've finished, and I'll borrow a car from Frank Griswold, or someone, and follow you on my own. I can be there by seven—it's just outside Aylesbury, isn't it?"

"That's right. Once you g-get to Aylesbury anyone will d-direct you. But are you sure you d-don't mind?"

"No, of course not." Judy stood up. 'That's settled, then. And now I must go back and do some work. So *au revoir*."

For a moment he did not reply, and in his silence there was something of that obscurely unsettling, incalculable quality she had glimpsed earlier. But then he, too, got to his feet—his delay in performing this courtesy was also vaguely discomposing—and nodded and slowly smiled.

"*Au revoir*," he said. "T-till this evening."

The picture of Judy that emerges from the foregoing conversation is, I suppose, rather mixed and ambiguous, and more particularly where her motives in accepting David Crane's invitation are concerned. But she was, as a matter of fact, a perfectly ordinary, straightforward young woman, and her predominant emotion, for the time being, was a perfectly ordinary, straightforward curiosity. Since Saturday the studios had been full of gossip about the Cranes—a tongue-wagging of epic scope which the *Mercury's* revelations had enormously intensified; and the opportunity of studying the Cranes at close quarters was one which in consequence she found quite irresistible. Woman-like, she was a great deal more interested in people than in facts, and it cannot, therefore, be asserted that her reason for contriving the invitation to Lanthorn House stemmed from any very avid desire to solve the mystery of Maurice's death and the attempted killing of Nicholas. But the Crane family were important, half-legendary figures in her world, and she was not intellectually sophisticated enough—or intellectually snobbish enough, if you prefer—to be convinced of their ultimate insignificance in the larger scheme of things. She wanted to stand at the very centre of the scandal and contemplate it from there; and David Crane's infatuation was her only passport to that dubious privilege. . . .

Vulgar curiosity, she told herself as she strolled back to the Music Department: that's all it is.

And at this stage she did not recollect that it was curiosity, in the proverb, which killed the cat.

2

It was when she was on her way to get lunch at the studio Club—a preserve of the Upper Orders which she sometimes used in preference to the overcrowded canteens—that she encountered Gervase Fen, who was carrying an old raincoat and had on his extraordinary hat.

"Hello," she greeted him. "Are you detecting?"

He shook his head. "Unluckily no. I've just come away from an *Unfortunate Lady* conference."

"Good Lord, are they still going on? I thought Saturday's was the last."

"So did we all. But Leiper didn't concur with the particular brand of nonsense we agreed on, and convened us again this morning."

"But the Cranes . . ."

"The Cranes were unanimous in staying away. Everyone else was there. A certain gloom was perceptible, I thought. I'm surprised, myself, that Leiper's going on with it."

"So am I. What on earth does he imagine is going to happen about Nicholas and Madge?"

"From what I heard him say to Stafford, he believes the whole affair to be a conscienceless newspaper stunt having no basis in fact whatever."

"Do you really mean to say he's so stupid as to think it's all lies?"

"Just that. And no one seems to have the nerve to disillusion him. I find it all," said Fen comfortably, "very pathetic. . . . By the way, you remember I asked you on Saturday what attitude the Crane family adopted towards Gloria Scott?"

"Yes."

"You said that about Nicholas you didn't know. Do you know now?"

"Yes. After all the talk there's been I can hardly avoid knowing. It seems he was always exceedingly nice to her—and not at all because she was bedworthy, or anything of that kind. Just pure altruism."

"So that people were a good deal surprised when the letter was published?"

"Lord, yes. Bowled over. . . . I say, is this important?"

"God knows," said Fen. "I'll tell you what it is, Miss Flecker," he went on rather balefully. "Humbleby is getting above himself. He's not keeping me *au fait* with the case. All he's done so far is to telephone me at some ungodly hour last night, gabble a few incoherent words at me, and then ring off before I had time to extract a single solid piece of information from him. Did *you* know that someone has tried to poison Nicholas?"

"Yes. I heard this morning. David told me."

"David. . . .? Oh, that's the dim brother, of course. I haven't met him yet."

Judy hesitated. "Professor Fen, you—you don't think *he* could possibly be the murderer?"

"My dear girl," said Fen kindly, "for the moment I

know of no cogent reason for eliminating any human being who is at present walking the earth. Why do you ask?"

"Well, he's invited me to his mother's house for dinner this evening, and I thought you might know if he was under suspicion, and if he had been I would have kept my eyes open, that's all."

"To dinner? At his mother's house?" Fen shook his head. " 'Tis ill pudling in the cockatrice' den," he murmured, "and they must walk warily that hunt the wild boar."

"This excursion into Bunyan signifying what?"

"Keep your eyes open in any case. . . . And now I must catch my bus. Good-bye. And look after yourself." He was gone.

Tea-time found Judy exceptionally busy, and she was not pleased to be interrupted by David Crane. On this occasion, however, he stated the pretext for his visit with unusual directness.

"I s-say, Miss Flecker, it's my c-car," he said. "N-Nick's car, I m-mean."

Judy said patiently:

"What's the trouble? Won't it go?"

"S-someone's s-smashed up the engine."

"*What*?"

"W-with an iron b-bar."

Judy stared at him. "David, are you sure you're not dreaming?"

"N-no, of course n-not. L-look for yourself if you d-don't b-believe me." He seemed quite distraught. "I t-tried to s-start her, and she w-wouldn't g-go, and then I l-looked to see if I could s-spot what was wrong, and—and there it w-was."

"It was all right when you arrived, though, wasn't it?" said Judy not very intelligently. "I mean——"

"Oh, yes. It w-was all right then."

"But in broad daylight, David! I don't understand how anyone can have *dared* . . ."

"It was in Nick's l-lock-up," he explained. "Only, of course, n-no one ever actually l-locks them, and I didn't. So you s-see . . ."

Judy did see. Adjoining the carpenters' workshop there was a row of lock-up garages (whose doors, as David had rightly observed, nobody ever bothered to secure) reserved for the use of the studio's Upper Twenty. And since from morning to night the carpenters' shop yielded an unintermittent uproar of hammering and mechanical saws, the noisy act of vandalism which David had reported could have been carried through, behind the garage's closed door, in reasonable safety. . . . Vandalism. Judy's heart sank. The car was Nicholas', not David's, and she knew that in certain quarters the feeling against Nicholas was running high. . . .

But this explanation had apparently not occurred to David; he seemed completely perplexed. "I d-don't understand it," he muttered haplessly. "I just d-don't understand it at all."

"What are you going to do?" Judy demanded; it could serve no useful purpose, she felt, to blurt out the theory she had just formulated.

"Oh, I'll hire a c-car in the v-village to t-take me home. That p-part's all right. B-but I w-wish I knew *why*. It seems so p-pointless, doesn't it?"

"Yes," Judy agreed. "Yes, it does."

"I know I oughtn't to be b-bothering you about it, n-not when you're w-working. B-but I just *had* to t-tell someone."

"You'll see the police about it, I suppose?"

"Yes. C-certainly I shall. Filthy rotten t-trick," said

David miserably. "Must catch the b-bounder who did it." He stood there shifting uneasily from one foot to the other, and now his self-consciousness, which the outrage had sent temporarily into abeyance, began to seep back. "Well. As I s-say. Thought I'd just t-tell you about it."

"I'd go to the police straight away if I were you."

David squared his shoulders. "Quite right. G-get it over and done with. Thanks for l-listening, Miss F-Flecker."

"Why not Judy?"

He made a gesture so preposterously bashful that she had the utmost difficulty in suppressing a gust of ribald and unseemly mirth.

"Thanks, Judy," he said. "I'll g-get along now. See you l-later."

And "Heavens!" thought Judy as the door closed behind him, "what have I let myself in for? Fathomless abysses of *nescier faire. . . .*"

"But it's damned queer," she murmured aloud, "about that car. I wonder . . ."

And after a moment's cogitation she reached for the telephone, put a call through to the College of St. Christopher in Oxford, and asked for Professor Fen.

Professor Fen was there. His voice sounded as if the telephone had awakened him from a particularly deep and agreeable bout of slumber; which in fact it had. What, he enquired rather surlily, was the matter?

But on hearing Judy's story he became audibly more complaisant and alert. "I'm sorry if I disturbed you," Judy said in conclusion, "but I thought it just possibly *might* have something to do with the case, and so . . ."

"Yes, you may very well be right. Will you do something for me?"

"What?"

"The car's still there, is it? It hasn't been towed away?"

"No, it's still here."

"Well, then, get a garage-man up from the village—or else someone at the studios who knows about cars—and have him look at the steering-gear."

"The *steering-gear*? But why—wait, though: I think I see what you're getting at. Only——"

"Don't theorise, please. Act. And ring me back, will you? as soon as you've found out."

This proved to be about an hour later.

"Well?" Fen enquired.

"You were right. Something essential in the steering had been filed almost completely through—I'm afraid I'm stupid about these things, so I can't tell you exactly what it was, but the man said it was a murderous trick, because if it snapped when the car was moving fast, there'd be an appalling smash."

"Quite so. Well, I continue to guess quite nicely, even if I don't actually deduce very much. Has David Crane told the police?"

"Yes. The local bobby came along and scratched his head over it. I told him he ought to get in touch with Inspector Humbleby and tell him about it. Was that right?"

"Perfectly."

"And *was* it meant for Nicholas?"

"It looks that way, doesn't it?"

"And then, I suppose, the person who'd done it found out *David* was driving the car, and didn't want to kill *him*, and put the engine out of action because that was the best way he could think up of cancelling what he'd done."

"Yes. Quite a plausible hypothesis, in the circumstances. Of course, there's one other possibility."

"I know what you mean: David did the whole thing

himself, after he arrived here, so as to create a—a red herring."

"You have a good, lively, sceptical brain," Fen commented. "But don't let it make you careless when you go to Lanthorn House this evening. Remember, we've none of us any idea what face this particular cockatrice is wearing. . . . Good-bye."

3

It was five past six, and the air was full of a slow, depressing drizzle, when Judy left the studios and set off for Aylesbury.

She had borrowed Griswold's car—a large, rather antiquated Humber saloon badly scarred by the destructive proclivities of its owner's innumerable children. Judy had commandeered it before, and it was not, in her experience, at all a reliable machine; but it was better than a sequence of buses, or the inordinate expense of hiring a taxi. It had the peculiarity, which Griswold freely admitted no one had ever been able to explain, of seeming on the point of petering out and then, at the last possible moment and quite without human intervention, suddenly revving itself up until the bonnet rattled, the cheeks of the passengers quivered as with an ague and an efflux of pastel-blue smoke shrouded it like dense fog. Griswold was accustomed to maintain (though not with much confidence) that this had something to do with the hand throttle's being caught up with the clutch, and in the course of time he had become inured to it, but it never failed to unnerve strangers, and it was with a good deal of wariness that Judy edged the eccentric vehicle out on to the road.

At the outset, however, it behaved tolerably well, and she made good progress until she was almost into Aylesbury. Then, just as she was rashly congratulating herself on this state of affairs, the front off-side tyre, which was worn wafer-thin at the sides, exploded resoundingly. Fortunately she was not travelling fast—the Humber, indeed, was not endowed with any great turn of speed—and she was able to come bumpily but safely to a halt at the road's verge. She climbed out and examined the tyre with dismay.

Aylesbury was still four miles off, and the rain, tiring of its earlier indecisiveness, had begun to fall more heavily. The road was deserted and there was no house in sight. Judy moaned faintly and groped in the car for the raincoat which luckily she had with her. Then, resigning herself philosophically to manual labour and to making her *début* at Lanthorn House looking like something the cat had dragged in, she fished out the tool-kit. She was an independent young woman who when professional help was not available believed in coping with her misfortunes herself.

Back in the early thirties some engineer had been visited with the inspiration of a Trouble-Free Jack, and for weeks had toiled to devise a tool capable of being manipulated (as the advertisements setting forth the thing's virtues presently announced) by a Child. All scientific progress, however, has its drawbacks; no bath water is ever thrown out without some species of baby goes down the plug-hole with it; and it proved that, in the case of the Trouble-Free Jack, Ease of Manipulation could not be achieved (by this particular engineer, anyway) without Extreme Difficulty of Assembly. The manufacturers did not, of course, overtly admit this depressing discovery; they were at pains to supply an Instruction Chart indicating how the Jack might swiftly and easily be put together. But as regarded the particular instrument which Judy now had in her hands, this *vade mecum* had long since vanished, and after ten minutes' uninterrupted toil the thing still remained as hopelessly unworkable as ever.

She beat a retreat to the interior of the car and sat there wondering sombrely what to do next. To walk into Aylesbury in the rain was an intolerable prospect—but there was likewise no future in sitting here till darkness fell, fiddling with the irreconcilable component parts of a Trouble-Free Jack. She must stop someone, therefore, and bespeak assistance or a lift to the nearest garage. Two cars had passed already. They had looked at first as if they might be going to stop, but as soon as they were near enough to make out that the penalty for this would be changing a wheel in what looked like developing into a cloud-burst, they had accelerated again and gone by. How, Judy wondered, could a subsequent motorist be effectively halted? The traditional formula was to be fixing one's suspenders and hence showing one's legs; but Judy felt sufficiently disgruntled and mistrustful of her luck to suspect that if she attempted this the first person to happen by would be some species of sexual maniac. And besides, she had on nylons and it was wet. She decided that the less blatant forms of allure would have to do.

At first they were notably ineffectual—and in view of her soaking hair and sodden raincoat Judy was not altogether surprised. Three cars in succession ignored her signalling. But the fourth stopped, and a large, jovial, middle-aged man emerged from it with massive cries of dismay at Judy's plight and unreserved offers of help. No trouble at all, he assured her heartily: he'd have it fixed in a jiffy, see if he didn't. Having taken one look at the Trouble-Free Jack, he produced his own; and in very little more than a jiffy the wheel was in fact changed.

Judy, her fears of sexual maniacs submerged in relief, informed the jovial man that he was an angel and that she could *kiss* him. And he, having in a brief, brotherly, pleasant fashion accepted and reciprocated this offer, assured her again that it had been no trouble, re-inserted himself, chuckling vastly, into his car and drove away.

By the time Judy reached Aylesbury it was twenty past seven; and in spite of David's optimistic prognosis, she had some difficulty in finding anyone who could direct her to Lanthorn House, and even when she had done so, continued on her way without much faith in the correctness of the route that had been indicated. Surely—she was asking herself twenty minutes later—this abominable cart-track I'm on can't be right? Or is it some idiotic short cut? At a small stone railway-bridge she pulled up and gazed bewilderedly about her. The twilight was closing in like an ambush, the rain fell monotonously, the rubber of the wipers creaked against the windscreen. In all directions there were dripping woods and fields and hedges and fences—but of a house, or a human being, no sign. The engine sputtered in a sullen, foreboding way; obscurely but unmistakably it conveyed to Judy the impression that it was not prepared to go on like this for very much longer.

Well, the only thing to do was to go on following the instructions of that palsied old imbecile in Aylesbury, and hope for the best.

Over the ruts and pot-holes of that unconscionable lane the car lurched forward. There appeared a succession of conspicuous landmarks for which Judy had no brief—a barn, a chalk escarpment blurred and ghostly in the rain and the dusk, a ruined church or priory. "He didn't mention this," she muttered crossly as each one hove in sight. "He never said anything about *this*." Presently she had to switch on the lights. And all at once, without quite realising what was happening, she found that the Humber was crawling painfully up a one-in-seven slope between cataracts of water which raced downwards on either side. She changed down; changed down again. But the engine was no longer in good heart for such stoic enterprises. Its pulse grew momently feebler; it began to knock; it developed, in its extremity, a sort of death rattle. In anguished auscultation Judy wrestled with the controls, but vainly. Long before the summit was reached a sudden explosion from beneath the bonnet delivered the *coup de grâce*, and the whole infuriating mechanism fell silent.

Judy crammed on the brakes, panicked momentarily when in spite of them the car started to slip back, and succeeded in bringing it to a halt by letting it drift against the lane's bank at an angle of forty-five degrees. The lack of optimism with which she plied the self-starter proved abundantly justified. In a final desperate effort she wound the handle until it kicked, and wrenched her arm so badly that she could not go on. Then she resigned herself, at long last, to the inexorable fact: the car was stranded.

"Damn," she said. "Damn, damn, *damn!*"

And standing there alone in the rain, while a small river of water gurgled round the Humber's back wheels, she wept hot tears of frustration.

As if its appetite had been whetted by its earlier, more gradual conquests, the darkness was coming on faster now, was licking greedily at what remained of the day. Judy stemmed her tears and a moment later turned abruptly, thinking that someone stood behind her. But it was only a scarecrow on the other side of the hedge—a scarecrow leaning backwards, rigid like a day-old corpse propped on a shooting-stick. . . . And *that* sort of simile, Judy told herself sternly, isn't calculated to cheer you up very much. Pull yourself together, girl; make up your mind what you're going to do.

And of course, there was only one answer to that: she could scarcely stay here all night. The car must be abandoned and she must find shelter. She had long ago lost faith in the directions given her in Aylesbury for getting to Lanthorn House, but she had followed them to the bitter end, and if by some remote chance there *was* any truth in them, she ought by now to be quite near her destination. There was, too, another feature of the situation which offered a pale, *faute-de-mieux* sort of encouragement: the rain was palpably slackening off, and in a minute or two might with any luck cease altogether. . . . She looked at her watch: ten to eight. But there was not the least possibility, as far as she could see, of finding a telephone whereby she might recite her mishaps to David and apologise for her lateness and, proleptically, for her drowned and unprepossessing condition. By this time she would naturally enough have been glad to waive the visit altogether, but there would, she realised, be no advantage to her in that, for to get back to Aylesbury and civilisation would probably be an undertaking even more formidable than the search for Lanthorn House. No, her best course was to plod onwards and once again hope for the best. She did what she could to immobilise the car and then set off.

At the summit of the hill she paused to get her bearings. According to what she had been told, this track ought to debouch in a main road, along which she must walk, northwards, for about a couple of hundred yards, and then turn off to the right. As far as she could make out at the moment, she was heading straight into a pathless wilderness, but none the less she pushed on doggedly between monotonous hedgerows and was presently rewarded by coming upon an isolated cottage, at whose door she knocked. A weedy, furtive-looking scion of the emancipated peasantry appeared to be the cottage's sole occupant, and the particular fashion in which he eyed her warned Judy that it would be impolitic to linger there; but the information she received was encouraging, for it revealed that her mentor in Aylesbury had not in fact led her astray: the main road was only a short distance away and Lanthorn House tolerably close at hand. Moreover, there was an hourly bus, she learned, which would take her right to its gates.

The hourly bus, however, swept maddeningly by before she was able to achieve the main road, and she was obliged in consequence to continue walking; by this time the condition of her shoes and stockings was incapable of deteriorating much further, and there was a kind of perverted comfort to be derived from that. With her long, athletic stride Judy marched on, devising conversational gambits suitable to be employed on arrival, and from time to time ruefully contemplating the indelible oil-marks which the Trouble-Free Jack and the starting-handle had imprinted on her slender hands. And before long she came to the branch road of which she was in search, and turned off along it.

The rain was still holding off, and here and there the canopy of cloud was splitting like stretched canvas, so that the encroachments of night were temporarily halted and reversed by the veiled illumination of the sun's dying rays. The road ran grey and ghostly into invisibility, hemmed in by beech trees whose bare wet branches gleamed wanly, like fading phosphorescence, and whose last year's leaves still lay in mouldering drifts against the grassy banks where now and then a primrose could be discerned. It was very quiet—so quiet that the sound of your footsteps began after a while to seem like a wanton profanation of some supernatural conspiracy of silence; and without being properly conscious of it Judy began to hum jauntily to herself, buttressing her independence against the insidious, pervasive hush. The road wound downwards and the trees that stood sentinel along it thickened and multiplied. There were deep dells among them, fringed with brambles and dead bracken except where the outcropping chalk prevented their growth. Probably a good place for bluebells, Judy thought irrelevantly; not a bad place for highway robbery, either. . . .

And was she never going to get to Lanthorn House?

But even as this rhetorical question presented itself, she rounded a bend and came within sight of the gates. At least, she *supposed* that these were the gates. Someone was entering them from the opposite direction, anyway—a man in a hat and mackintosh; and there was that in the way he walked which suggested to Judy that it might be Nicholas Crane. He had not, however, seen her or heard her steps, for he went on in ahead of her without looking round.

Arrived at the entrance to the drive, Judy paused to take stock of the situation. In the heraldically carved stone gateposts there was nothing to indicate that this was her destination, and the lodges, where she might have enquired, were patently uninhabited—looked, indeed, uninhabitable. But there had been no other house in this particular road, and it was a fairly safe bet that this was what she was seeking. No harm in finding out, anyway. Judy walked through the gates into the estate.

The continuing downward gradient was vaguely disconcerting; in the dusk you had the sense of descending into positively troglodytic depths. The trees and grass and bushes and undergrowth grew rankly here, unchecked by cultivation—though, as only the evergreens were in leaf, there was an impression of barrenness, too; the small buds on the tangled stems were invisible, and they looked dead. Distantly a night-owl cried, and a clock chimed half-past eight. There was a cold wind stirring in the foliage, and as it fingered her sodden clothes and hair Judy shivered and quickened her pace.

The man (Nicholas?) who had preceded her was not in sight; but the drive twisted incessantly, and unless he had turned off it into the grounds he could scarcely be very far ahead. He might, of course, be waiting for her among the bushes—and the vision which that possibility conjured up was not wholly agreeable. None the less, Judy went forward steadily. Soon, surely, she was bound to come in view of the house, and there would be lights and food and hot fires and cheerfulness. She pictured herself demurely wrapped in a dressing-gown while her outer clothes dried, humorously reciting the tribulations she had gone through. Even now she was capable of looking back on them fairly tolerantly; so in an hour's time——

And it was at this point that she heard the voice.

It came from beyond the bend confronting her, and she knew it at once for Nicholas's. It said: "Hello! Enjoying the weather?"

And then, in an altered tone: "What are you—so *you're* the——"

And then a shot.

Birds flew up out of the trees with a whirr of wings, calling distractedly. The echoes of the explosion resounded through the hollow in which the house lay.

And beyond the bend in the drive a man cried out feebly and fell.

It was all over in a moment. And Judy, who had her share of courage, quickened her steps and ran—not *away* from whatever ghastly thing had happened, but *towards* it. She came round the bend and stopped short at what she saw.

Nicholas Crane lay sprawled on his back at the drive's verge. His lips were curled back from his teeth in a kind of snarl; his hat had dropped off and his immaculate fair hair was spattered with mud; his eyes were open but sightless; beside his right hand lay an automatic pistol. A long knife had been driven upwards through his ribs into his heart, and even in that faint and waning light it needed no more than a glance to tell Judy that he was dead.

No more than a glance; and since the moment of the attack scarcely twenty seconds had passed. That meant that the attacker must still be near at hand—and no sooner had Judy realised this than her blurred senses became sharply focused as she tried to determine which way he had gone. Though her heart was beating fast, she was for the moment queerly devoid of both fear and repugnance. To *pursue* seemed somehow natural and inevitable, in spite of the appalling peril it must certainly involve; and long before this primordial instinct had taken conscious shape she found that she was, indeed, pursuing.

Hearing guided her. Nicholas Crane's murderer, who had obviously heard her running up, was plunging noisily away through the undergrowth in blind flight. Racing frantically after him, Judy was conscious that the automatic was in her hand—though she had no recollection whatever of having picked it up—and conscious, too, that the butt was still warm where Nicholas had held it. It gave her immeasurable confidence, and that despite the fact that she had never fired any sort of gun in her life. In an Amazonian frenzy she ran recklessly ahead.

And now, as if at a signal, darkness had shut its jaws over the last remnants of day, and its annihilating conquest was complete. The rain was falling again—but Judy was past caring about rain, was transmuted, indeed, into a creature wholly compounded of impulse, wholly devoid of calculation. Her heart pounded; the salt sweat dripped from her forehead into her eyes; in a dozen places her clothes were ripped and rent by brambles, and there was scarcely a square inch of her stockings that the brush had not mauled. A Mænad figure, physically splendid, she fled through the unkempt grounds of Lanthorn House like an arrow, stumbling sometimes but always recovering, beating against hardly visible obstacles yet never falling, oblivious of reason, stripped in a second of the veneer with which centuries of civilisation had overlaid what was natural in her. . . . And Chance, rejoicing in the overthrow of its age-old enemy the considering intellect, took her into its special care, driving her along the track of her quarry, whenever sense faltered or doubted, as unrelentingly as a ravenous brute in pursuit of its prey.

The terrain was rising as she ran, up towards the rim of the bowl in which Lanthorn House lay secluded; and presently the chase led out of the trees and thickets on to bare turf which ascended, at the last steeply, to what was apparently a flat, grassy terrace of some description. Judy's foot struck a fragment of submerged masonry and she fell. She was up again instantly, but by wretched bad fortune the automatic had flown out of her hand, and her helpless groping failed to discover it again. If she lingered to search for it her quarry would irrevocably elude her; she must not, therefore—the decision was made at once and unhesitatingly—linger to search for it. And she was running again even before that decision was made.

The person she hunted must be tiring, for she was closer to him now—so close that she could hear his frantic breathing above the sound of her own. What she was to do on overtaking him she never once paused to consider: it would be a hand-to-hand fight now, and she would have to be extremely lucky to get the best of that. But circumspection had altogether deserted her. She dimly sensed that, once undertaken, an affair like this must in honour be carried through to the end, however mortal its issue might be. Her stride lengthened; her breath and pulse grew quicker; and she knew she was gaining ground fast.

The distance between the two of them cannot have been more than a couple of yards at the moment when the high hedge—at least two feet higher than a tall man—loomed up out of the obscurity and the ground became overgrown again. For an instant Judy paused, feeling for the gap through which her quarry had blundered. Then she found it and followed. A second hedge immediately confronted her, and after briefly listening for the sound of her quarry she turned right between it and the first. It had been a gruelling run and her energy was flagging now, but so also must be the energy of the person she pursued, and she pushed on, grimly determined to make up the leeway she had lost in seeking a breach in the hedge. To the left she turned, to the left again, to the right; and was obscurely though incuriously aware that hedges were all about her. But presently, at a bifurcation, she halted, the better to choose her direction, and for the first time realised that she could no longer hear the attacker's movements; which meant, of course, that he had gone to ground and was lying in wait. . . . Judy took a few uncertain steps along the left-hand fork; stopped, bewildered, when she saw that this alley forked again. . . .

Then, somewhat belatedly, she understood where she was.

4

In an emergency the human mind is apt to function in odd, incalculable ways. Into Judy's, as she stood there a little dazed by the sudden knowledge that she had plunged unwittingly into the Lanthorn House Maze, there drifted with the sharp clarity of a lesson learned by heart certain words that she had encountered long ago.

"I have heard or read . . . of a man who, like *Theseus*, in the *Attick Tale*, should adventure himself, into a *Labyrinth* or *Maze* . . . but as the Night fell, *wherein all the Beasts of the Forest do move*, he begun to be sensible of some Creature keeping Pace with him and, as he thought, *peering and looking upon him* from the next alley to that he was in . . ."

And Judy shivered. Somewhere in this maze, as in that, there was a tomb.

At heart Judy was superstitious—and let no one mock at her for it. Superstition is not mere intellectual error; it is a part of the emotional life, and the worldly-wise who suppress it do so at the risk of impoverishing their souls, an eventuality which for the most part they do not succeed in avoiding. So the words of the story (*only* a story, she told herself fiercely: nothing *more* than that . . .) wrought in Judy an effect which in the circumstances was very far from being beneficial. They shattered, suddenly and horribly, the spell of frenzy which the hunt had cast upon her, and as her normal perceptions returned, she realised that she was exhausted and that it would be futile to attempt more. . . .

And as a matter of fact, she reflected sombrely, it had been futile to attempt as much. Worse than futile: crazy . . . and the recognition of her folly in attempting to tackle a desperate murderer single-handed came upon her like a douche of ice-cold water. Mad, *mad*! She had been possessed, she now saw, possessed by those devils whose name was said to be Legion; and after propelling her headlong down the most appropriate local equivalent of the Gadarene slope, they had deserted her, left her to fend for herself in a condition of physical and spiritual exhaustion, the virtue—so to call it—gone out of her, all passion spent. Common sense, the more insistent for its temporary exile, returned to plague and rebuke her from every side. What *ought* she to have done? Hurried on to the house, of course, and reported the killing. No one would have dreamed of blaming her for not embarking on this fantastic enterprise, and she would long ago have been safe, with light and warmth and company. . . . Company; Judy was beginning to feel a longing for that, as she stood there in the darkness, between the high hedges, with water dripping off her ruined clothes on to the bumpy, cluttered ground underfoot. Yes, company, she thought, would be a very pleasant thing at the moment.

In the meantime, what strength she had left must be devoted to getting out of this atrocious place and as far away from it as possible.

She was not, as yet, badly frightened. That was to come later. But she knew that somewhere a killer lay in ambush; and a maze, ordinarily an innocuous plaything, can in certain circumstances begin to seem like a trap. With a wry grimace Judy recalled the pleasurable anticipation of just this exploration which she had expressed to David Crane only that morning. Æons ago, it seemed; and now——

Well, now the thing to do was to make a move, and that as furtively as might be.

Direction? Easy enough. She must go back the way she had come, and fortunately she remembered the turns she had taken. Right at the entrance, then left, left, right. That meant left, right, right and the entrance would be on her left.

What she did not remember was that mazes are designed specifically to confuse people who have made a note of the way they came.

After ten minutes of anguished searching—the more nerve-racking in that her progress was necessarily far from noiseless—Judy realised that she was indeed trapped. In a Maze with a Murderer, she thought, and because the springs of hysteria were starting to trickle inside her, she giggled inanely to herself. Unless, of course, the murderer had succeeded where she had failed, and got himself out somehow or other. But that was unlikely. Perhaps he was as afraid of her as she was of him—and as this possibility occurred to her Judy giggled again. More loudly, this time. And "My God," she thought, as with an effort she got control of her nerves again, "if I'm going to go on like this I might just as well shout and tell him straight out where to find me."

(". . . So he stood still and hilloo'd at the Pitch of his Voice, and he suppos'd that the *Echo*, or the Noyse of his Shouting, disguis'd for the Moment any lesser sound; because, when there fell a Stillness again, he distinguish'd a Trampling (not loud) of running Feet coming very close behind him, wherewith he was so daunted that himself set off to run. . . .")

Not loud. No, of course it wouldn't be. That was to be expected.

. . . But you must make up your mind, Judy my girl, just what it is you're frightened of: on the one hand, M. R. James-plus-tomb, or on the other Mr. *X*, who pushed a knife into Nicholas Crane. You can't have it both ways. Or can you? It rather looks as if you can. . . . Well then, put it like this: which would you rather have waiting for you round this corner you're coming to, *X* or—or the inhabitants of the place, whispering in conference? Take your pick, ladies and gents: a guaranteed triple-proof homicidal maniac or a group of fine spectres, jewelled in every hole. . . .

But this won't do. It won't do at all. Stand still, Judy. Stand still, get a grip on yourself, and do some hard thinking.

As soon as her own movements ceased, it was very quiet there. There was the unrelenting patter of the rain, of course, but beyond that, nothing. Really nothing? Well, sometimes the hedges rustled, as though there were a person fumbling at them on the other side.

"And, indeed, as the Darkness increas'd, it seemed to him that there was more than one, and, it might be, even a whole Band of such Followers: at least so he judg'd by the Rustling and Cracking that they kept among the Thickets. . . ."

The rustling was due to the rain. Of course it was due to the rain. Or—since this was a neglected, abandoned place—to animals. Small animals.

". . . *wherein all the Beasts of the Forest* . . ."

Rats?

Judy put two fingers into her mouth and bit them till the blood came. It wouldn't do to scream, wouldn't do at all, not with Mr. *X* lying doggo perhaps only a few feet away. . . . Cats, presumably, lay *catto*—and despite all she could do to prevent it, Judy giggled again, and went on giggling. The imbecile noise of it got out of hand, continued (as it seemed to her last surviving outposts of caution) interminably.

Then, when at last it stopped, the silence that replaced it seemed even more horrible than before.

All at once black misery overwhelmed her: misery bitter and intense beyond guessing, seas of it millions of fathoms deep. It was—had she known it—a reaction altogether healthier and more salutary than the half-wit facetiousness in which her shaken mind had earlier been indulging; but to her it was far more ghastly than that, was the ultimate abyss beyond which there could be nothing, *nothing* worse. On all sides the high, abominable hedges hemmed her in, their unpruned summits just perceptible as a ragged line against the night sky. She was cold, soaked, inexpressibly tired and terribly afraid. And careless, now, of what might happen to her, she fell to sobbing like a lost child.

How long that lasted she was never afterwards able to say, for this was the point at which her mind grew numb and refused—last prophylactic against its own impending ruin!—to accept any longer the messages of her senses. She was vaguely aware that when the sobbing ceased she started to move again, but what impelled her to do this, and how long it lasted, remains unknowable. Probably her blind wandering about that unspeakable labyrinth did not continue for so very long, but to her it seemed like days. She remembers—remotely, like something in an almost-forgotten dream—that whenever she turned into a *cul-de-sac*, which was often, she would emerge from it again without any sense of frustration or disappointment; and the truth is that at this stage she was a mere automaton, as bereft of will and cognition and conation as a robot, without the least consciousness of what she was looking for, or why. Days, it seemed; no, months, centuries. . . .

So that when at last she came out from among the hedges she did not immediately realise what had happened.

But something made her hesitate, staring blankly into the darkness. And at that hesitation her brain began painfully to function again. She was in the open. She was no longer penned in. She had escaped, at last, out of the crazy, bewildering sequence of alleys and bends and *impasses*.

So it was all over. For a moment she could hardly take

it in. After what she had been through it seemed impossible to assimilate. But it was true. It was true. She could *feel* that she was free. . . . She gave a choking gasp of relief.

And quite near her, something moved.

Judy's throat went dry; she tried to cry out and could not. Her hand, jerking in a nervous spasm against the pocket of her raincoat, rattled something there. Matches. She did not pause to reflect that the cold rain would extinguish a flame almost instantaneously. With trembling fingers, in a last frantic snatching at courage and reason, she dragged out the box and struck one of the matches.

For an instant it flared up brightly. And Judy's heart sickened at what, in its brief and wavering illumination, she saw.

She was not out of the Maze at all. On the contrary, she was in the clearing at its centre. And a short distance in front of her was the tomb. . . .

Only it wasn't a tomb. It was a grave, a humped mound with a decaying headstone askew at one end. And something that might or might not have been human was crawling across that mound.

The flame went out.

So then Judy did scream.

5

Gervase Fen, Professor of English Language and Literature in the University of Oxford, was restless that Tuesday afternoon. Term was over: for the vacation he had no specific plans, and he felt—which was uncommon in him—very much at a loss for something to do. Moreover, he could not disguise from himself the fact that his criminological amusements were beginning to display the ominous characteristics of an addiction, or at the very least of a settled habit, and in consequence of this he fretted at being kept out of touch with the Crane case by Humbleby's deplorable uncommunicativeness. Sherlock Holmes, when circumstances omitted to supply pabulum for his febrile intellect, had soothed himself with doses of cocaine, but the Dangerous Drugs Act had put a stop to all that sort of thing, and such lawful alternatives as remained—alcohol, for instance—would be only very doubtfully efficacious. It was not—said Fen, addressing himself to the impassive quadrangle outside his first-floor rooms at St. Christopher's—it was not that he had any ideas about the Crane case, as things stood; it was simply that he feared Humbleby might have overlooked some clue germane to its solution. And although he knew that the C.I.D. are not fools, and that this was therefore very unlikely, such considerations failed to soothe him. Mistrust of experts, in spite of all that the apologists for technocracy can advance against it, is deeply rooted in the English character, and Fen, whose habit of mind was not cosmopolitan, shared in it abundantly.

His restlessness was accentuated by Judy's report on the tampering with Nicholas Crane's Bentley, and its odd sequel. A scrupulous murderer, Fen thought—scrupulous, anyway, where the lives of those he considered innocent were concerned; and that attitude might prove to have its importance. . . . But more facts were needed, more *facts*. A dozen times Fen had examined and analysed the data he already possessed, and he was convinced, by now, that no enlightenment whatever was to be derived from them; but somewhere or other the significant, the vital, indication must be awaiting discovery. Fen had no faith in the absolute dogma that such ciphers as man can create man can also solve, since he was aware that the history of crime exhibits a number of instances to the contrary; but he did believe that in ninety-nine out of a hundred cases mysteries are susceptible of explanation, and that this was the hundredth case he was not at all prepared to assume. So he prowled and pondered and grew peevish, and the afternoon waned into early evening, and still there was no news from Humbleby.

At seven-thirty Fen decided to take the initiative, and telephoned to Scotland Yard. But Humbleby was not there, and they either did not know, or else from policy refused to say, where he might be found. Fen's irritation increased, and he rang up Lanthorn House. Eleanor Crane, who answered, was civil and appeared to recognise his name, but no, she said, Inspector Humbleby had not been there since the previous evening, and he had not said when, if at all, he proposed returning.

"Ah," said Fen. "Well, thanks very much, Mrs. Crane. I thought it just possible that he might be with you. I hope I didn't interrupt your dinner."

"Not at all. David's guest"—the husky voice was ever so slightly sardonic—"David's guest hasn't turned up yet, so we're keeping dinner back."

A little cloud of obscure foreboding—for the moment no larger, certainly, than a man's hand—took shape at the back of Fen's mind.

"I suppose," he said, "that that would be Miss Flecker."

"Yes. I didn't realise you knew her. To judge from my son's not over-subtle allusions, I'm afraid he may have been pestering her rather."

"Is she very late, may I ask?"

"It seems that she said she would be here by seven definitely. I hope she hasn't had an accident. But we're rather out of the way here, so it may just be that she's not able to find us. She hasn't been here before."

"Just so. Thank you again, then." Fen said good-bye and rang off.

An accident. . . . But in forty minutes' lateness there was no reasonable ground for misgiving, and Fen had no cause for thinking that Judy stood in any danger from the unknown *X*—the more so since *X* had apparently gone to such trouble and risk to prevent David from driving home, and probably smashing himself up, in Nicholas Crane's car. None the less, Fen found that he was oddly perturbed, and after a short interval of vague and futile worrying he telephoned the Long Fulton Music Department. He had not much hope that at this time of day anyone would be there, but it happened that Johnny, who was currently engaged in the composition of an immense and vacuous symphony, had decided that the Music Department was a convenient, quiet and sympathetic place in which to score this opus during the evenings, and he was consequently available and able to give Fen the information required. Yes, he said, Miss Flecker had left for Aylesbury, in Mr. Griswold's car, shortly after six.

And that being so, Fen reflected as he rang off, she ought certainly to have arrived there by seven; the distance between the two places was not great. But no doubt Eleanor Crane's explanation was the true one: she had simply lost her way. . . . Fen confabulated with his soul and discovered that his indistinct anxiety on Judy's behalf derived in the long run from nothing more subtle and altruistic than the desire to *do* something. It was largely a sham, a pretext—all else having failed—for purposive action of some sort. That fact elicited, he felt a good deal easier in his mind. Judy had probably arrived at Lanthorn House by now, but there was no reason why he should not drive over there and make sure of it, and the excursion would keep him occupied for a while. Having dressed himself for rain, he left his rooms and went out to his car.

It was a small red sports model, exceptionally strident and dissolute-looking, which he had purchased from a cashiered, impoverished undergraduate years before. A chromium nude leaned forward from the radiator cap, and the name LILY CHRISTINE III was engrossed in large white letters across the bonnet. A leaky hood shielded the car's seating rather perfunctorily from the elements. Fen ascertained that he had enough petrol for the eighteen- or twenty-mile journey and noisily set forth.

It was completely dark, and raining hard, when at a quarter to nine he drove in through the Lanthorn House gates; and he came upon the body of Nicholas Crane so suddenly that only the gleam of the knife's haft in the headlights prevented him from running over it. He stopped the car, climbed out, and made a brief, melancholy examination. "Poor devil," he muttered. "But I don't suppose he had time to be much afraid." To judge from the flaccidity of the limbs, death was still only somatic—which meant that it had probably not occurred earlier than four hours ago; but it was not possible, he thought, to make a more definite estimate than that. He took a torch from the car and by casting about discovered with its aid a crumpled, muddy handkerchief lying near-by, with the initials J.A.F. embroidered on it. And at that his anxiety was abruptly renewed. From what he knew of Judy he thought it very unlikely that she had killed Nicholas Crane, but it looked as if some time this evening she had been on the spot, and if by any chance she had witnessed what happened. . . . Fen's investigation of the area became notably swifter and more purposeful as soon as this possibility occurred to him.

And it did not take him long to find what he was looking

for; Judy's reckless pursuit was imprinted in mud as plainly as any zealot for footprints could desire. The small, sharp impression of the shoes were superimposed on the impressions made by the person she had followed—and that showed that at any rate she had not gone with him under duress. But there was more: both persons had been running fast, since the impression of the heel was consistently deeper than the impression made by the ball of the foot and the anterior edge of the sole was in every case prominently etched. And since *Judy* had been running, she had been tracking the other person not by his footprints—to follow footprints in tangled undergrowth while continuously running fast is an impossibility—but by his actual presence; in other words, she must have been chasing him close behind. More yet: by comparing the amount of water which had collected in the footprints with the amount which had collected in the natural hollows of the ground, it was feasible to make a rough guess at how long ago the chase had taken place; not more than an hour previously, Fen estimated, and probably rather less....

These observations occupied him for scarcely more than half a minute, and they left him seriously alarmed; much as he admired the girl's courage, he could scarcely commend her wisdom, and what the issue of the chase might have been he did not at all care to imagine. He began to follow the tracks, taking care not to tread in them and moving as rapidly as he could. And until he came out of the trees and bushes on to an open slope, he made good progress. Here, however, he was obliged to pause uncertainly, swinging his torch this way and that, for at this higher level the turf was springy and porous, and in spite of the rain one's steps, as an experiment speedily proved, left no marks on it. Without much optimism Fen walked slowly upwards; at this stage the only thing he could do was to look about at random. And presently he came to the terrace of flat ground where Judy had tripped and fallen, and where he was able to make out the scanty, ground-level remains of a dismantled or ruined house. He paused irresolutely, listening, but apart from the steady hiss of the rain the silence seemed absolute. A moment later, however, his eye was caught by a dull metallic gleam in the torch-light, and he stopped to pick up a small automatic pistol from which, as the contents of its clip demonstrated, a single shot had been fired. Though admittedly equivocal, it was not, he felt, a very reassuring discovery, except in so far as it indicated that he was still on the right track; and there remained the problem of what direction he should take now. For a few minutes he walked in continually widening circles centred on the spot where he had come on the gun, but without finding any trace that would help him. And he was just setting off in the upward direction, on the not specially cogent but unimprovable grounds that this would be a direct continuation of the line that Judy and her quarry had taken thus far, when he heard the scream.

It was not a loud scream, or a long one, but it was enough to indicate the way he must go, and a few moments hard running through ruin and darkness brought him to the Maze. With the help of his torch he was able to make out immediately what it was—the more immediately in that he already knew that such a place existed in the Lanthorn House grounds; but for all that, his fears for Judy's safety were so intense that he needed the exercise of all his will-power to restrain him from the idiotic course of plunging heedlessly in. He must go in, of course: here the footsteps were visible again, and like the spoor of the animals in Æsop's fable they pointed exclusively inwards—they did not emerge again. Other ways of egress were a possibility, but he would have to accept the likeliest hypothesis, that Judy was still in the Maze, and hope that it turned out to be correct. Should he call out? If he did so, it might have the effect of scaring Judy's assailant away from her (supposing that she was being attacked, which at the time seemed probable), but on the other hand it might conceivably provoke him to an even greater ruthlessness. Fen decided against it. Stealth and surprise were useful weapons; if the intention was to kill Judy his bawling would hardly impede it, and if that intention were absent he would simply be giving the enemy warning of his presence, a needless handicap. So he kept silent—and in the meantime the thing to do was to devise some means of marking his route into the Maze so that when the need arose he might readily get out of it again.

All this takes long to tell, and, moreover, savours of cold-blooded calculation in the face of another person's peril. But in fact it occupied only a few seconds' thought, and even that necessary delay Fen bitterly grudged. Then, blessedly, he remembered something. In the pocket of his raincoat was a huge ball of thin string, bought the previous day, and that, plainly, was exactly what he wanted. He tied one end of it rapidly to a sapling which grew just outside the Maze's entrance and then, unrolling the ball as he went, strode forward into the warren of damp, rank, weed-cluttered alleys. The string would almost certainly not last out to the Maze's centre, but it would be useful as far as it went. He was in two minds as to whether to keep his torch alight or not. It would infallibly mark out his progress, but that would help the girl as well as the murderer, and in the end he elected to keep it on. In an affair like this, he reflected grimly, there arrived fairly early on a point at which reasoning became valueless and one simply had to trust to luck.

Fen was well-read in the more interesting by-ways of human activity, and he knew a certain amount about labyrinths—knew, for instance, that their basic plan is always very simple and that in almost every case their centre can be reached by the application of some brief, straightforward formula. He was not, accordingly, so much at a loss as a less-informed person would have been, and his preliminary explorations were of a methodical sort, aimed at eliminating the more palpable blind alleys and false trails. Unreeling his string, and rewinding it whenever a cul-de-sac obliged him to go back on his tracks, he fairly quickly whittled the possible routes down to two, and on noting that one of them involved a symmetrical plan—first right, second left, first right, second left—while the other did not, followed it unhesitatingly. By choosing his turns according to this prescription he would probably be working towards the perimeter of the Maze, which his initial survey had told him was rectangular; at some point, therefore, he would have to vary the formula—or, more accurately, deduce for it a second part—so as to be able to move back towards the centre. And since mazes are essentially no more than large-scale toys, it was tolerably obvious that the second part of the formula would be significantly related to the first—second right followed by first left, for instance, as against first right followed by second left. The devisers of such places, having thoroughly bewildered their victims, had liked to be able to point out how extremely simple it was once you knew. And although Fen was aware of the grave warning against over-confidence contained in the adventures of Mr. Jerome's Harris at Hampton Court, he did not believe that this particular maze would turn out to be any exception to the overall rule.

He had, of course, no reason for supposing that Judy would be at the Maze's centre when he got there; she might be anywhere. But the route from the entrance to the centre, once established, would provide a point of reference from which lateral excursions could be made, and prevent him from roaming about at random and getting lost himself; moreover, even his errors constituted a part of the search which had to be made. He has confessed since that he was far from liking the atmosphere of the place, and that although for obvious reasons he was not so strongly affected by the story as was Judy, Dr. James' ill-advised jewel-hunter kept incongruous company with the egregious Harris in the literary quarters of his mind. He was, however, methodically active, and this kept his imagination in check, as also did the much more tangible danger of an assault by *X*. To proceed soundlessly was, he soon discovered, quite impracticable, and he therefore abandoned caution in favour of speed. This made him unpleasantly vulnerable, but there was no help for it. Often he stopped still and listened before pressing on again between the interminable high hedges; twice—in view of the fact that his presence must long ago have been perceived—he called Judy's name. Silence alone answered him; and he grew sick with misgiving.

Though he attempted to apply it too soon, and was temporarily led astray in consequence, his guess about the second part of the Maze's formula proved to be correct, and in due course he came to the centre. Against all expectation, the string had lasted wonderfully—there seemed to be miles of it, and Fen blessed the ironmonger who had pressed it on him with sophistries about the most expensive being always the cheapest in the end. He was, indeed, negligently blessing the ironmonger at the moment when, on the point of investigating the Maze's centre, he was struck down by a blow on the back of the head.

He estimates that he was probably unconscious for

between five and ten minutes. In retrospect his view of this episode is cool and detached, but he is not the man to suffer pain stoically, and there can be little doubt that at the time he was mightily aggrieved. When he came round, dazedly and painfully, among the soaking brambles and weeds, his first coherent thought was for his life-line, and he was not much surprised to find it gone: *X* had beaten a retreat and taken it with him to delay pursuit. He was not, however, excessively upset by this circumstance; it was an eventuality which he had all along considered possible, and having grasped the principle on which the Maze had been planted, he was confident of his ability to get out of it again. His torch remained, and after collecting it he got dizzily to his feet, fondling the back of his head and noting with a certain sour gratification that there was no blood. In another half-minute he had found Judy.

She was lying unconscious, her face muddy and paper-white, but as far as he could see she was not injured in any way. Presently, having sat down beside her for a minute or two in order to give his head a chance to spin itself to a standstill, Fen put her across his shoulder and tottered away with her. Before searching for her he had taken the precaution of marking, by means of a handkerchief tied to a twig, the particular alley by which he had come to the centre, and with that initial signpost there was, as he had anticipated, no serious difficulty in finding the way out. The Maze behind him, he was guided back to the drive by the headlamps of his car, which he had left burning. And by a quarter to ten he and Judy were in sanctuary at Lanthorn House.

All that night the windows of Lanthorn House blazed with light, and there was a confused, interminable coming and going of doctors, policemen and, in the last stages, newspaper reporters. Fen, having made sure that Judy was safe and unharmed, grew irritable at the inconclusiveness of what was being done, and departed in Lily Christine shortly after midnight; his adventure had left him feeling distinctly unwell, and his interest in the case was submerged in an overwhelming desire to go home and to bed. But the routine of investigation went on until daybreak. At the start, Humbleby was in charge of it; he had been summoned from London and had driven to Aylesbury with all possible speed. Latterly, however, he was absent, since at two in the morning a distraught Inspector Berkeley telephoned through from Doon Island to tell him that Madge Crane was dead.

6

At five o'clock on the afternoon of the following day, which was the Wednesday, Fen sat and drank tea with Humbleby in Humbleby's room at New Scotland Yard.

It was a small room, solidly but austerely furnished. Its windows, high up in a corner of the building, looked towards Parliament and the river. A small but vehement gas-fire warmed it. Humbleby was in the swivel-chair behind the broad oak desk, and Fen, his head bandaged in a needlessly dramatic and elaborate fashion, was in the chair reserved for visitors, his long legs resting irreverently on a corner of the desk. Fen is exigent in the matter of sympathy for his afflictions, but he knew that at the moment it was Humbleby who deserved commiseration, and he did not, therefore, as in minor discomforts he normally does, adopt the air and hollow tones of a man precariously convalescing after a severe operation. Instead, he eyed Humbleby compassionately, noting the pallor of his face, the strained lines of his mouth, the blue suffusions of sleeplessness under his eyes, the dishevelment of his usually neat grey hair and the soiled, creased condition of his clothes. Humbleby had laced their tea with rum, and he drank greedily, exhaustedly, gazing out over sooty roofs into the grey March afternoon.

"I've just been to see the A.C.," he said. "He was extremely pleasant, but now Madge Crane has been murdered the case will be front-page news until it's solved"—he nodded towards the heap of evening papers in front of him—"and in those circumstances I quite realised they'd have to take it away from me. Nothing less than a Chief Inspector will do now. Chichley. Do you know him?"

Fen shook his head.

"A nice fellow, and very able. Still, it's disappointing. The A.C. made it clear that the transfer didn't constitute any criticism of me; as he said, I simply haven't had the time to get down to anything yet. But just the same——"

"Dispiriting, yes," said Fen; he was fond of Humbleby and thought it a great pity that because of Madge Crane's stardom he should have to be elbowed out. "How long have you got?"

"Before Chichley takes over? A few hours, I dare say. I really can't discuss the details with him till I've had some sleep."

"It might," said Fen, "be possible to wind up the case today."

"I wish I could believe that, but I'm afraid you're too optimistic."

"Perhaps. But shall we make the attempt? Or are you too tired to discuss things for half an hour or so?"

"No. I'm not too tired. We'll do that. And if you can throw any light on this business, I'll be eternally grateful. It's not a question of promotion—I could have had that years ago if I'd wanted it. It's just that I *detest* leaving any job half-done."

Fen nodded. "Understandable," he said briskly. "Let me get my information up to date, then. Nicholas first, and then Madge."

"Right." Humbleby finished his tea, leaned back and lit a cheroot. "As far as I can see, I've uncovered all the really important facts. I left Doon Island at midday today, you understand, and called in at Lanthorn House before coming back here."

"And you talked to the girl?"

"To Miss Flecker, you mean? Yes, I did."

"How is she?"

"Quite recovered, I'm glad to say. And very anxious to see you and thank you for rescuing her. She's gone back to her flat, and a woman friend is going to sleep with her for a few nights, until she's recovered from the shock."

"Her unconsciousness *was* just a faint, I take it."

"Yes. She must have been horribly overwrought, so it's not surprising. Brave of her to chase after this fellow, but scarcely sensible. However. . . . She hasn't, I'm afraid, the smallest notion who it was."

"And Eleanor Crane—did you talk to her?"

"Not a chance of it. The doctors were—um—adamant. Extraordinary, the way she collapsed when she heard Nicholas was dead."

"She was very fond of him, then?"

"Doted on him, it seems, though she took care never to show it. And the consequence is that now she's a dangerous hysteric."

"Yes," said Fen. "Let's get down to business, then. I gather that Nicholas returned to Lanthorn House shortly after eight. Where had he been?"

"Getting an early dinner in Aylesbury. Apparently he travelled there and back by bus. Eating out, you realise, was one of the precautions he was taking against poison."

"Quite so. And now, the murder and the business in the Maze. Alibis, to start with. How about the people at Lanthorn House?"

"Except for the servants, they're none of them exempt. Eleanor Crane is assumed to have been indoors all the time, but there's no proof of it, or, rather, so little that it's almost valueless. Medesco left at half-past seven to drive back to London, and——"

"Medesco?"

Humbleby explained Medesco's status in the household, a status of which Fen had not hitherto been aware. "It seems," he said in conclusion, "that the fellow wasn't actually staying there, but he'd developed the habit of travelling down quite often and spending the day. . . . I don't know where these people get all their petrol from." Humbleby sighed. "Or, rather, I do."

"And David?"

"He left the house, on foot, shortly after Medesco, at about twenty to eight. According to his own incoherent account, he jumped idiotically to the conclusion that as Miss Flecker hadn't turned up punctually she wasn't coming at all—had deliberately stood him up, in fact. So he went out for a walk in the rain, ostensibly to nurse his wounded pride, and didn't get back from it, as you know, till just before ten. Not at all a reasonable way to carry on, but then, he strikes me as being an exceptionally stupid person."

"M'm. . . . Well now, the murder itself. What about the knife?"

"An oversized boy-scout affair, not specially uncommon. It had been ground razor-sharp. No fingerprints."

"Nicholas fired a shot. Do you think he wounded his man?"

"I'm certain he didn't. We found the bullet in a tree-trunk."

"A pity. The footprints?"

"Size nine in men's—a very popular size, unluckily. I'm still waiting for the detailed report to come in, and it's our best bet at present, because it will certainly give us height and weight, and that will mean only a few hundred thousand suspects instead of several million."

"Come, come," said Fen. "That's surely far too gloomy a view. One can assume, I imagine, that it was someone Nicholas *knew*."

Humbleby gave him Judy's account of the incident, and ended by saying:

"Yes, I suppose Nicholas's shout of 'So *you're* the——' does suggest someone he knew."

"And his casual 'Hello! Enjoying the weather?' must mean it was someone he wasn't surprised at finding in the grounds."

"Well, no, there's a snag there, I'm afraid. According to Miss Flecker those words weren't spoken casually. They were spoken *nastily*, as if Nicholas knew straight off why the person was waiting there. So if you think about it you'll realise that it needn't necessarily have been someone who had a right in the grounds."

"Yes, I see," said Fen slowly. "Do you think it was a man?"

"There's no conclusive proof—unless you count the footprints, which after all *might* have been made by a woman wearing a man's shoes—but in view of the head-on way Nicholas was knifed I can't believe any woman did it."

"I quite agree. We do make progress, then. A man whom Nicholas knew, of the height and weight the footprints report will specify."

"It's a start," Humbleby admitted without enthusiasm.

"And now," said Fen, "tell me about Madge."

Humbleby's narrative was clear and to the point. Like Maurice, Madge had been killed by colchicine, but in her case the poison had been introduced into a decanter of gin, some of which she had drunk at about nine o'clock the previous evening; and she had died at one-thirty a.m. It seemed that in spite of her protests she had secretly been glad of the surveillance organised by Inspector Berkeley; and the strictness of that surveillance made it quite certain that after nine p.m. on the Monday, when the watch was inaugurated, there had been no opportunity whatever for poisoning the gin. Moreover, at lunch-time on the Monday it was certainly innocuous, since some of it had been drunk without ill-effect. That left some eight hours of the afternoon and early evening to be accounted for. For most of the period Madge Crane had herself been in the sitting-room where the gin was kept, but between six and seven she had gone out for a walk, leaving her secretary, Miss Oughtred, in charge.

"The Oughtred woman," said Humbleby, "is a sad case. I'm tolerably certain Madge Crane bullied her abominably, but in spite of that she's horribly upset by the girl's death. And since in a way she was *responsible* for that death, you see——"

"I don't see at all," Fen interposed. "How was she responsible?"

"Well, she gave Madge to understand that the cottage hadn't been left unguarded for a second, when in fact it had been—and for very much more than a second. And Madge, as I've told you, was a great deal more nervous of being poisoned than she pretended: Maurice's death must have shaken her up. So if the Oughtred woman hadn't lied to her, stating that she'd never left the cottage, Madge would probably never have touched the gin, *or* any other food and drink that could have been tampered with while the cottage was empty. She fooled Berkeley into thinking that she didn't believe in the possibility of an attempt to murder her, but from what the Oughtred woman says, she was really rather frightened."

"But why," Fen asked, "did Miss Oughtred lie to her?"

Humbleby groaned. "Believe it or not, Miss Oughtred was having an affair with the Doon Island butcher. . . . If you'd *seen* the poor plain creature—she must be forty at least—you'd find that barely credible; but I've checked it and it's true. So as soon as Madge went off for her walk, Miss Oughtred slipped out, met her butcher and stayed with him at least half an hour. She was supposed to be getting the dinner, but apparently it was the sort that doesn't need watching while it cooks. She got back to the cottage ahead of Madge, and not unnaturally didn't mention her rendezvous; she knew Madge would not only sneer at her pathetic liaison, but also put a stop to it. Madge was that sort of person. So she kept silent. And now Madge is dead, of course, and as Miss Oughtred realises that the colchicine must have been put in the gin while she was away spooning between six and seven on Monday evening, the poor wretch is in a terrible state about it."

"Our murderer does get about the country, doesn't he?" said Fen thoughtfully. "Do you think it's possible he has an accomplice?"

"I think it's very unlikely indeed."

"So do I. Do you think he has a private aeroplane?"

"An *aeroplane*?"

"I'm not being facetious."

"No, of course I don't think he has a private aeroplane. Or if he has, he certainly wouldn't use it for flying about from murder to murder. Too conspicuous altogether."

"Yes. I quite agree. How long does it take to get from

Doon Island to Lanthorn House, or *vice versa*—aeroplanes apart?"

"Three hours," said Humbleby, "would be the minimum."

Fen took his feet off the desk and stood up.

"And that being so," he said, "you can arrest a certain gentleman straight away—provided, of course, that you ignore the possibility of an accomplice, which I think you'd be quite right to do. The point is——"

He broke off as a new thought occurred to him,

"No, I'm being a bit previous," he said. "It's not *quite* watertight. . . . What time did you get to Lanthorn House on Monday evening?"

"About eight."

"And David Crane was there at that time?"

"Yes."

"So he couldn't possibly have been on Doon Island between six and seven, poisoning the gin decanter."

"No. Nor could Medesco, nor Nicholas, nor Eleanor Crane."

"Then it *is* watertight. And the answer——"

The telephone rang, and Humbleby picked it up in no very good humour at the untimely interruption. But as he listened, his impatience vanished; and when, after a few words of warm commendation, he rang off, his tiredness had vanished and he was exultant. "Got him!" he said.

Fen smiled. "A confession? He's been so careless that I've often wondered if he meant to give himself up as soon as Gloria Scott was avenged."

"No, not a confession. Something even more conclusive. You remember you advised me to circularise the stewardesses of passenger-ships which berthed in this country about two years ago in the hope that one of them would recognise Gloria Scott's photograph?"

"I remember," said Fen sardonically. "At the time, you gave it as your considered opinion that my brain was softening."

Humbleby grinned, his cheroot at a rakish, triumphant angle between his teeth. "I apologise," he said unapologetically. "I abase myself. . . . And that's very generous of me, because as a matter of fact I did act on your suggestion. And it's worked."

"All my suggestions work," said Fen smugly.

"Gloria Scott," said Humbleby, with the air of one who recites intoxicating poetry, "landed at Liverpool on February 19th, 1947, from the s.s. *Cape Castle*, which had brought her and her mother from South Africa. The stewardess who looked after them on the voyage retired a year ago and went to live in the Western Highlands; and since she reads no newspaper but *The Scotsman*, and *The Scotsman* was not one of the papers that published Gloria Scott's picture, she wasn't in the least aware that she knew anything which could help us. Mother and daughter kept to their cabin almost the whole time, so the other passengers saw next to nothing of them. But this Mrs. MacCutcheon, the stewardess, necessarily saw a good deal of them, and she remembers the couple perfectly. On that voyage, I need hardly tell you, Gloria Scott's Christian name wasn't Gloria and her surname wasn't Scott."

"As to her Christian name," said Fen equably, "you have the advantage of me. But I can tell you what her surname was." And he did so.

"Yes, yes!" Humbleby was vastly pleased. "You're perfectly right. I don't at the moment understand how you arrived at it, but you're perfectly right. Good enough for a warrant, don't you think?"

"Quite good enough," Fen assented gravely. "But

before you go, don't forget to see your Assistant Commissioner and tell him that Chichley's services will not now be required."

"Such pleasures," said Humbleby in a judicial manner, "come rather low on the moral scale, but they're not the less alluring for that. . . . Do you want to accompany me?"

"No, thanks. I'm squeamish about creatures in snares, however much they may have deserved it."

"Yes, you're right," said Humbleby more soberly. "It's never a pleasant business." He stood up. "But if you'll meet me later, we'll discuss it all."

"I'll be at the Athenæum," said Fen. "Dine with me if you have time. And come there anyway."

"*Explicit.*" Humbleby moved to the door. "*Explicit* the Crane case. From now on the lawyers take over. . . . Till this evening, then."

An hour and a half later he was knocking at a certain door. It was opened to him by a maidservant—a slatternly, full-bosomed girl, irresistibly suggestive of the low-life episodes in an eighteenth-century novel. No, sir, she said, the master 'adn't been 'ome not since morning. And no, she 'adn't a notion where 'e might be. Bin out a lot the last few days, 'e 'ad. Funny goings-on, if they asked 'er. Oh yes (sniffing haughtily), they could come in and 'ave a look round if they didn't believe 'er. . . .

They went in and had a look round, and the house's owner was certainly absent. Humbleby posted two men there against the contingency of his return, and drove off resignedly with his sergeant. The sergeant was not moved at being personally involved in the *dénoûment* of a case which the whole country was discussing. He was of the old school: as far as he was concerned, a murder was a murder, whether the victim was a film star or a vagrant, and all arrests were alike in representing an ethic vindicated and job done. Having cleared his throat loudly, he did, however, permit himself to address a sociable question to his superior. "Think 'e'll be able to slip out of the country, sir?" he enquired conversationally.

Humbleby grunted. "I hope not. And nowadays it isn't easy, is it?"

"Not with all these Government regulations it isn't, sir. I know they 'elps us in some ways, but I'd as soon be without 'em, just the same. The more red tape you 'ave the more petty wangling there is for us to dirty our fingers on. And there's a lot too much of it, if you ask me."

Humbleby concurred in these strictures. "Still, red tape's useful in this case," he observed. "The odds on our fellow's escaping are—oh, at least ninety-nine to one. . . ."

But unless natural death claims him, Evan George will no doubt still be congratulating himself, many years hence, on the fact that it was the hundredth chance which came off.

CHAPTER V

I

To Professor Gervase Fen, c/o Leiper Films Inc., Long Fulton Studios, England.

"Mexico, April 1949.

"MY DEAR PROFESSOR FEN:

"You'll be surprised, I dare say, that I should write to you rather than to the police; we were, after all, only very briefly and slightly acquainted. But I've always felt a great admiration for your talents in the criminological as well as the scholarly field, and I should like you to be the legal owner of my confession, which I don't doubt will earn some little notoriety in the history of crime. You will of course pass it on to the police, so that the affair can be definitively wound up and any remaining uncertainties cleared away. . . . As you can see, I'm not repentant: those three odious young people deserved to die. But it's strange how spiritually empty I feel now that the job is done.

"My one regret is that it wasn't possible for me to follow the course of the investigation. I should like to have known whether you had any inkling of the truth *before* my flight gave the game away. In view of your ability, and of my own deliberate carelessness, I imagine you had much more than an inkling.

"Please note that I say *deliberate* carelessness. I flatter myself that if I had chosen to do so, I could have covered my tracks so effectively that even you would never have suspected me. But of course, the one thing I could not hope to conceal for long was the identity of 'Gloria Scott', and since that in itself was bound to incriminate me, the precautions I took as regards the actual killings were never more than sketchy, never intended to do more than give me time to finish what I had set out to do.

"One thing at least will be clear to you by this time: the girl you knew as 'Gloria Scott' was in fact my daughter Madeline.

"And I adored her.

"Note the tense of the verb. I don't use that tense merely because Madeline is no longer alive. Something—a quite unexpected psychological *volte-face*—happened to me when I saw Maurice Crane die that Saturday. . . .

"But you shall hear all about that in its proper place.

" 'Gloria Scott' was my daughter. And to make you understand why I killed the Cranes I must take you back to the time of my marriage, nearly twenty years ago.

"I suppose there never was a less sensible union. Dorothy and I were incompatible in almost every respect. I met her in Johannesburg, where I was born and where I spent the first thirty-seven years of my life. And looking back on it, it seems incredible to me that I could ever have thought her attractive in any way. None the less, I did. You must realise that I didn't begin writing, didn't acquire a reputation and a decent income, till quite late in life. At the time I first encountered Dorothy I was a very insignificant person, earning a wretched pittance as a clerk in the Johannesburg office of the De Windt Diamond Company, and Dorothy came from a higher economic level altogether. Her parents, like mine, were dead, and she had a private income—nothing enormous, but quite adequate to live on. Even at that time I was hankering after a literary life, and if I was to write, I needed unearned money to keep me going while I established myself.

"So you see how it happened. It wasn't Dorothy I married, but her Deposit Account at the bank.

"She was a slim, tall girl, very fair, with washed-out blue eyes. As you know, I'm small and dark, and I've noticed that men of my physical type are often infatuated with women of hers. And in some obscure fashion she must—since she did marry me—have been attracted to me, outwardly unimportant though I was. I should like to think that she divined my talent, but that would be to flatter her. Actually, I believe she regarded the marriage from the first as a licence and an opportunity for unrestricted bullying. And I was stupid enough to fall into the trap.

"After the first few weeks my married life was a hell. With my physical smallness and my absolute dependence on Dorothy for money, I was impotent, hamstrung. Little men who are maltreated by big wives are normally matter for farce, but I can assure you from personal experience that the situation is not funny. . . . If she had had any respect for my writing I might have put up with the other things, but at first I was very unsuccessful, and she never missed an opportunity of jeering at my work. And sexual intercourse, when she allowed it at all, was a condescension, an unspeakable mockery.

"But then Madeline was born.

"Artistic creation apart, Madeline provoked in me the strongest emotions I've ever known. Love, as other people experience it, has never come my way, and I've had no deep, enduring friendships, and so emotionally I was frustrated, bottled up, and all the affection I was capable of was available for Madeline when she came. I doted on her—it was a love so strong that nothing, not even my work, had a chance against it. I can't pretend to myself, now that I'm able to look at things more clearly, that it was a healthy state of mind; on the contrary, it was an obsession which intensified as the years went by to the point, almost, of dementia. But I'm not writing this letter in order to justify my feeling for Madeline—only to explain how it came about that I embarked on anything so melodramatic as a career of vengeance.

"My wife hated and despised me. And because I worshipped Madeline, my wife came to hate and despise Madeline as well. She was not physically cruel to the child—though I think she would have been, and enjoyed it, if she'd dared—but she thwarted Madeline in every way she possibly could, so that even when Madeline was an infant I could see that she was becoming secretive and twisted and mistrustful. I understand that Madeline was not popular at the studios, or at the Menenford theatre where she worked. But can you wonder that she wasn't frank and free and straightforward, after the upbringing she'd had? I believe that if she had not died she would have fought off, in time, the effects of that upbringing, because she had a naturally sweet and candid nature; but you can't chain a girl for seventeen years to a mother who hates her without warping her character badly.

"I can manage to look at Madeline objectively now. She grew up to be rather conceited and silly and wild. I wouldn't say these things about her if they had been her fault. But Dorothy was responsible, Dorothy and——

"I was going to add 'no one else', but that wouldn't be true. Indirectly, *I* was responsible, too.

"Because, you see, Dorothy divorced me and the court gave her custody of Madeline. And that meant that from then on Dorothy was able to indulge in her subtle beastliness to Madeline without any restraint at all.

"I needn't go into detail about the divorce. All I need say is that my home life was abominable, and I slept with a girl and Dorothy found out about it. Of course, she jumped at the chance to get rid of me, and but for Madeline *I* would have been delighted to get rid of *her*; by that time I'd sooner have starved, or given up writing, than lived on her detestable money any longer. But I adored little Madeline—she was six then—and the thought of parting with her was unbearable to me. Dorothy knew that, and obtaining custody of Madeline was her great triumph, the most succulent and satisfying part of her revenge on me. I did everything I could to get the decision reversed, but it was impossible. I went so far as to contemplate suicide, but I felt that would be a betrayal of Madeline, because there was always the chance that one day, however far distant, I might be able to be of service to her. What I did in the end was to get drunk and leave South Africa. I was drunk continuously for three weeks, and then when my money ran out I worked my passage on a boat bound for England. I had the right to see Madeline once a month, but I thought it would be better to make a complete break.

"In England my talent was recognised, and I prospered; it was for Madeline's sake that I worked and saved, and there wasn't a day when I didn't think of her. Sometimes I got news of her from friends in South Africa who knew how I felt, but I never mentioned her to anyone in England, and I doubt if anyone in England knew that I'd ever been married; somehow it wasn't a thing I wanted to talk about. I brooded a lot, no doubt, and worried a lot, and it's arguable that on this topic I got to be a bit unhinged. But in a fragmentary way I was kept informed about Madeline, and what I wasn't told I could visualise or imagine. I was sent an occasional photograph, too. . . .

"And that was how I was able to recognise my daughter at Nicholas Crane's party.

"I'd heard that Dorothy and Madeline were leaving for England—that Dorothy had developed cancer of the lungs and wanted advice from Harley Street. And I'd tried to trace them after their arrival in England, and completely failed. That meant that for two nightmarish years I'd had no news of them whatever, and didn't know whether they were alive or dead. I'd intended attempting to make it up with Dorothy, so that I could see Madeline again, but both of them seemed to have just stepped off the ship and vanished into thin air. I suspect now that the detective agency I employed was grossly incompetent.

"I was sounding the ultimate depths of human misery when Leiper asked me to write the script for *The Unfortunate Lady*. My first instinct was to refuse—all work was an atrocious penance at that stage—but then I decided that a new kind of job might alleviate my depression slightly, and eventually I accepted. I'd not the faintest notion, of course, that Madeline was in the film business, and though I heard 'Gloria Scott' referred to once or twice, the name naturally conveyed nothing to me; and as her part in the film wasn't important enough to justify her attending our script conferences, there was no opportunity for me to meet her.

"But then came the night of Nicholas Crane's party.

"I was talking to someone when she came in, and didn't immediately see her. But when I did, I recognised her instantly; and I think that if I hadn't already had a good deal to drink I'd have made something of a scene. As it was, I could hardly believe I wasn't dreaming.

"And she recognised me, of course. Caroline Cecil told your Inspector Humbleby that as soon as Madeline entered something startled her; and that something was the unexpected sight of me. She knew who her father was, and my photograph has appeared on the dust-jackets of various of my books; but apparently she'd had no idea, till that moment, that I had anything to do with films in general or *The Unfortunate Lady* in particular. So seeing me there was a shock.

"We were introduced. We spoke to one another like strangers. She wasn't sure that I'd identified her and I wasn't sure that she'd identified me, and I think we both felt that a rowdy party wasn't the place for a reunion like ours. I was dazed, too. It was like inventing an island or a continent and then discovering that in all its imagined detail it actually existed. The party dragged on and I drank a lot more. Madeline stayed behind to talk to Nicholas Crane and I went out to wait for her on the pavement. One or two others, as it happened, waited with me.

"It's odd how one's mind works. I'd been assuming that because I wanted so passionately to be with Madeline, she'd want to be with me. But she didn't, of course. I'd been out of her life for so long that I was nothing but a name to her—and God knows what lies Dorothy had told her about me. Anyway, she'd been on her own in England for two years and yet had never made any attempt to get into touch with me. . . She would have done, perhaps, if she'd ever been utterly wretched, but until Mr. Nicholas Crane came along she'd escaped that.

"And in the end it was to me that she turned for comfort. As we walked to Piccadilly that night, the whole story poured out: how she'd grown up to detest Dorothy; how Dorothy had died in their Liverpool hotel the night after they landed and how, being still only seventeen and thinking that a particularly odious brother of Dorothy's would now be appointed as her guardian, she had run away to Menenford that same night, without telling anyone of Dorothy's death, and had there taken a job at the repertory theatre under an assumed name. She was afraid, it seems, that the police would find her, but there was no photograph of her in Dorothy's luggage, and although the Missing Persons Bureau got one from South Africa, she was never located. The ration-book difficulty she solved by eating in cafés. That was how she began a completely new life. . . .

"She was distraught that night in Mayfair, almost hysterical. Small wonder. In addition to all the other things, she told me what Maurice and Madge and Nicholas Crane had done to her.

"You can guess how I felt. As for her, her one thought was to run home and hide her head under the bedclothes. I consoled her as well as I could, and after arranging to call for her at her new lodgings in the morning to talk things over, I put her into her taxi. She wasn't in the mood for company, even mine.

"Naturally I lied about this episode to the police. By that time, Maurice Crane was dead, and I could hardly admit that I was Gloria Scott's father.

"I stood in Piccadilly for a few minutes after the taxi had gone, fretting. It had occurred to me, rather belatedly, that Madeline's mood was such that she really ought not to be left alone. So after a while I hailed a second taxi and told the man to drive me to the Stamford Street address.

"And by the time we reached Waterloo Bridge they were just pulling my daughter out of the river.

"I noticed the little crowd that had gathered, and I told the driver to stop. Somehow I had a premonition of what had happened. I stayed there only long enough to make sure I was right. Then the taxi took me back to my hotel.

"I didn't sleep at all that night. I was a little mad, I expect. There were two lines of Pope's Elegy which chased one another interminably round the inside of my skull. '*On all the line a sudden vengeance waits, And frequent hearses shall besiege your gates . . .*'

"There was only one thing I wanted to do, and that was to kill.

"And there were three people whom I thought the world would be well rid of.

2

"As you know, colchicine was what I used, and it was a more or less arbitrary choice. I was limited to the vegetable poisons, of course—I've never been able to understand why murderers insist on buying packets of arsenic at the chemist's when the fields and woods and gardens are smothered in things that are quite as deadly—but it might just as well have been aconitine or belladonna. Perhaps I was influenced by the fact that to me the autumn crocus is one of the most beautiful of flowers. . . . I hadn't the resources—chloroform and what not—for isolating the pure principle of the drug. But my amateurish distilling turned out quite well—didn't it? And if it had failed to work, I could always have employed some other method.

"The distilling was done immediately before lunch on the Friday. Earlier that morning I had been to Stamford Street to remove any evidence there might be there of Madeline's real name. In case you should think me stupid—which most certainly I am not—I must emphasise that this was never intended to be anything more than a delaying tactic; I knew that my daughter's true identity was bound to be established in the end. But as a delaying tactic it was useful, for I could not at that stage foresee what opportunities I should have for getting at my victims, and I needed a few days' immunity in which to work.

"A few days, I say; the point is that I intended quite honestly to give myself up as soon as the job was done. Does that surprise you? Probably not. You must have perceived that *X*'s recklessness—in the matter of leaving footprints, for instance—could only be explained, in a person who in other respects was so obviously intelligent (for example, I invariably wore gloves), by some such hypothesis as that. In the end, however, the habit of being alive proved too strong for me. It was not lack of courage which prevented me from surrendering myself; it was the intellectual conviction that such an act would be socially valueless, and hence merely irrational and superstitious.

"When I was at Stamford Street I took the opportunity of removing, for sentimental reasons, one or two mementoes of Madeline. I have them with me here—but it's strange how little they move me now.

"I poisoned Maurice Crane's medicine that Friday afternoon. The grounds of Lanthorn House provide perfect cover, and I was spying out the land when I happened to glimpse him at his bedroom window. So that enabled me to find the right room without too much difficulty. The house is large, rambling and completely vulnerable, and it was simple to get in. To roam about it uninvited, with a tincture of colchicine in my pocket, was of course tremendously risky, but I have never been averse from danger, and the gods protect those who act boldly. Certainly they protected me, then and throughout. At Stamford Street, at Lanthorn House, on Doon Island, at Nicholas Crane's London flat—on each and every occasion I escaped undetected. A guardian angel—or devil, as some will be sure to say!—looked after me, and my confidence increased hugely as success followed success.

"I went home and waited for what should happen. You know how things turned out. Maurice Crane did die, and in front of my very eyes. And that was when, quite suddenly and without warning, Madeline ceased to be important to me. I must not say too much on this subject, or stupid people will misconstrue me. But I can tell you this, that at the moment of Maurice Crane's death my love for Madeline was blotted out, or thrust aside, by an even stronger emotion. Till then, I had not believed that any stronger emotion could possibly exist. But I was wrong. What I felt then was the strongest and deepest and most intoxicating of all the emotions—and I've wondered since how on earth I managed to conceal it! However, I'm an excellent actor, and manage I somehow did.

"Nicholas Crane was the next on my list, and until early on the Monday no opportunity of dealing with him presented itself. But after that the Fates were kind. I visited his flat at half-past seven that morning on a fictitious pretext. *Not* a very plausible hour for visiting! But I was devouringly impatient and scarcely cared whether he found my irruption suspicious or not. My excuse for knocking him up was to have been that I was leaving London early for the North, and wanted before I went to consult him about certain technical details—camera-angles, panning and so forth—in my script. He might or might not have believed that; and an opportunity for leaving some poison behind might or might not have occurred. But in the event, such considerations turned out to be irrelevant. By a blessed coincidence he had gone out, inadvertently leaving his door unlatched. So I was able to do what I pleased.

"That afternoon I drove down to Doon Island. There I was obliged to wait an hour or two before it was possible to enter Madge Crane's cottage, and when between six and seven I did succeed in doing so, I was somewhat perplexed as to where my poison should be put. Let me make one thing very plain. Although Maurice Crane's death changed me psychologically, so that from then on the driving force behind my actions was no longer my devotion to Madeline, but something rather different—in spite of all that, I never allowed myself, however strongly I may have been tempted, to kill indiscriminately, just for the sake of it. If I *had* succumbed to that temptation, the girl who chased me into the Maze would no longer be alive. Nor would you. Nor, probably, would several other people. But I have a good deal of self-control, and I kept myself in check. The mere pleasantness of an experience, however intense, does not justify one in over-indulgence, I consider. So you see, I'm not really the conscienceless monster some people will probably represent me to be!

"All of which is by way of explaining the difficulty I was in after I'd climbed through a window into Madge Crane's cottage. There seemed to be no medicine in this instance, and whatever else I poisoned the secretary might have eaten or drunk as well. In the upshot I had to fall back on the very unsatisfactory compromise of putting my colchicine in the gin. And again it worked exactly as I had intended—though not, of course, until thirty-six hours later.

"That night I went again to Lanthorn House, and there operated on the steering-gear of Nicholas Crane's car. I thought it very likely, you see, that as soon as the cause of Maurice Crane's death was discovered Nicholas and Madge would be on their guard against poison; so additional plans had to be made. As you'll remember, there was a script conference the following day, the Tuesday morning, and I was horrified when I saw David Crane drive up to the studios in Nicholas' car. I had no grudge against David, no wish to see him die. After lunch, therefore, when the carpenters' shop started work again, I disabled the engine as best I could with an iron bar I found in the garage. So tell that to anyone who's stupid enough to think of me as a homicidal maniac!

"On Tuesday evening I killed Nicholas. I'm sorry to say that he took me unawares—otherwise it would not have been such a head-on encounter. I have the right to be a little proud of myself, I think. He realised at once why I was there, he was bigger and stronger and younger than I, and he had a gun, while I had only a knife which I'd kept from my South African days. But I went for him baldheaded, and he was so flustered that his shot missed me by yards. The moment when the knife went into him was the best moment of all. . . . You'll be thinking, of course, that what I experienced was just a commonplace blood-lust. If you *are* thinking that, you're wrong. I can safely say that my excitement was of an altogether more subtle and intellectual variety than *that*.

"Unfortunately, I lost my head as soon as the deed was done. When I heard someone approaching, I fled, not realising that it was only a solitary girl. You'll have heard about our game of hide-and-seek in the Maze. Needless to say, I didn't blunder into it intentionally! And there were times when I wondered if I should ever get out! The girl and I must have got to the centre, unbeknown to each other, by different routes. At the moment when she lit that match and screamed and fainted I'd just fallen over the mound of that grave in the darkness, and I was crawling about trying to discover if I was on the edge of some pit or other. . . . Doubtless it was a little unnerving for her. Further scruples, you see! I must apologise to you for felling you and removing your guide-string, but you'll appreciate that I was somewhat anxious to delay pursuit. . . .

"Well, the story's nearly told. The stop-press columns in the late editions of the Wednesday morning papers informed me that Madge Crane was dead and my job completed, so I decided it was time for me to be moving on. At Brixham, in Devon, I stole a motor-launch, and by night crossed in it to the French coast near Cherbourg—a neighbourhood I know well. At Cherbourg I boarded a boat bound for Mexico; and here I am. Ever since the end of the war I've been investing my money in diamonds—it's a precaution I advise you to take in these days of shaky currencies—and I was able to bring a quantity of the stones with me. They'll enable me to live in comfort, here or elsewhere, for a long, long time to come.

"So now you know all about it. But there's one additional thing I must say, and that is . . ."

(*Here the manuscript breaks off.*)

3

"In a mild way," said Fen, "one wishes one knew what the 'additional thing' was. The usual claim to have been unique, I expect. I don't suppose the murderer has ever lived who didn't imagine his mental processes to be unprecedented in the world's history."

Judy Flecker nodded.

"But he wrote other confessions, didn't he?" she said. "You could perhaps fill in the gap from those."

"Dozens of them," Humbleby agreed. "For all I know he's writing them still. But most of them are almost completely fantastic. I understand that latterly they've been addressed to church dignitaries for the most part—the Moderator of the Methodist Assembly being a particular favourite."

"And is it always Mexico he imagines he's escaped to?"

"No, it's Labrador sometimes, or the Sahara. Neither of those places bears much resemblance to the inside of Broadmoor, but that doesn't seem to worry him at all. No, the point is that Fen's letter, which was the first of them, is the only one that's both coherent and—um—substantially true. Its statements have been checked, as a matter of routine, and apart from the penultimate paragraph they're all correct."

"Is he completely insane now?"

"I believe so, yes."

"And do you think he was insane at the time he committed the murders?"

"Probably. Not on the surface, of course, but certifiably, none the less. To judge from what he says himself, it was seeing Maurice Crane die that finally pushed him over the edge."

"I go cold down the spine," said Judy, "whenever I think of him standing over me in that ghastly Maze. . . . It's funny: I never met him in the normal way, you know, or even set eyes on him. You actually arrested him in London, didn't you?"

"Yes. In a Tottenham Court Road pub, at lunch-time

on the Thursday. His picture was in all the morning papers, you remember, and the pub's proprietor recognised him and telephoned us. God knows what he was doing there, or what he intended to do. Mentally, he was pretty far gone by that time, and I saw at once that he'd be much too mad to come up for trial. . . . Just as well, I suppose."

They were in the lounge of the Club at Long Fulton studios. It was a long, low, raftered room with chintz-covered armchairs, brass ash-trays, and at one end a well-stocked bar. Their drinks were on a low glass-topped table in front of the settee they were occupying. Bright May sunshine shone in through the windows, and since it was midday, and the studio people were almost all at work, they had the place to themselves. Fen and Humbleby were there at Judy's invitation; it was only during the past week, at a date nearly two months after the *dénoûment* of the Crane case, that they had succeeded in arranging a meeting convenient to all three of them.

Judy turned to Fen.

"And now," she said, "what about the logic of it all?"

"Simple enough," he replied, "if once you were prepared to grant that the murderer hadn't an accomplice who was on Doon Island while he was at Lanthorn House—or *vice versa*." He became aggrieved. "But from the deductive point of view it wasn't at all a satisfactory case, for the simple reason that there were so many *alternative* ways in which the mystery could have been solved: with the aid of the footprints report, for example—or by any one of numerous combinations of mere chance and mere routine. . . . Still, one can't, I suppose, expect life to conform with the pattern of detective stories, in which but for pure reasoning no criminal would ever be caught. I sometimes think——"

"Get on with it," said Humbleby, "and don't ramble so much."

Fen regarded him rather coldly.

"The vital clue," he said, "didn't appear till right at the end. It consisted of the information that Madge's gin could only have been poisoned between six and seven p.m. on the Monday. Now, Nicholas' medicine could have been poisoned either between six and seven p.m. on the Monday or between seven and eight *a.m.* on the Monday. Even to an intelligence as tardy as Humbleby's it was clear that between six and seven p.m. the murderer could not have been *both* on Doon Island (poisoning Madge's gin) *and* at Lanthorn House (poisoning Nicholas' medicine), for the excellent reason that the two places are a good three hours' journey apart. And that meant that Nicholas' medicine must have been poisoned between seven and eight on the Monday *morning*.

"Now there was never any question but that the murders were purposive, that the victims were exclusively people who had harmed Gloria Scott. And therefore the interesting thing about the time Nicholas' medicine was poisoned was the fact that that time was hours previous to the publication in the *Mercury* of Nicholas' letter to Madge. In other words, *X* was gunning for Nicholas long before the world at large knew Nicholas had ever harmed Gloria Scott at all—at a time, indeed, when the girl was thought to be his particular *protégée*. I'd *guessed* at the contract business, but *X* wouldn't have killed Nicholas, to judge from his scruples about David and the car, on the basis of guess-work."

"Wasn't there the possibility, though," said Judy, "that the business of the car was a red herring contrived by David?"

"Yes, certainly. But that possibility was only acceptable on the hypothesis that David was the murderer; and

Humbleby was witness to the fact that he couldn't possibly have poisoned Madge's gin."

"Oh, yes, I see. . . . Go on."

"*X*, then, was scrupulous about not harming the innocent. And since he poisoned Nicholas' medicine early on the Monday, that meant he must have had inside information about the contract trickery. From whom did he get it? Up to 8.20 a.m. on the Monday, when Snerd gave the letter to Rouncey, there were just four people who knew of it: Madge, Nicholas, Snerd—and Gloria Scott herself.

"Now it was demonstrable, of course, that none of those people was *X*. Snerd might have been; but when Nicholas was knifed Snerd was safely in gaol, so that eliminated *him*, even if there'd been no other grounds for doing so. So one of the four had clearly told some other person about the trick that had been played on Gloria. Snerd? No, inconceivable; he admitted so much when Humbleby caught up with him that he couldn't possibly have done himself any further harm by admitting *that*; and he's not the sort of man to lie in order to protect someone. Madge and Nicholas? Equally inconceivable. It was as much as their jobs were worth to let any whisper of their shabby little deception get abroad.

"That left Gloria Scott.

"And there was only one person Gloria Scott talked to between the moment when Nicholas told her what she'd let herself in for and the moment when she committed suicide."

"Evan George," Judy murmured. "Yes, I *see*. . . . But look here, mightn't he have passed the information on to someone else?"

"He might, yes. But in that case, why should he have lied about his talk with Gloria? Why should he have denied (his silence on the subject was an obvious denial) ever receiving the information?"

"Well, if he admitted to being Gloria Scott's father, he'd be suspected of Maurice Crane's murder. So even though he was innocent of that murder, he didn't *dare* admit it."

"No good, I'm afraid. At the time he lied, it wasn't clear that Maurice Crane had been murdered at all. He might quite well—as far as, if he was innocent, George knew—have died a natural death."

"Oh yes, of course. . . . There's still another loophole, though. Evan George might have been lying about his conversation with Gloria to *protect* someone—someone he'd told about the conversation."

Fen raised his eyebrows. "But in what way could his lying possibly have protected anyone? At that stage Nicholas' medicine *hadn't yet been poisoned*, and until that had happened, this whole business of who knew about the contract trickery was completely irrelevant: it just didn't incriminate anyone. No, I'm afraid the conclusion was unarguable: Evan George lied; and his motive in lying can *only* have been to protect himself. . . . I could only guess, of course, at how he was related to Gloria; but that he was her father seemed to be by far the likeliest thing."

There was a long silence; all of them were looking back on the case, and on the part they had severally played in it. Then Judy said:

"Poor David. . . . I'm afraid it'll take him a long time to recover from it all."

"Is he still working here?" Fen asked.

"No, he's left. He was never any good, and anyway he'll be thirty-five in August and come into the money his father left in trust for him. . . . He asked me to marry him the other day."

"And are you going to?"

"I'm afraid not. He's a very nice soul, but he'd only make about a quarter of a proper husband. One would have to marry others as well to make up, and polygamy isn't legal."

"Polyandry," Fen corrected her mildly.

"Polyandry, then. . . . Though I'm not at all sure," said Judy dreamily, "that having several husbands at a time mightn't be rather piquant."

"The plural of mouse is mice," Fen observed, "but I doubt if it can be maintained that the plural of spouse is . . . " He broke off. "By the way, what's going to happen about *The Unfortunate Lady*?"

"Shelved," said Judy. "Shelved *sine die*. I gather that Leiper suddenly got tired of it. At the moment he's contemplating a film about Sir Philip Sidney."

"Which purports to prove, no doubt," said Fen acidly, "that the entire *corpus* of Sidney's poetry was fabricated in 1909 by Mr. T. S. Eliot."

Humbleby looked at his watch. "Well, I must be off, I'm sorry to say. I have an appointment with some burglaries in Hammersmith."

"Just one more thing before you go." Judy leaned forward earnestly. "Do you think that what George says about Gloria's miserable childhood, in his confession, is true?"

"As far as I've been able to check it, it is. Why do you ask?"

"Oh, I don't know. . . . I really did like her, you know. And when I look back on it all, it's always her I think about most. And she had such rotten luck—a cruel mother and perhaps a hereditary taint from her father, too."

"Yes," said Humbleby seriously, "she did have rotten luck. For anything mean or vicious that she did one can hardly blame her."

Fen nodded. "So our final toast is inevitable. With Gloria Scott the case began, and with her it should close. . . ."

He raised his glass, and they theirs.

"To the memory," he said, "of an Unfortunate Lady."